ESCAPE FROM A DARK CAVE

Science Traveler Series

Book 12

ESCAPE FROM A DARK CAVE

Science Traveler Series

J. L. Greger

Bug Press

Bernalillo, New Mexico

Escape from a Dark Cave

Bug Press
An imprint of IngramSpark
Bernalillo, New Mexico 87004
http://www.jlgreger.com

ISBN (paperback): 9781735421483
ISBN (EPUB): 9781735421490
Library of Congress Catalogue Number: 2023920337

DEDICATION

This book is dedicated to the irregularities in all of us that make us interesting.

Perhaps we may can be more tolerant of the limitations in others if we accept our own imperfections.

CHAPTER 1: Sara Almquist Begins a Case

Monday, April 24

Sara Almquist sailed east along state road 165 for ten miles before she came to a sign: *Unimproved Road*. The sign was an understatement. The paved two-lane road suddenly narrowed. It couldn't be called a cow path because no cow would be dumb enough to amble along the almost continuous series of potholes with only sharp rims in between. The sides of the road weren't an option. A small creek trickled along one edge. Rocks stretched upward on the other.

Normally she would have turned around when she saw the sign, but her destination—Sandia Man Cave—was only a mile farther. Paul Carbonne, the special agent in charge of the Albuquerque FBI office, had called this morning and recruited her to investigate an apparent murder near the Sandia Man Cave.

"Did you know there's a national historic landmark less than twenty miles from your home?"

She had recognized immediately he was trying to build a bit of suspense to lure her into accepting an assignment. Sara consulted for several federal agencies on cases which had a scientific bent. However, she'd noted on her calendar in the Albuquerque FBI office she was unavailable this week. She had planned to be continuing an assignment for the State Department, but Carbonne must have discovered that assignment had ended early. She decided to let him continue.

"I'm not surprised. Spanish settlers founded the town of Bernalillo in the 1600s."

"I'm talking about a much older site near Placitas called the Sandia Man Cave in the Cibola National Forest. It's believed to have been used by humans at least ten thousand years ago.

Scientists have found evidence of butchered, ice age mammoths in the cave along with ancient hunting junk."

"Wow. I thought the only site in New Mexico with that type of history was in Clovis in southern New Mexico." Sara imagined Carbonne was grinning. He always was pleased when he could surprise her with a bit of scientific trivia. "But you didn't call me to talk about science or history. I know a dead body is going to appear soon."

"Yep, a ranger found a body in the canyon below the cave three days ago. He assumed it was a tourist who overestimated his climbing skills and the medical examiner claimed the body for identification. The medical examiner just called. The man had a deep gouge in his skull, which could have been caused by a cave axe. He'd been dead for at least a week already last Friday."

"So, why call me? I'm an epidemiologist and know nothing about archaeology. Moreover, I dislike being in caves."

"Is it claustrophobia or fear of bats?" Carbonne snickered. "Or are you afraid of the dark?"

Sara recognized their relationship had deteriorated to that of a bickering brother and older sister a long time ago. "All three. I can tolerate walking around Carlsbad Caverns as a tourist, but I don't like squeezing through narrow passages or crawling in bat guano. The moldy smells in caves make my nose itch."

"No problem. The cave has only a few fruit bats. I want you to talk to the new sheriff for Sandoval County more than I want you to search for evidence in the cave. He has the mistaken belief that this is his case, but I think he'll trust you."

Sara thought Carbonne's request didn't make sense. The Sandoval County Sheriff had died in an auto accident a month ago. "When did the county commissioners appoint a new sheriff? Besides as an administrator, you get paid big bucks to handle jurisdictional debates." She laughed. Carbonne had complained to her frequently that he'd gotten a minor pay raise for the hassles of dealing with "the spitting matches" among agents and agencies as the Special Agent in Charge of the Albuquerque FBI office. Generally, the person in this type of position was called the derogatory-sounding title of SAC.

Carbonne was silent for a moment. "Our friend Chuy Bargas was appointed Sheriff of Sandoval County while you were consulting in Brazil."

Sara gulped. She'd met Chuy years before when he was starting out as a police officer in Mercado. She'd worked with him on several cases and had seen him make several spectacular arrests. She'd also seen him fail miserably twice—both times endangering her life. Sara suspected she was the last person Chuy would want to work with in his new job. "Are you using me to send him on a guilt trip? Poor guy doesn't deserve it. Why don't you send him an email pointing out the cave is in a national forest and hence under federal jurisdiction?"

"You know you're a mouthy employee."

Sara suspected Carbonne hadn't told her the whole story. "I'm an independent contractor who demands honesty from the supposed boss."

Carbone sighed. "You know my reasons. The last time Chuy and I cooperated didn't end well. I got promoted in the FBI—if you can call being the SAC of an FBI office a promotion—and he got demoted from being the temporary police chief in Mercado and was forced to go to a rehab clinic for months. When you enter the scene, he'll realize this must be a complex case."

***

Her thoughts were drawn from the past to the present when her car hit a particularly deep hole and lurched toward the stream at the side of the road. She tightened her grip on the steering wheel and glanced at her speedometer. Fifteen miles per hour was too fast on this road. For the next ten minutes she maintained her speed at ten miles per hour, put all thoughts of the past out of her mind, and concentrated on the road. She sighed in relief when she saw a small wood sign for the Sandia Man Cave.

The dirt path into the parking area for the cave was smoother than the state road. An SUV emblazoned with the Sandoval Sheriff's crest and a pickup truck with the U.S. Forest Service insignia were already parked in the lot.

She decided the Sandia Man Cave didn't attract many visitors. The parking area had more clumps of weeds than gravel.

She recognized the thin, ramrod straight man standing by the sheriff's vehicle as Chuy Bargas. His thick, wavy hair was now gray, although he was only in his early thirties.

J. L. Greger

CHAPTER 2: Into the Darkness of Sandia Man Cave

Chuy's lower lip trembled slightly. "Dr. Almquist. I didn't expect to see you. Carbonne said he would send someone to talk to me who could explain the situation clearly."

Sara studied the man for a second and then gave him a hug. "I guess I should congratulate you on your new position." She stepped back and smiled. "It takes guts to accept an elected position like that of sheriff. But you are certainly more qualified than the last sheriff who ran for office on his name: Butch Cassidy Smith."

Chuy licked his lips as he often did when nervous and said, "Neither political party could find anyone who wanted the position, so the county commissioners appointed me until the regular election in six months."

"Don't underestimate yourself. You know solving a crime requires thought, hard work, and luck. Unfortunately, the public seldom recognizes the relative importance of these factors as they read or listen to news stories."

Chuy looked down as he ground a large bug into the dirt with his boot. "Boy, do I know that." He didn't look up. "Why didn't Carbonne have the courtesy of talking to me?"

"As he would say, he's up to his hips in rattlesnakes and figured I'd be a good judge of the importance of the physical evidence." She shrugged. "I doubt his assumption because I know nothing about caves, except they contain odd types of fungi, bacteria, and bats." She didn't pause. "I've also seen the medical examiner's preliminary report. Have you?"

"No."

"The man died of a deep wound in his skull. The likely murder weapon is a cave axe. I understand a ranger called your office last Friday and requested help in investigating the scene."

She handed him a sheet of paper. "Here's what the ranger sent the FBI:"

> *The body was found below the Sandia Man Cave on Friday, April 21. It was in a black garbage bag and covered with leaves. The body was too decomposed to handle. The medical examiner removed it.*

Chuy glared at her. "The ranger didn't want to waste the time of FBI agents on an apparent accident but felt the time of my staff was less valuable."

Sara thought the last two years had embittered Chuy, but it was understandable. "I'm not going to argue with you. We both know many FBI agents are arrogant. No one knows that better than Carbonne." She noted Chuy's defiant stare. "That's why he sent me to look at the evidence in the cave with you. We can decide together what technical help to request."

"Okay, let's go."

She grabbed his arm. "Just remember—I'm a great walker at fifty but not a real hiker."

Chuy's face softened. "I know Carbonne did me a favor when he sent you and not a regular agent to talk to me." He pointed to the two women in U.S. Forest Service uniforms. "These two rangers will be our guides. They think no one has entered the cave in the last three days because they boarded up the entrance when the body was found."

"We both know a couple of boards across the entrance wouldn't stop anyone intent on entering, and the cave was open to everyone until the body was found."

He gave a wan smile. "I brought a deputy along to photograph everything."

***

Sara stood at the start of the dirt path and stared up at the cliff. She wondered how ancient men and women or even archaeologists in the 1930s had found the entrance to the cave at the top of the sheer cliff. The trail from the parking area to the foot of the cliff was about a half-mile walk. At first, it was a gentle slope. It quickly became steeper and was lined by tall trees growing from the canyon below. Metal guard rails and the side of the cliff lined the final part of the path as it turned into stone steps.

Sara was thankful the two rangers slowed as they mounted the steep steps. She tried not to gasp for breath and instead turned to look out over the canyon to the distant slopes. They were covered by trees. She knew she hadn't fooled anyone.

Chuy asked, "Do we need to slow down?" The rangers silently stared at her.

She pointed to a metal double helix suspended by the side of the cliff. "I guess that spiral staircase leads to the mouth of the cave." She stared at the heavy metal poles supporting the platform over the staircase. She was glad the stairs were encased with metal mesh but wished the steps of the spiral had been wider and less steep. "You all can go at your own pace. I'll take my time."

As Sara climbed the spiral, she took occasional brief glances at the distant hills. She noted the rangers and Chuy's deputy seemed to enjoy leaning over the railing and studying the canyon below.

Sara avoided looking down.

Chuy stopped about halfway up the spiral and turned to Sara, "Ever since my fall at the L.A. Airport, I dislike heights. That was only thirty feet. A fall here would be hundreds of feet."

Sara laughed nervously. "Don't feel bad. I don't have an excuse, but I'm not enjoying this climb."

When Sara and Chuy reached the open platform at the top of the spiral staircase, the rangers were already removing boards and chains to reveal the gaping mouth of the limestone cave. The floor of the cave was gray and uneven. She suspected the rocks in the cave were shades of beige, like the side of the mountain, but everything looked gray in the gloom.

The foresters turned on spotlights and gasped. In a far recess of the cave, plastic water bottles and empty soda cans littered the floor. One ranger opened a large plastic garbage bag nearby. The stench of banana peels and rotting tuna wafted through the cave. The ranger shook her head. "Someone holed up here for days. Usually, a ranger checks the cave daily, but not when it's boarded shut."

Her partner smiled and stepped closer to Sara. "Most of the rangers only give a cursory glance at the entrance and wouldn't notice anything at the rear of the cave. We rely on a local group of cavers to clean it once a month."

Chuy's deputy rushed forward to take pictures. He reached into a crack in the wall to support himself as he leaned forward into an indent in the wall. The indent was about four feet wide, four feet deep, and three feet high. "Hey, this is almost a cave in the cave." He moved his hand and a blue polyester coverall fell from the crevice.

"Don't touch anything else." Chuy looked nervously at Sara.

"I'll arrange for experts from the FBI lab to check out the junk in this cave. Chuy, I don't think you and I need to inspect the cave further." She turned to the foresters. "Please board up the cave again. Maybe, even block off the path to the cave. Winslow Red Feather from the FBI lab should be contacting you within the next two hours."

CHAPTER 3: Sara's Path to the Cave

"You owe me. I don't want to go into that cave again." Sara plunked herself down in a chair in front of Carbonne's desk while Bug, Sara's Japanese Chin, quietly seated himself at her feet.

Carbonne frowned. "I'm sorry. Was Chuy... unpleasant? I thought he'd be courteous to you of all people." He turned and foraged in the under-the-counter refrigerator behind his desk and pulled out two diet colas. "Does Bug need...?" Carbonne stopped in mid-sentence when he saw Sara had already poured water into a glass bowl for the black-and-white dog.

"Chuy was a perfect gentleman."

Carbonne handed her one of the cans and frowned. "Did you take Bug to the cave?"

"Of course not. He couldn't handle the spiral stairs. And it was too hot to leave him in the car." She opened the can and took a big draught. "I don't think Chuy cares for caves. As we climbed the stairs, he commented on his fall at the airport a couple of years ago. I don't know why, but I then looked down. I shouldn't have." She gulped her cola again. "I never enjoy those tourist opportunities where you can stand on plexiglass and look down into a canyon either. And they're all shiny; the metal mesh surrounding the stairs was rusted. It didn't inspire confidence."

"Okay, but what makes you think he doesn't like caves?"

"When we left, he said he didn't want to be sheriff enough to fight for jurisdiction on this case even if might please some sects of his constituency."

Carbonne eyed Sara as she gulped her soda. "You know you're the only visitor to my office who doesn't ask for a glass or a straw when I hand him or her a can. I like that you're not fussy or temperamental. *But* today you're nervous and... your arm is in a sling." His stare softened. "Brazil, especially

Manaus, was in the news daily last week. I called you today because I wanted to see if you had been evacuated from Brazil and were okay."

Sara smiled slightly.

"And I needed help. You could have told me you were injured and weren't up to climbing into a cave."

Sara touched her sling. "Two bullets passed through my upper arm—just the soft tissue. I wore the sling to prevent me from overusing my arm. It wasn't a problem today. And doctors say the eardrum in my left ear doesn't need surgical repair. It's healing nicely. Nothing wrong with me but..."

"It's normal to be edgy after a gunshot wound. I always am. The aches and flashbacks make it hard to sleep."

"I can ignore the ache when I'm busy. That why I thought an assignment might be good for me."

"You should have told me. Did Chuy comment on your arm?"

"No, he probably thought I'd been clumsy and didn't want to embarrass me by asking about the sling."

"Do you want to talk about it?" He paused. "Or is everything you did in Brazil classified, except for your participation as a scientist at the World Health Organization conference on tropical diseases?"

She replied honestly. "The conference was rather routine. No major scientific breakthroughs were announced, but it was interesting to see clinicians interact with entomologists and climatologists. You know with global warming, the types of mosquitos that transmit tropical diseases, such as malaria and dengue fever, are spreading into Florida and California."

Carbonne tapped his fingers on his desk. "I'm surprised you had time to attend the conference. What's more, I'm not going to let you dismiss me so easily. It's not every day that a friend is involved in a major international incident. One day last week—maybe Thursday—the press mentioned a shootout in a convent when drug dealers ambushed an American scientist and consulate staff, who successfully defended themselves." He pointed to her arm. "I assume that's when you were wounded. Sanders must have had you under heavy guard."

"Actually, only two women were with me, until Sanders brought in reinforcements—none too soon."

"Scary?"

"I was too busy to be as frightened as I should have been."

He nodded. "That describes the worst situations I've faced. I was always too busy to be scared." He stared into space before he looked at Sara. "Back to my questions. The pictures on the Friday six o'clock news of the attempted takeover of the U.S. consular offices in Manaus by drug gangs and rogue police were ghastly. Then it was announced on the ten o'clock Friday news that our president has recalled acting U.S. Ambassador Eric Sanders from Brazil." Carbone drained his can of soda and stared at Sara. "Surely you can tell me something."

Sara was amused by Carbonne's attempt to learn details. She always enjoyed bantering with him. Carbonne had worked for Sanders as an information specialist when Sanders was trying to stem the movement of drugs from Cuba to the U.S. Accordingly, Carbonne understood the intricacies and nuances of "information collection."

However, Sara was reticent to say much. "My appointment as the U.S. representative to the scientific conference sponsored by the World Health Organization was my cover. As usual, I was given gobs of scientific data not only on tropical diseases, the theme of the conference, but also on the drug trade in Brazil. Little of it was classified."

Carbonne snickered. "Yes, but as Sanders's..." He seemed to be thinking. "...helpmate, you know how he thinks and how to use scientific data to extract more information for him."

Sara shrugged. "Don't be naughty. You'll hear more in a few days if Sanders's efforts succeed."

Carbonne frowned. "I saw a clip on the TV news on Saturday morning. Sanders was departing from a private jet at Andrews Air Force Base. I figured he was still in Washington. Was that some sort of ruse? Did he go back to Brazil?" He walked around his desk, squatted, and petted Bug. "Barbara and I looked but caught no sight of you during the clips on Sanders."

Sara finally saw a way to change the direction of the conversation. "It's about time you talked about Barbara. How is the mother-to-be? Does she like her new job?"

Barbara Lewis was Carbonne's significant other and an FBI agent, who had recently transitioned from being an investigative agent to the administrator of a program to recruit more minorities, particularly Native Americans, into the FBI and other federal law enforcement programs. Much of Barbara's efforts were focused on children and teens now. Data indicated many indigenous teens learned too late that a criminal record lessened career opportunities in law enforcement or underestimated the educational requirements to be an FBI or DEA agent.

"She's fine and insisted I check on you. She was worried Sanders had gotten out of Brazil but hadn't protected you." He turned and fumbled with papers on his desk. "One of the ways she disciplines me is to say: Don't be like Sanders."

Sara shook her head. "You win. I can't let Barbara think my relationship with Sanders is that bad. I was on the jet out of Brazil with Sanders, but I exited with the crew from the back." She smiled. "We lucked out. The jet was usually used by the Secretary of State. So, it was comfy with a shower, bed, and a good galley. I was checked out at Walter Reed Medical Center before I roughed it on a military transport headed for Kirtland Air Force base here in Albuquerque. I usually prefer to take commercial flights, but Sanders thought I should avoid potential encounters with reporters in airports."

"Wow, Sanders really wanted to keep you out of view."

Sara pulled two files from her tote bag. "No more questions. Let's get down to the business of the murder near Sandia Man Cave. I talked to the medical examiner. He said the autopsy had its limits because the man had been dead more than a week, and April has been warm. The man had on gray shorts and a gray T-shirt. The killer wrapped the body in a black garbage bag. We agreed that info shouldn't be mentioned in any press release." She thought for a moment. "We assume the killer knew the victim because he took time to wrap the body."

Carbonne picked up a file from his desk and motioned Sara to join him at a small conference table. "You always get special treatment from lab crews, including the medical examiner's office."

"Not true. I appreciate their expertise, and they know it." Sara pulled a page from her file. "The examiner had an artist render a drawing of the victim's face." She shoved the page to Carbonne. "I doubt it will be of much use. The victim had short, sandy brown hair, was slightly over thirty, five-ten, and weighed about a hundred-forty pounds—well, before bloating. Neither his fingerprints nor DNA matched anything in the national databases. He wore no rings but sported a glow-in-the-dark-watch. The examiner said cavers often wear that type of watch. He's already sent the watch to the state lab for determination of the type of dust embedded in it."

Carbonne studied the picture. "The artist depicted a handsome man. Perhaps the cave was a rendezvous spot."

"Ugh, the floor of the cave is a series of uneven slabs of limestone." She sighed. "Of course, tastes vary." She reviewed the page in her hand. "Oh, I forgot the most important clues. The medical examiner said the victim's T-shirt was emblazoned with *Sandia Grotto*."

"A tourist item?"

"No, I did some checking." She paused. "Did you know those exploring caves prefer to be called cavers not spelunkers? I wonder why. Cavers have a national spelunking association. The local clubs are called grottoes." She pulled a half sheet of paper from a file and glanced at it. "The local Albuquerque club is called Sandia Grotto. I lucked out. They're meeting tonight at seven."

"In a cave?"

"No. I thought I might attend the meeting with an agent." She pushed the half sheet with information on the spelunking club's meeting toward Carbonne. "Someone might recognize the picture. I might also learn a bit about the Sandia Man Cave. Evidently this group has helped the U.S. Forest Service maintain it for the last fifteen years." Sara tucked the pages back into her tote. "That's all I've got."

"It's a lot for a gimp."

Sara ignored him and stood. "I asked the foresters to keep the cave closed to the public but to allow the FBI lab crew access." She petted Bug and noticed Carbonne was beginning to laugh. "Don't laugh at Bug. He had a hard week in the pet spa and needs a little extra attention." Without stopping for breath, Sara added, "Oh, I stopped by the lab before I came to see you.

I requested Winslow be assigned to this case because he's the most adventurous and athletic of the lab crew."

"You know you could take it easy. A couple more days won't make any difference to the victim."

Sara's jaw dropped. "You say that now after sending me to that awful cave." She leaned down and picked up Bug's water dish. "I need to go home and take a nap. The last few days tired me out."

Carbonne rose and sauntered to the door. "Why don't you meet us for supper tomorrow night? Barbara will want to hear about the Amazon jungle and won't ask prying questions." He laughed. "She's more ecologically correct and less nosy than I am."

As Sara and Bug stepped into the hall, she said, "Almost everyone is more proper than you. That's why you're a good undercover agent. Don't forget to tell an agent to meet me at the meeting tonight."

"None of the agents would dare boss me around like you do." He laughed.

CHAPTER 4: Sandia Grotto Club

Sara studied the crowd milling around the refreshment table in a conference room at the Central Methodist Church in Albuquerque. All the men had on T-shirts or short-sleeved casual shirts and khaki shorts or jeans, except one man in a sports jacket. Sara figured he was the FBI agent. Carbonne had emailed her that Agent Jack Drum was "inexperienced but trainable" and would be at the meeting. She wondered what Carbonne was hinting in his comment, but it was unimportant now.

Everyone in the room looked athletic. Only two in the crowd had gray hair. With one exception, all the cavers wore their hair short like the victim's or long and in a braid. Three of the women in the crowd were dressed like the men. Two others wore low cut tank tops. She guessed these two were more interested in male cavers than caves per se, but then she felt ashamed for making the assumption. She suspected the attendees looked like typical cavers.

She recognized a lanky man with short gray hair wearing a navy plaid shirt. "Ralph, I talked to you this afternoon. You look like your picture on your department's website. I'm Sara Almquist from the FBI. Thank you for letting me bring Bug along." She pointed to the dog, who waved his tail sightly. She pointed to the man in the sports jacket as he stepped to her side. "This is Agent Jack Drum."

Jack extended his hand. "I want to..."

Ralph glanced at Jack and focused on Sara. "Sara already explained the purpose of your visit. I put you on the agenda after the basic business. This way, late comers won't miss it." Ralph shook his head. "Sad. Sandia Man Cave doesn't need more bad publicity. A woman was bludgeoned to death near it in 1999. The murder was never solved. Now another murder."

Sara shoved an artist's rendering of the victim at Ralph. "This is the artist's guess at the man's appearance."

Ralph studied it. "It could be any of several men in our group—young, athletic, white with short hair."

Jack sighed. "I figured this was a long shot. I'll make my announcement. If no one comes forward, I'll leave."

Sara tried to not show her annoyance. This young agent was over-rating his importance.

She and Carbonne had discussed the problem of the arrogance of the FBI agents in the Albuquerque office several times. Carbonne had accepted his current administrative position because he had found his fellow agents' attitudes obnoxious. He'd seen the contempt they showed for the poor and the homeless when he'd worked undercover as a homeless vagabond in Albuquerque. He'd also observed several agents snub and harass his Native American girlfriend when she was training to be an agent. Sara guessed he'd probably selected Jack to attend the meeting because he hoped she would "teach" him humility.

"I'll stay for the whole meeting and mingle afterwards because sometimes people recognize the victim if given a little time to think."

Ralph nodded. "I can always recognize an experienced professor. We in academia learn to squeeze answers from unwilling audiences. You know my students in mining engineering at the University of New Mexico aren't a talkative bunch. I must prod them to get them to participate in class discussions." Ralph wended his way through the group. The crowd was seated and relatively quiet by the time he reached the podium.

After the minutes and the treasurer's report were approved, Ralph introduced Sara. She introduced—graciously she thought—Jack Drum and allowed him to announce the murder of a man near Sandia Man Cave. He described the victim's characteristics and said, "Does anyone know him?"

The group was silent. Jack started to walk to the door.

Sara rose. "The victim and his family need your help. It's unlikely the FBI can catch the killer if we can't identify the victim. Think how you would feel if a loved one went missing." She picked up Bug and cuddled him. "Think how his pets must miss him. Jack omitted a couple of points. The victim wore a T-

J. L. Greger

shirt with a Sandia Grotto decal. That means several of you are likely to know him. The medical examiner noticed clues during the autopsy suggesting the victim might be autistic."

Sara decided not to explain that the victim's brain was a little heavier than typical for his size. That phenomena could be due to swelling after death, but the examiner also had noted cortical deviations often found in patients with autism. Those clues were technically debatable and could lead the audience into an interesting scientific debate, which would not be productive for Sara's purposes tonight. She noted no one responded. "The autism was probably mild. He might have seemed socially inept or slightly awkward physically."

The two women with the scoop neck tops began to whisper to each other.

"You might have thought he was science geek or a loner."

Now five in the audience were staring at her.

"It's okay if you guess wrong. There are always false leads in missing persons cases, but often other leads eventually yield positive results." Sara smiled. "What do you think?"

One woman, who had been whispering, stood. "We..." She looked at her friend. "...we think it might be Toby Collins." She twisted her hands and looked around the group for encouragement.

After thirty seconds, Ralph rescued the woman. "You might be right. Toby Collins is an enthusiastic caver, but he sometimes teeters on ledges." He scratched his jaw. "Makes me nervous."

The other women with a scoop neck top raised her hand. "I never could get him to talk much to me." She blushed. "He was geeky."

Sara pushed down on Jack's shoulder to prevent him from standing. "Jack and I will stay and talk to any or all of you after your meeting. The more we know about Toby Collins the better."

Ralph seemed to study the crowd. "I think your investigation is more interesting that the program—a lecture on mineral composition of the Fort Stanton Cave. Why don't you start your interviews now."

"Won't the speaker be hurt?"

"No, it's not one of my better lectures."

***

Sara had misjudged the two women in low-necked tops. They were sisters: Valentina and Valeria Perez. Sara suppressed a smile when they gave their names. The alliteration of their names was cute, but it must have created constant confusion in school and at home. Perhaps that was why the sisters wore their hair so differently. Valeria wore her hair in short spikes dyed various shades of red. Valentina's hair was black and looked like it hadn't been cut in years.

Valeria was the more talkative. "Toby didn't talk much when I first met him three years ago, but he became more friendly when I was pregnant." She frowned. "That was strange. Most guys talked less to me when I had the baby bump."

Valentina nudged her. "You also asked for help."

Valeria paused. "I guess I changed when I was pregnant. I didn't want to go on difficult explorations." She looked down at her trim body. "It's hard to squeeze through narrow passages when you're pregnant."

Jack coughed violently.

Valeria ignored him. "Ralph convinced me that I could remain an active caver in a different way. I could participate in the maintenance of Sandia Man Cave. It's close to my home in Mercado, but even that was a problem. I didn't want to handle the chemicals we used to remove the graffiti on the walls of the cave."

Sara suppressed the urge to ask questions about the chemicals. If the murderer was a caver, he or she might know about these chemicals and have cleaned the site well.

Valeria continued, "Ralph introduced me to Toby who had overseen the maintenance of Sandia Man Cave for ages. After that Toby was chatty with me."

Valentina shrugged. "If you consider, constant question and comments about wall cleaners to be conversation."

Valeria scowled at her sister. "Toby always started a conversation with me by commenting about the cave, but he also asked me questions about how it felt to be pregnant and later about my son Miguel." She paused and closed her eyes. "I don't remember any other man asking questions like that. I didn't think the questions were strange because he worked in a lab at the university and liked to know how things worked."

Sara noticed others were waiting to speak to her. Jack was frantically recording his conversations with other cavers. "Valeria, I or someone else from the FBI lab may need to talk to you more about cleaning the cave. Would you mind coming to the FBI offices off I-25?"

Valeria's eyes widened. Valentina stepped back.

"Oh, you're not suspected of anything." Sara knew that wasn't true. At this point everyone in the room had to be considered a potential suspect. "I could even give you a short tour of the facility, especially the lab, after we talk."

Both women smiled. Valeria said, "I'm a nursing assistant in the clinic in Mercado. I'd like to see the FBI lab."

Sara had a brainstorm. She stepped back and announced, "Jack and I want to talk to all of you tonight but probably can't listen to all your stories about Toby. Would your group be willing to come to the FBI headquarters in Albuquerque—you know the facility off I-25? I'd give you the tour of the lab and evidence room afterwards. That's a real opportunity because it's hard to get clearance to the building otherwise."

Jack's face turned gray. Many in the group, including Ralph shouted, "Yes."

Ralph got the names, addresses, and emails, of all those at the meeting. Jack learned when the cavers were available for interviews during the next two days. Sara focused on those who didn't seem enthusiastic to visit the FBI headquarters by standing with Bug near exit to the room and questioning people as they tried to leave.

The first two she stopped were annoyed but showed her their state driver's licenses and allowed her to extract information after she insisted. She mentally noted their appearances. One was tall, dark haired, with a narrow face. The other was short with a dark braid down his back. Both insisted they'd "seen enough labs." Their comments suggested they didn't trust anyone in law enforcement.

***

As she drove home, Sara knew she'd not done a good job. She hadn't brought a recorder. Jack had been more prepared and had brought one for her as well as one for himself. She had allowed a non-vetted individual—Ralph—to help collect data, but she was desperate for help. In general, she hadn't assessed the situation correctly beforehand. Thank goodness, she'd brought Bug. As usual, he'd made up for her deficiencies by entertaining those waiting to speak to Jack or her. All she'd say to Carbonne tomorrow was: "Who knew so many people liked being in caves."

CHAPTER 5: A Tentative Identification

Tuesday

Sara started her day as she usually did—talking to Sanders on the phone at six. Sanders began by saying, "Did a staffer from the Senate or House call you yesterday?"

"No." Sara felt stomach acid rising in her throat. She didn't like the thought of being the prey in a Congressional investigation.

"You were wise to keep out of view on Saturday. I was notified yesterday around noon that I was to appear before the Senate Committee on Intelligence tomorrow. If you'd been seen, you might have been expected to attend the hearing, too."

Sara could tell from his voice that he was tense and let him continue with only a "Hmm" of acknowledgment.

"That didn't give me and others in the State Department much time to prepare. My boss—the undersecretary—convinced the chair of the committee that the hearing should be behind closed doors and without any public announcements before or after the meeting."

Sara felt her blood pressure rise when Sanders said, "my boss—the undersecretary." The woman was a wily politician and knew Sanders's loyalty to the State Department was boundless. Hence, his boss could manipulate him to do tasks more self-serving diplomats would avoid. Sara admired Sanders's patriotism but distrusted his boss. She didn't voice her opinion because she knew it would irritate Sanders.

Sanders seemed not to notice Sara's silence and continued, "A staffer from the House Committee on Intelligence called at four and said the members of her committee would also be present."

"They must want answers." Sara thought, *Or sensed this could be good publicity for them.* "It's not often the House and Senate work together on anything."

"No, these two committees often cooperate. Members of both committees were apprised of the situation in private sessions before I went to Brazil. The conservatives had urged for more aggressive U.S. actions against the drug gangs. The liberals had wanted the U.S. to protect the jungle and the indigenous people more forcefully. All agreed they liked keeping Brazil out of the headlines in the U.S., except for sports."

She tried to be a good cheerleader. "You can convince reasonable senators that your actions were necessary. You have congratulatory emails from Brazilian officials, which show they didn't view your attack on the gang's headquarters as inflammatory. *And...*" She emphasized the last word. "... this hearing isn't a surprise. You started preparing your comments on the plane as we flew back from Brazil."

"My boss and I didn't think they'd call the hearing until the end of the week. I will have to give your name if they ask. It will be apparent to them that you were more than a scientist invited to represent U.S. interests at a WHO scientific conference in Manaus."

"I'm prepared. You know I keep a diary of my all my consulting activities. I updated it on the plane while you were busy with your notes. But I hope they don't ask questions about our private lives."

"It wouldn't be a problem if you had accepted my marriage proposal last year in India."

"Quite the contrary, then I would have moved to Brazil with you when you were appointed as the chargé d' affaires." She attempted to change the topic and embarked on a point of contention between her and Sanders. "I hope the undersecretary and the secretary for once do the right thing." She noted her pitch was raised and she tried to lower her voice. "They knew they sent you to do an impossible task and that things would blow up. They even appointed you as chargé d' affaires rather than ambassador to Brazil so they could recall you with less fuss."

Sanders sighed. "And that is why I had you whisked back to Albuquerque. You say what you think."

"I'm sorry, but my testimony would certainly emphasize how dire the situation in Manaus was. Remember, I'm always in your corner."

Sanders's voice softened. "I know. I needed your pep talk. I'll call you tonight to rehash the hearing. Love you." He hung up before Sara could respond.

Sara scooped Bug up. He had nestled at her feet as he often did when she was upset. She wasn't sure how he read her so accurately. It could be her voice was raised. More likely, he smelled pheromones in her sweat when she was tense.

***

Carbonne's secretary waved Sara and Bug into his office at eight-fifteen. "He read your email from last night and expected you at eight-thirty."

Sara didn't wait for Carbonne to look up. "Sanders is appearing before the Senate Intelligence Committee this morning. I may be called to Washington. So, you'd better use me on the Sandia Man Cave case while you can." She then proceeded to pour water into a cup for Bug and make him comfortable near the small table.

Carbonne said nothing until he set two diet colas on the table and then placed his hand on her shoulder. "I'm sorry. Are you sure you want to work today?"

"I worry less when I'm busy. Besides, Jack and I turned up clues last night—more than I was prepared to handle. It never dawned on me there were so many who liked being in caves."

"I already talked to Jack. By now, he should have the search warrant for Toby's small condo near the UNM campus."

"Jack must have been annoyed to have already been in your office."

"No, impressed would be a better word. He'd never seen an agent whip up the crowd so completely. Evidently, your hokey act of cuddling Bug and noting how the victim's pets must miss him was effective." Carbonne snickered. "It's like Sanders told me several years ago: 'Never underestimate Sara's nosy mother routine.'"

"Every investigator has his own schtick. Mine is being a folksy busybody. Yours is being an invisible homeless man." Sara shrugged. "What do you want me to do?"

"Talk to Toby's mother. Winslow has already agreed to be your driver and to collect the lab data." He tapped her shoulder. "I see you don't have the sling on today."

"My arm didn't ache much last night. I thought I'd see how I did without the sling today. Are you sure it's a good use of Winslow's time to drive me?"

"Knowing you, you'll want someone from the lab to collect samples. Besides, Winslow claims his field trips to Santa Fe with you for the botulism murders were the best." Carbonne winked. "There's no accounting for taste."

"How about Jack?"

"No one is better at questioning grieving parents than you, but I don't think Jack, as a guy, could learn to imitate your routine. His time is better spent following up on the cavers from last night." Carbonne returned to his desk. "Jack didn't like your idea of bringing them here as a group." Carbonne winked. "So, he can track them down individually."

"It will take longer."

"I know, but he must learn from his decisions."

Sara rounded up Bug and his paraphernalia and was about to leave, when Carbonne said, "Unless I hear differently, Barbara and I plan to meet you at the Range Café at six tonight."

***

The house was of territorial design with a porch shading the front of the tan, flat-roofed, stucco house. The yard in front was designed to reduce water usage and was mainly artfully placed red and beige gravel accented with yucca and red sage.

Sara rang the buzzer by the sturdy red front door. No one answered. She heard a morning quiz show on a television and punched the buzzer again.

Winslow walked to the side of the house, peered into a window, and returned to the front door. "There's a TV on and someone appears to be slumped in a chair. Can't we announce we're FBI and enter? We can claim we thought the person slumped in the chair needed help."

"You've watched too many TV shows." Sara thumped on the door. "Mrs. Collins, it's the FBI. Please answer the door."

A dog barked. Sara thought she heard, "Go away."

Winslow knocked harder on the door and yelled, "Mrs. Collins. This is an emergency. Let us in."

J. L. Greger

Sara heard more barking and then shuffling steps. "Junior, be quiet." The door opened slightly. The nose of golden retriever protruded into the gap.

Sara pushed her card from the FBI forward.

"Go to the chair."

The dog retreated. The door opened slightly wider. The old woman's henna-colored hair with gray roots was wrapped around soft pink rollers on both sides of her face. The hand that grabbed for Sara's card was deformed with arthritis. "Did you find Toby?"

Sara had checked missing persons reports for Albuquerque before she left the FBI offices. No one had reported Toby Collins missing. She decided not to pursue the issue now. "Mrs. Collins, we want to talk to you about Toby. May we come in?"

The old woman sighed and hobbled back to her recliner.

Sara assumed the sigh was a yes and walked into a great room with a ceiling of stained dark vigas that matched the wood floor. The heavy mission-type furniture had probably once been top-of-the-line but now looked shabby. The golden retriever was sprawled by the recliner. "Mrs. Collins, when was the last time you saw Toby?"

The old woman ignored Sara and focused on her television show.

"Mrs. Collins, would you mind if my associate turned off your TV?"

"Why?"

"We need to discuss Toby. It's important." Sara sat down on the edge of the sofa closest to the recliner.

Winslow didn't wait for the woman to respond, grabbed the control, and turned off the television.

"Where was Toby this time? He keeps forgetting to tell me when he goes off to explore another cave."

Sara placed her hand on Mrs. Collins's knee. "When did you last see Toby?"

"I don't know… but he didn't stop by on Saturday. I told the police officer, who lives across the street, that Toby was missing on Sunday." She pushed Sara's hand from her knee. "You certainly took your time in getting here. I have a list of things I need done."

Sara didn't think she should show a picture of Toby in the morgue. It would be hard for anyone to identify the bloated face. "I'm sorry to tell you, but we think Toby is dead." She waited thirty seconds for the words to sink in. "We know Toby sometimes stayed with you on weekends. This man…" She pointed to Winslow. "…would like to collect items from the bedroom Toby used for lab analyses." Sara thought it useless to explain that Winslow wanted to collect objects that might have Toby's DNA. "Where did Toby sleep when he stayed with you?"

"Upstairs in the gray bedroom. Toby could never be normal like my other son and like real colors. He wanted his bedroom to have gray walls." She was silent for thirty seconds. "Are you sure he's dead?"

"No, that's why my associate needs to collect samples for lab analyses. We're sorry to bother you."

"Do I have a choice?" She pointed at Winslow. "Will he steal anything valuable? I don't like men who wear their hair in braids."

"He'll only collect things such as a toothbrush, a comb or brush, and maybe clothing."

The old woman shrugged.

Winslow raced up the stairs with a case of supplies.

"What am I supposed to do while he pokes around my house?" The old's woman's blue eyes seemed vacant as she stared at Sara. "My husband took care of everything. He died more than a year ago. Toby…" She shrugged. "Toby's not much help, and my other son—Ben—has a family and runs our family business." She smiled. "He's an ophthalmologist—like my husband."

"Where does Ben live?"

The woman looked confused. "Why? I can't bother him. He's with patients now. Ben is successful. The business has tripled since he took over. His wife and daughters are beautiful. But Toby just works in a lab at the university and never keeps a nice girlfriend." She paused. "Toby only has the job because my Jacob convinced a professor in the medical school to hire him. Toby always disappoints me."

Sara noticed Mrs. Collins was using the present tense as she referred to Toby. She evidently hadn't heard *or* hadn't accepted the reality of his death. Sara decided she'd address the problem later and repeated her question, "Where does Ben live?"

"Here in Albuquerque. You've heard of Collins's Eye Associates. That's our family business, but Toby is no good at business." She stopped and gazed in the distance. "People complained when Toby as a teenager worked in the reception area of our business. I was annoyed, but my husband—Jacob— didn't mind. That's when Jacob and Toby started going to meetings with those odd people who went to caves."

The golden retriever put his head on the woman's lap.

Sara texted the new information on Ben Collins to Jack and asked him to get a search warrant for the Collins home. She wasn't sure Mrs. Collins could legally approve the removal of samples from the house. That was unlikely to be a problem if the only objects Winslow collected were a toothbrush, a comb, or clothing, but she wanted to be optimistic. Winslow might find something interesting. She sighed because extracting answers from Mrs. Collins was tiring. She bet Toby had found being around his mother tiring, too. "Mrs. Collins, what is your first name?"

"Lydia."

"Do you mind if I call you Lydia?"

"In our business, all the employees called me Mrs. Collins."

Sara guessed Lydia preferred to be called Mrs. Collins. Sara wondered what was taking Winslow so long upstairs. She wanted to check on him but was afraid what Mrs. Collins might do if she left her alone. "Did Jacob like caving?"

The old woman waved her hand toward the stairs. "What is that man with the braids doing upstairs?"

"He's collecting samples for analyses. We need to be sure the man we found is Toby. You were going to tell me whether Jacob liked caving."

"I asked Jacob why he went to meetings with strange people. He said Toby fit in with them, and he liked being with people whose greatest passion wasn't money. You know most of them work other jobs. Playing in a cave is a hobby for them. Strange."

Sara felt slightly chastised. She had learned that caving was a volunteer activity for eighteen of the twenty at the meeting last night. Many of the cavers believed their adventures were scientifically worthwhile and thought they were pioneers in the frontier of caves. Sara reluctantly admitted to herself that Jacob had been wise to seek friends for Toby among the cavers.

Mrs. Collins interrupted Sara's thoughts. "My Jacob liked to see Toby happy. It made Ben jealous sometimes when all Toby and Jacob talked about over dinner was their caving experiences." She paused. "It wasn't fair to me either."

Winslow was whistling as he walked down the stairs.

"Mrs. Collins is worried that you might take something valuable. Let's show her what you collected."

Winslow stopped whistling and placed his survey case on the dining table. He pulled out four bags and motioned Sara to come closer.

Sara choked. One of the bagged items was a photo album. A wrinkled note was in a second bag. She read the note carefully:

Mom,

It's my money. The lawyer said I can do with
it as I wish.
It's my life. I don't have to obey you.
Stop threatening me.

Toby

"The note was crumpled and lying on the floor near the bed. The album was on the bed."

"Show Mrs. Collins the bags with the comb and the T-shirt while I call Carbonne. I think the note might be too important to risk it being classified as incorrectly collected."

Winslow winked and presented the two bags as if they were part of a guessing game to Mrs. Collins. He made her guess what was in each of the bags he held behind his back and where he'd found it. The game seemed to entertain Mrs. Collins and she was eager to learn where Winslow had found the items. She said several times, "I thought I'd checked his room."

Sara decided one way to prolong their visit until Jack arrived with the search warrant, which Carbonne thought she needed, was to collect a sample for DNA analysis from Mrs.

Collins. The old woman would not allow Winslow to swab the inside of her cheek but decided Sara could do it when faced with alternative of having to go the FBI building.

The door buzzer sounded. Sara rushed to the front door and stepped outside to speak to Jack. "Winslow collected a potentially incriminating note."

"I know. Carbone called me. Sounds like I had a better morning than you did. Two of the cavers, I interviewed this morning, saw Toby argue violently with a man, whom they believed to be his brother. Both thought the argument was about family money." Jack flashed a search warrant at Sara. "I'll serve it."

***

The old woman growled when Jack handed her the search warrant, "When am I going to see a real policeman?"

Sara and the two men looked at each other in disbelief and stepped into the next room. Winslow laughed. "I don't think she understands Native Americans can work for the FBI. I'll search the house with the one who wins the coin toss, while the loser talks to her."

Jack assumed a thick drawl. "The ole miss won't talk to no colored man."

Sara sighed. "She's old…"

"And a racist." Jack whistled as he climbed the stairs behind Winslow.

"You owe me."

***

Sara showed Mrs. Collins the note, being careful to not let the woman touch it. "When did Toby give you this note?"

"I don't know?"

"Try."

After five minutes of dithering, Mrs. Collins admitted Toby had moved his possessions out of the house in March after a blowup. "Disabled people like Toby don't talk much. They explode when angry. He said dreadful things to me."

"Like what?"

"I don't want to repeat them."

"Give me an example."

"I don't know. Nasty."

Sara watched her laptop for messages from Winslow during the fruitless exchange. Finally, one arrived:

"Mrs. Collins, why did Jacob withdraw from being a co-owner of Toby's bank account five years ago?"

"Don't know."

"I think you do."

The woman fiddled with a button on her blouse. "Jacob thought Toby should be independent after he turned thirty. He bought Toby a condo and helped him furnish it. It was silly. Toby had a perfectly nice room upstairs."

"Okay. What happened in March?" Sara expected more dither.

Mrs. Collins answered immediately. "Toby moved out completely."

"Why? Were you arguing about the money in Toby's endowment?"

The woman eyed Sara suspiciously. "No."

"I expect you got Toby to do what you wanted for years by acting confused." Sara thought it sounded better than saying Mrs. Collins was manipulative. "For some reason he finally moved his stuff out completely a couple of months ago. Why?"

Mrs. Collins stared open mouthed at Sara. Her voice was hoarser when she spoke. "He decided to marry... He'd met a girl at work."

"Her name?"

"Candy... No one decent uses a name like that. She isn't pretty. One of those who liked caves."

"Candy what?"

"I... don't know."

"Stop the act You can be charged with obstructing an investigation." Sara decided to act a bit herself. She stood and yelled up the stairs. "Do either of you have a pair of handcuffs?"

"Candy Lopez."

CHAPTER 6: Clues Lead to More Clues

Sara called Sanders as soon as she left the Collins home. It was almost noon in Washington, D.C., and the morning hearing should be over. She got a busy signal. She texted him. She called the undersecretary's office. Once Sara identified herself, she was told the undersecretary and Mr. Sanders were still in conferences on the Hill.

Sara wondered whether she should go home and start packing a case with her best suit in preparation for having to go to Washington to be grilled by senators. She decided it was a defeatist attitude and instead returned to Bug waiting for her in her office in the FBI building.

Soon, Sara and Bug were sitting in the shade of a tree outside the building. "Mrs. Collins claimed Junior listened to her better than Toby. That's not surprising. You're the best listener I know."

Bug had stopped grooming himself and licked her hands.

"But Mrs. Collins called Junior 'dumb' and kicked him whenever she wanted him to fetch something for her."

Bug pulled on his lead. He was bored with the conversation. Sara was bored, too. Mrs. Collins wasn't worth more thought. She might not be sad Toby was dead, but she hadn't killed him. She wasn't strong enough to have landed the fatal axe blow to Toby's head.

***

Sara reviewed Jack's notes and tapes from the morning. The cavers he'd spoke to on the phone said Toby was a "loner with an odd stare" but he was the main reason the Sandia Man Cave looked "so good" during the last fifteen years. Several noted Toby was helpful after he understood your needs, but "you had to state your needs clearly. Hints and gestures didn't work."

Only two—Ralph and Valeria—admitted knowing anything about Toby's personal life. They both noted Toby planned to marry a woman he worked with, but his mother didn't approve of the union. Both claimed they only knew the woman's first name: Candy.

Ralph's taped comments were insightful. He said, "Toby is the typical well-functioning individual with Asperger's Syndrome—compulsively organized and focused. Anyone who *messes*—that's the word Toby uses—with his gear or routine will rile him. Two cavers quit our grotto three years ago because they couldn't work with Toby. His brother goads him into fights. For example, his brother spray-painted graffiti onto the walls of Sandia Man Cave as a joke." Ralph also provided the name of Toby's boss—a professor named Levine in the medical school.

Sara called Sanders's number again. She didn't get a busy signal, but she didn't get an answer either. She left a message.

***

"Dr. Levine, I'm so glad you could make time in your schedule for me to visit your lab."

Sara had arrived at the appointment early and walked by Levine's laboratory before coming to his office in a small complex of faculty offices at the intersection of two hallways. She'd observed three individuals either actively involved in bench activities or huddled over desks at the ends of the benches in his lab. No one was on either side of another bench. That coincided with data she'd gotten from university records. Irwin Levine was the principal investigator on an NIH grant "*Paenibacillus* as a source of new antibiotics." He was a co-investigator along with Toby Collins on contracts with the U.S. Geological Survey and U.S. Forest Service to survey microorganisms in caves. The grant and the contracts provided salaries for five employees.

Sara studied the professor as she entered his office. He was in his forties and appeared to be more athletic than most academics. She deemed him to be attractive even though his dark hair was now a fringe around his skull.

She extended her hand. "I'm Sara Almquist. As I explained on the phone, the FBI is investigating a murder near Sandia Man Cave. We suspect it might be Toby Collins."

Sara was surprised that Levine didn't gasp at the mention of Toby' name or express any sadness. Instead, he said, "I thought I recognized your name. After your call, I checked you out online. Your work as an epidemiologist is first class. How did the FBI convince you to consult on this case?"

His smile seemed sincere, and Sara suspected he would be talkative if she encouraged him. "I live near Albuquerque and enjoy consulting."

"I'm sure we could find a faculty position for you at UNM."

"I was faculty member for years at Michigan State and enjoy my freedom now."

"The bureaucracy got you."

Sara was eager to turn the focus from herself to the victim. She shrugged. "Bureaucracy is a thorn to all scientists until they need salaries and funding for their research."

He nodded and sighed.

"Tell me about what Toby did in your lab."

"Toby was officially a lab tech. He performed routine analyses on microorganisms—both bacteria and molds—for their antimicrobial properties."

Something didn't jive. Sara was sure Toby had been listed in the university records as a co-investigator on two contracts. "If he was only doing routine analyses, why did you allow him to be named a co-investigator on two of your contracts?"

Levine's lip trembled and his neck and face reddened slightly. "I see you checked details with our VP of Research. You should have told me."

Sara thought that was a strange response. "That's why the FBI uses scientific consultants. We try to be thorough."

Levine's lip no longer trembled, but his neck still was red. "It's a long story. Toby's father, Jacob, was an affiliate faculty member in the med school. After he'd been caving with Toby for several years, Jacob recognized that caves could be the source of many unique microorganisms. He encouraged Toby to earn a degree at the university in biology with an emphasis in microbiology. Jacob and I got contracts from the geological survey and forestry service for identifying microorganisms— both bacteria and molds—in caves. We focused on the Fort Stanton Cave because spelunkers were convinced its newly discovered passages would be a rich source of unique organisms. In time, Toby took over from his father on the contracts."

"Did Jacob have a real interest in caves or was he trying to find a niche for his son?"

Levine cocked his head. "You must have talked to Mrs. Collins." He paused.

Sara tried not to convey clues and kept her face still.

"Good poker player, too." He shrugged. "I think Jacob was trying to protect Toby from Lydia and Ben. By the time Toby was thirteen, it was apparent Toby was bright but would never be the acceptable to Lydia and her friends."

"Why do you say that?"

"Toby is—I guess was—not socially adept. He didn't talk a lot and had limited interests. Lydia considers herself a socialite as a member of an early pioneering family."

"Okay." Sara frowned. "What did Jacob say about Lydia? I want to understand your earlier comments."

"Not much. His comments were always the same. 'Lydia was so sweet when I met her, but she changed when Toby was diagnosed.' And his explanation for everything he did with Toby was 'Lydia will see that she and Ben do well.'"

"Okay, what did Jacob say about Ben?"

"Jacob took Ben, as well as Toby, caving for a while. That ended quickly. I don't know why. After that, Jacob occasionally commented on Ben's progress through medical school and residency. He sadly noted that Ben's wife was more of a southern belle than Lydia. That's about it."

Sara scanned her notes. She wasn't satisfied with Levine's answers regarding how Toby became a co-investigator on two contracts. She thought it strange that Levine's comments on Toby's family had been more expansive than those on his research. She tried to sound casual as she reintroduced her initial question. "I'm still confused. What did Toby do to deserve being a co-investigator on two contracts?"

Levine's upper lip trembled again. He stood, opened a file drawer, and handed two files to Sara, "He had control of the sources of several interesting microorganisms."

Sara thumbed through the first file. It was a proposal to the U.S. Geological Survey and involved identification and characterization of bacteria and molds in the Fort Stanton

Cave. Nothing she saw clarified Levine's answer. "What do you mean?"

"It will be apparent when you look at the second file." Levine shifted in his chair. "About twenty years ago—when Toby was teenager—Sandia Man Cave was in sorry shape. Spray-painted graffiti hid the petroglyphs. Litter all over. Jacob made a deal with the U S. Forest Service and convinced the Sandia Grotto cavers to take on the project of saving the cave. Jacob and Toby led the efforts to cleanup the cave about fifteen years ago and maintained it ever since."

Sara browsed the proposal as Levine spoke. "Okay, I see Toby's foci are cave conservation and reclamation."

"Yes, fifteen years ago he did an independent research project as an undergraduate in my lab. By then, Jacob and I already had a contract to study microorganisms in the deep recesses of the Fort Stanton Cave." He looked at the ceiling. "Toby was too awkward to spelunk in the Fort Stanton Cave, but Jacob had strong ties with those controlling the exploration of the cave."

Sara figured a smile was enough to encourage Levine to continue. She wondered why he used the term spelunk because the cavers at the grotto meeting hadn't used the term. Now wasn't the time for that question. Levine was on a roll.

"I don't know how, but Toby and Jacob, with the help of an experienced spelunker in the U.S. Forest Service, gained access to a remote section of the Sandia Man Cave."

Sara straightened in her chair. *What remote section?* She thought she'd seen the whole cave. The two forest rangers didn't mention a remote section. Sara tried not to show her surprise and nodded as Levine continued.

"Toby quickly identified bacteria with antimicrobial properties on the walls of the remote area. Jacob convinced the forest service to keep the remote area in Sandia Man Cave a secret because it was a perfect uncontaminated—but easy to reach—source of cave bacteria and molds."

Sara hated to admit how poor her inspection of the cave had been. "Have many people have seen this remote area of Sandia Man Cave?"

Levine licked his lips. "Only Jacob, Toby, a senior ranger—I don't even know his name—and Candy. I've seen pictures, but Jacob and Toby never told me how to access the area."

Sara tried hard not to smile. Jacob might have been a nice man, but he had taught Toby how to be a shrewd entrepreneur. "What makes the remote area so special?"

"Jacob and Toby hypothesized that most caves in New Mexico harbored potentially valuable bacteria if you could get into areas with little—or at least controlled—human traffic."

"What constitutes valuable bacteria?"

"Any that have antimicrobial properties towards other bacteria."

"Back to my earlier question. What makes Sandia Man Cave unique?"

"Toby hypothesized that after the caves were cleaned properly, useful bacteria would again grow on the walls. His last contract was to determine how long it took one wall in the remote section of Sandia Man Cave, which had been cleaned, to regenerate and harbor the bacteria found on the other walls in the remote area of the cave."

Sara noticed that Levine spoke faster as he talked about his and Toby's work. "It sounds like exciting stuff."

"We thought so."

One thing still bugged her. She decided to blurt out the question. "Weren't you worried when Toby didn't come to work during the last two weeks?"

Levine looked surprised. "Well no. He was on his honeymoon."

Sara lost her cool. "Are you kidding?"

"No. He got married on a Monday." Levine checked his calendar. "It was April tenth at the Central Methodist Church. I was Toby's best man. Ralph Edwards stood up for Candy. Neither Toby's mother nor brother attended." He shrugged. "I doubt they were invited."

"How about her parents?"

"Her mother raised her alone and died two years ago. Candy has no siblings."

The wedding sounded pathetic. Sara readjusted her thinking. "Don't you think it strange that Candy didn't report him missing?"

Levine leaned back in his chair and closed his eyes. "Are you sure she's not missing, too?"

Sara straightened. This case had taken another twist. Before she contacted Jack, she needed to see how Levine answered a question for which she already knew the answer. "How did Candy function in your lab?"

"She was good at culturing finicky bacteria." He shrugged. "Many of the bacteria from caves are difficult to culture in the lab."

He'd evaded the question. Sara tried again. "What was her title?"

"She was a graduate student." As Sara stared at him, he added, "Officially, she is a dissertator and should be completing her dissertation this summer." He shrugged. "But I doubt she will."

"Do you have her phone number and address? We need to talk to her."

He rummaged in a file drawer and handed her a card before she finished the question. "Here's her contact information."

Sara grabbed the card and stood. "I'll be right back." She rushed from the room and called Jack. The medical examiner had estimated Toby had been killed between the seventh to the fourteenth of April. Levine's comments—if they were to be believed—had shortened the period to four days—the eleventh through the fourteenth of April.

***

As soon as Sara returned to Levine's office, he said, "Candy might not be at the address I gave you. She wanted to move in with Toby. I think his condo was nicer than her apartment."

"My partner found only men's clothes in the closet in Toby's condo." She didn't add Jack had found several pieces of women's underwear in a bureau drawer in the bedroom. "Seems strange that she didn't move in after the wedding. Don't you think?"

Levine coughed. "You didn't know Toby. He kept his lab bench orderly and became irate if anyone messed with anything on the bench. He probably wouldn't let her move in. Candy said that Toby couldn't understand why she spread papers out on the floor of her apartment as she wrote the review of literature for her dissertation."

Sara frowned. "Candy's system sounds antiquated but logical. I sorted reference papers on the floor of my office when I was writing reviews, but most of my grad students sorted everything electronically."

"You're showing your age." Levine laughed. "Toby was like your grad students. Candy was a hybrid. She electronically sorted reference papers on the computer when she wrote research manuscripts for journals but spread papers out on the floor as she wrote the review of literature for her dissertation because she had hundreds of references. Hence, she worked at home much of the last month."

Sara again thought Levine was purposefully withholding info. "So, when was the last time you saw Candy?"

"At her wedding." His face twisted a bit. "She called the day after and said she'd have a draft of her review of literature to me this week. I was surprised because I expected her to have other interests on her honeymoon. When I asked, she replied, 'Toby needs some time out.'" He shook his head. "I didn't ask; I guess I should have."

CHAPTER 7: Nothing Goes as Planned

Sara guessed that Candy would need some comforting, and no one was better at the task than Bug. After she left Levine's office, she picked up Bug from her office and headed for Candy's apartment on Montgomery Boulevard.

When she neared the Donut Mart on Montgomery, she decided many people craved sweets when they were upset. Besides, she'd missed lunch and was hungry. She bet Jack was too. Winslow was always hungry. She pulled into the lane for curbside pickup.

Today was her lucky day. No one was waiting in line. She pulled up to the window. Seeing no one, she leaned over to get her wallet out of her purse. She heard a crashing noise and looked back at the window. A man was pointing a gun at a clerk.

Sara pushed the gas pedal and tore forward to the rear exit of the parking lot. She punched 9-1-1 on her phone and shouted, "Armed robbery at Donut Mart on Montgomery!"

She looked around and realized her mistake. A black sedan was careening toward her. She was in its way.

She dropped the phone and pulled left onto the sidewalk, but not fast enough. The black sedan grazed the right rear of her Subaru SUV. Bug, who never barked, emitted a series of high-pitched yips. The sedan kept going. She focused enough to get the first five letters and numbers of the six on the license plate of the fleeing car.

She wrote the numbers down and undid the seat belt around Bug's carrier. He jumped into her arms. As she hugged him, she assessed the situation. She'd been lucky—she and Bug were okay. She hoped the same was true for those in the Donut Mart.

She thought she smelled gas, grabbed her purse, and climbed from the car with Bug still in her arms. She avoided stepping on the splintered red plastic from her taillight as she surveyed the damage. There was a dent on her right bumper and the right taillight was a bare bulb, but she decided the smell of gas had been her imagination. She thought it best not to try to open the SUV's tail gate because it might not close easily.

She ran toward the shop as she heard sirens. No one had emerged from inside. She lowered Bug to the ground as two patrol cars swung into the lot. She knew the policeman were apt to shoot if she moved quickly or tried to extract anything from her purse. She hoped no one was bleeding inside, but thought it unwise to rush in. The Albuquerque Police had a reputation for shooting first and asking questions later.

Two officers jumped from the car with their guns pointed at Sara. They shouted, "Hands up."

She lifted her arms. The left arm hurt, and she wished she'd worn the sling today.

"Higher." One officer focused his gun on her as the other opened the front door of the shop.

"I can't. It's injured." She thought if she mentioned it was injured when she was shot in Brazil, it would raise their suspicions. "I was the one who called from the drive-through. My car is in back. The get-away car hit it as it left through the parking lot and went into the Walgreen's lot."

The officer continued to wave his gun at her.

"I got their license plate number—well most of it. I work for the FBI. Do you want to see my ID?"

"Stand still."

The other officer yelled, "A man inside was shot."

"I could apply a tourniquet to an arm or leg."

The officer with the gun pointed at Sara lowered it slightly. "Be careful as you show me your ID and tell me the license number of the car."

He studied her ID card carefully and called to the other officer. "She's okay. Let her see the victims. I'll phone in the license number." He shook his head and stared at Sara. "Are you sure you don't know the last number?"

"It was a letter."

Bug resisted when she stepped forward. She scooped him up and entered the shop. The waiting area at the front of the shop looked normal.

Then she stepped to the counter. A teen-aged girl sat on the floor next to the body of a man. Blood pooled on the floor.

The police officer now in the back shouted, "There are two locked in the storage closet. It's padlocked."

Sara heard a gunshot. She suspected the padlock was no longer a problem. Sara tied Bug's leash to a chair. As she went around the counter, she asked the girl. "Are you wounded? Can you stand?"

"Not sure."

Sara grabbed the girl's arm to pull her up. The girl moaned but managed to stand and stagger away. Sara felt the man's neck but couldn't find a pulse. She decided she couldn't help him and guided the girl to the front as EMTs rolled a stretcher in. "The man behind the counter hasn't moved."

The EMTs began to work on the man. Sara looked at the teen. "Are you okay?"

The girl started to choke and then vomited on the floor.

Sara collected a handful of paper napkins from the counter and opened a bottle of water from the shop's self-service beverage center. She placed the napkins and bottle on the table next to the girl. As the girl cleaned herself up, Sara called Carbonne's office and left a message.

New officers arrived. They quickly ascertained that Sara had nothing to add because she couldn't describe the robbers. Their next question was less than friendly. "Why didn't you try to stop the robbery?" Sara explained she was scientist who consulted for the FBI, not an agent and seldom carried a gun. They didn't believe her and searched her purse and car and didn't find a gun. They still didn't believe her and called the FBI switch board. After a short discussion with Carbonne, a police officer announced she could leave once he logged in the damage to her car.

She took pictures of her car, called her insurance agent, and waited for the police to log in the damage to her car. Sara thought the wait was excessive. The officer didn't write the report on the damage to her car until all the employees at Donut Mart and the other police officers had left.

***

Jack greeted Sara at the door to Candy Lopez's apartment two hours after she left Dr. Levine's lab. He winked and said, "Where's the donuts? Carbonne said you were bringing donuts." He reached down to touch Bug's ear. "The pup looks more ready to work than you do."

J. L. Greger

Bug wagged his tail and marched into the apartment.

"I won't bore you with my problems. I'm sure Carbonne said enough. To cap it off, the police at the Donut Mart wouldn't let me take a dozen donuts if I left ten dollars."

"No wonder they didn't trust you. A dozen donuts cost more than ten." Jack low voice rumbled into a deep laugh. "You know Carbonne worries about you. He was ready to personally come down to the Donut Mart and rescue you."

"I know. Those police were convinced I was in on the robbery. They didn't even apologize when they captured the get-away car because I gave them the license number. Strange."

Jack nodded. I'll tell you something stranger." He whispered, "Candy's story has lots of holes, but I believe she didn't harm Toby." He massaged his head. "I think Mrs. Collins biased my thinking. Anything that contradicts Mrs. Collins's statements seems logical." He grinned. "I sent Winslow back to his lab. I could leave, too."

"Don't even think about leaving." Sara placed a hand on his shoulder and pushed him toward the table past piles of papers and books on the floor. "You're in charge here. What do you want me to do?"

He whispered. "Get Candy to trust you as a woman and a scientist. Winslow and I found nothing to indicate strife between Toby and Candy." He shrugged. "Actually, we found little to suggest Toby was here much."

The woman sitting at the table in the sparsely furnished apartment fit Levine's description more than Mrs. Collins's portrayal of Candy Lopez. She had muscular shoulders, but not "manly" ones as Mrs. Collins had said. Her nose was aquiline, not "horsy." Her dark hair pulled back in a ponytail was neat, not as "dirty as a nag's tail." She looked about thirty-five and wasn't "haggard." However, the woman's eyes were red, and her eyelids were swollen.

Bug marched up to Candy and brushed against her leg. Sara extended a hand to Candy. "I'm Sara Almquist. I hate to bother you with more questions but Jack..." Sara pointed at the agent. "He doesn't understand why you didn't report Toby missing. Most grooms don't disappear the day after their wedding."

Candy's eyes widened. "I told him. We both needed more space. I'm under a time deadline. My funding runs out at the end of the month. Toby felt his father would want him to... mend bridges with his brother, even if that was impossible with his mother."

Sara sat down and started the recorder on her phone. "I had a long talk with Dr. Levine. He tells me that you're almost through with your dissertation." It wasn't exactly what Levine had said, but it was close enough. "You've got two manuscripts published and two more submitted. He said you planned to submit a draft of your review of literature to him this week. Then you only have to write a summation with a discussion of future research for your dissertation. Is this how you would describe your situation?"

Candy waved her hand over the piles of papers and books. "You don't understand. I'm not sure I can finish the review this week. I can't concentrate. The summation chapter will be a challenge. It's like outlining a proposal for future research based on my work for the last five years. Then there's the papers I've submitted. What if they're rejected?"

Sara put a hand on Candy's shoulder. "I always found my graduate students were nervous, sometimes hysterical, as they finished their dissertations. There are so many unknowns. I bet you've grown close to Dr. Levine and the others in the lab and wonder if you'll be happy in your next position."

Candy stared at Sara. "Are you kidding? No one in the lab, besides Toby, cares whether I live or die. Why are you here?"

Sara thought there were several ways to interpret Candy's questions. She'd start with the most naïve response first and settled Bug on her lap. She hoped the action would make her appear motherly to Candy. Besides both she and Bug needed each other's company after their rough morning. "I used to be a professor of epidemiology at Michigan State. Now I consult. He..." Sara pointed at Jack. "...thought as a scientist I would understand your situation."

Jack leaned forward. "I have no idea what's in a dissertation. The longest paper I ever wrote was fifteen pages."

Candy blinked back tears.

Sara pulled a tissue from her purse. "Dr. Levine described you as a capable scientist."

"Did he add he doubted I could finish a dissertation?"

Sara avoided lying by not answering the question. "I'm sure with help, you can finish it."

Candy whimpered. "Yeah, sure."

Sara suspected Candy and Levine didn't have a good relationship. Now she needed to assess the bond between Toby and Candy. "I'll bet your tears are more about Toby than your dissertation. Did you two have an argument?"

"Toby had problems. As Toby's widow, I must solve his problems now."

Sara thought Candy's response was odd. She seemed more concerned about Toby's business problems than about Toby. She also seemed to have adjusted too easily to being a widow not a wife. Perhaps she could get more answers from Candy if she focused her on something pleasant. "You must have pictures from your wedding. May I see them?"

Candy shook her head. "We didn't hire a photographer. No one wanted pictures."

Sara stroked Candy's arm. "Well, are you framing your marriage certificate?"

Candy pulled her arm away. "No, I didn't keep a copy, but Toby kept three. He said, 'Our marriage certificate made me his heir.'"

Sara was surprised by the coldness of Candy's answer. "Why was it important?"

Candy stared at Sara. "Have you met Toby's mother? He didn't want his mother messing with his stuff."

Jack snickered.

Sara was uncertain how to proceed. "I don't understand. Besides his condo, what other property did Toby own?"

Candy closed her eyes. "Can't you stop with the questions? I've got things to do."

Jack snorted. "Candy, we'll leave once you answer our questions. You told me earlier that Toby had business obligations to his family. You mentioned the Collins Eye Associates several times but didn't explain how Toby functioned in the family business." He motioned Sara to join him in the kitchen alcove.

Jack placed his back toward Candy. "She said repeatedly that Toby felt it was urgent to solve these unnamed business problems immediately."

"Remember the empty file that Winslow found at Mrs. Collins's house. The one labeled the *Collins Family Trust*. I'll see if she knows anything."

As they returned to the table, Sara said, "Candy, we found an empty file labeled *Collins Family Trust* at Mrs. Collins's house. Did Toby ever mention it?"

Candy's eyes widened. "No." She bit her lip.

Sara doubted Candy's answer. "Okay, did Toby talk to a lawyer lately?"

"No."

"The lawyer might have been a friend of Jacob's. Ralph Edwards from the Sandia Grotto hinted Jacob had made financial arrangements for Toby."

"Why did you bother Ralph?" Candy rose and went to the bathroom.

Sara heard clattering noises. She stepped to the bathroom and saw Candy rummaging behind the mirror in the metal medicine cabinet.

Candy shrieked, "It's missing."

CHAPTER 8: Is Carbonne a Reluctant Groom?

Carbonne liked the Range Cafe. The food was good, and its Southwestern motif with lots of folk art was funky enough to appeal to him. He especially like the chandeliers made of barbed wire and the horns of longhorn steers. More importantly, Barbara liked the restaurant.

Barbara had been less grouchy lately. She'd been nauseated during most of the first trimester of her pregnancy. Then she'd been a field agent. The stress of insults from macho male agents and the fear of injuring the fetus had kept her tense. However, two months ago she'd been named the regional supervisor of FBI minority recruiting. She liked the job and seemed to think it was "more consistent with her Native American heritage." He wasn't sure what she meant by the statement, but he was smart—or cowardly depending on your perspective—enough not to ask.

Currently their biggest problem was setting a wedding date. After listening to endless lectures from her mother, Barbara thought they should marry before the baby was born. He agreed it would simplify life for the child, according to amniocentesis a girl. In truth, he had not planned to marry ever. He thought Sara and Sanders had the perfect relationship—a committed relationship mixing professional and personal interests. Barbara had pointed out she was twenty years younger than Sara, and she wanted children. Carbonne had noted Barbara had said children, not a child. He thought two children were too much, but again wisely—more like cowardly—had not argued. He figured a year from now Barbara would be too tired with a baby and a career to remember her original preference.

His thoughts were interrupted when the hostess led Barbara and him to a table. He was glad the hostess had agreed to seat them even though Sara hadn't arrived yet. At this stage of her pregnancy, Barbara tired easily. Tonight, there were gray shadows under Barbara's eyes and her voice was flat.

It wasn't like Sara to be late. Just before he left the office, Jack Drum had called Carbonne to complain. Jack hadn't complained about Sara per se, but he wanted more help with the case. Carbonne had laughed. "Don't be fooled by Sara's slow—sometimes tedious—interview style. You'll be amazed in a couple of days by how she weaves the seemingly insignificant details into a solid case. She'll tell me if you two need more help."

Carbonne suspected Jack might be right when he looked at his watch. Sara was a stickler for punctuality, and she was late. Perhaps, Bug was traumatized by the holdup at Donut Mart, but the little dog usually seemed oblivious to stress if Sara was nearby. More likely, Sanders wanted Sara's sympathy after the Senate hearings. He guessed Sanders's skills as an information specialist had been taxed to their limits in Brazil.

As Carbonne helped Barbara into her chair, he realized she'd asked him a question. He knew it was time to punt. "I don't know, Dear. What do you think?"

Barbara's dark eyes flashed annoyance. "I told you I think sooner is better."

She was beautiful when she was slightly annoyed. It made her eyes look blacker. Then they matched the color of her long hair. Carbonne decided to start the evening well. "Why don't we stop by the county clerk's office tomorrow at lunchtime and get a marriage license?"

Barbara mouth flew open.

Carbonne couldn't decide if he'd pleased her or made a mistake. He proceeded confidently anyway. "Aren't you leading a recruiting program at the Mercado High School tomorrow? We could meet at the Sandoval County Courthouse. It's not far from the high school. That clerk's office in Mercado is always calmer than the one in Albuquerque. When will you be finished with your recruiting program?"

"At last, a decision from you." Barbara paused. "Did Sara lecture you?"

"No. A marriage license is good for ninety days. I thought it might be good to have it on hand."

"That sounds like Sara's practical advice."

Carbonne didn't want to admit the truth and was thankful when he spied Sara at the entrance of the restaurant. He stood and waved his hand.

Sara rushed to the table. "Sorry I'm late" She pulled out a brightly colored turquoise and yellow chair and fell onto the chair. "I was on the phone with Sanders. The Senate hearing went well today, but he's facing one or two more days of hearings." She studied the menu.

"What does that mean?" Carbonne thought Sara owed him more of an explanation. It would also distract Barbara.

"Reason prevailed. They thought Sanders's use of violence in Manaus was unfortunate, but there was no other way to capture key drug leaders." She put down the menu. "I don't know why I look at the menu. I always order their chili rellenos. Barbara, what are you having?"

"Chile rellenos. I like the batter they use here. It's how my mother makes them."

***

Carbonne wished Sanders had been present as Sara encouraged Barbara to share her plans for the wedding. Another man might have helped him divert the discussion to something more interesting.

He hadn't realized how extensively Barbara and her mother had planned the event even though a date hadn't been set. They planned to hold the ceremony in the old mission church atop the mesa at Acoma.

The adobe church had been built in the early 1600s. The original—now mainly ceremonial—homes on the mesa dated back to the 1100s. Because the church and hilltop community were a national historic landmark, Carbonne suggested Barbara might not be able to get permission to use the church for the wedding.

Barbara had glared at him. "My family is a member of the pueblo. We can use it unless it's a feast day."

Barbara had assured him previously only her family members and his guests would be present at the wedding ceremony. He hadn't thought to ask about any other events associated with the wedding.

For example, Carbonne had not known Barbara's mother planned to invite everyone in the pueblo to the family's ceremonial home atop the mesa after the wedding. Barbara explained, "My mother and aunt will prepare the food in their homes in nearby McCarty the week before the wedding. The men will transport the food to the mesa on the morning of the wedding while the women finish decorating my family's ceremonial home and the church. The wedding will be around seven—at sunset. The feast will continue for hours."

Originally, Carbonne had been glad he and Barbara were meeting Sara at the Range Café on a Tuesday because there were no musicians on Tuesdays. As he listened to the plans for the wedding, he wished a blues or a country group were playing. The music would have drowned out some of the wedding planning. A rock group would be even better, but the Range Cafe was quiet on this night.

As Carbonne looked at Barbara's animated face, he realized he was being unfair to her. She was twenty-five and had a right to want a proper wedding. On the other hand, he was forty and didn't want to look like a necessary accessory at a large event. He cleared his throat. "I hate to interrupt, but I need to do a bit of business. Sara, Jack sounded discouraged when he called at five."

Sara looked surprised. "It's too early to be concerned until we talk to Toby's brother and the cavers who argued with Toby a year ago. We also need to determine whether someone stole a bottle of pills from Candy's apartment."

"Why?"

"Toby and Candy hid something, which Candy thinks is important, in a brown pharmaceutical vial." She shrugged. "That didn't seem logical, but I didn't pursue Candy's reasoning because Winslow may have collected the vial already." She sighed. "Then we can start worrying. Well, after we've exhausted leads that Winslow generates in the lab."

Carbonne shook his head. "You think the case is progressing logically?"

She shrugged. "Not great, but okay."

"Good. Anything more you can tell me about Sanders's activities?"

"The Senate Intelligence Committee is talking to Brazilian officials, U.S. embassy staff from Brazil, and three Americans arrested for participation in the Brazilian gangs tomorrow and maybe Thursday." She smiled. "So, Sanders should be here by Friday, if you need him as a best man."

                                                    J. L. Greger

Barbara reached across the table and grabbed Carbonne's hands. "We could get married this Saturday or Sunday. It would be a rush, but we could do it."

CHAPTER 9: Is Winslow Under-Appreciated?

Wednesday

Winslow felt a kinship with Toby Collins They were both young—although Toby was a bit older and in his early thirties—and they were both science geeks and outsiders. Winslow loved being able to use the cool equipment in the lab to explain what happened to the agents who strutted into the lab in tight pants. Those know-it-all agents were his father's age but still tried to act like studs. Almost funny.

Unfortunately, none of the guys he grew up with on the pueblo had ended up with a job like his. They thought he was bragging when he tried to talk about his work. The crew in the lab were nice but they were older and rushed home to their families at the end of their shift. Accordingly, Winslow spent much of his free time alone playing computer games. His search of Toby's home computer had shown that Toby was a gamer, too.

Now at seven a.m. on Wednesday morning, he was drinking a diet cola and organizing the data he'd collected. Sara would probably stop by in a couple of hours for an update. He didn't make a list of lab evidence in a case for most agents, but he did for Sara. He liked Sara. She appreciated the efforts off the lab crew, explained how she would use the data, and asked for suggestions. Most of the agents didn't.

Although Winslow felt a kinship to Toby, they differed in one way. Toby was disgustingly neat. There was nothing out of place in Toby's condo. Winslow knew his mother would cry with delight if he kept his apartment as neat. Mrs. Collins had trained Toby well. Of course, Toby's neatness could reflect his condition. Winslow had checked the web. Autistic individuals were prone to "pathological" neatness.

DNA from the victim in the morgue matched the DNA on the toothbrush in the condo and on the comb and T-shirt found in Toby's bedroom at Mrs. Collins's home. There was no doubt. Toby Collins was the victim.

On the crumpled page found under the bed in Toby's old bedroom at the Collins house, Winslow had found traces of three individuals' DNA. Toby was the source of one partial fingerprint and one spot of DNA. Mrs. Collins was the source of most of the prints and DNA. He hoped Ben, Toby's brother, would be the source of the other partial print and DNA. He texted Sara to remind her to collect DNA from Ben.

Winslow thought the most interesting item he'd found in Toby's bedroom in the Collin's house was a photo album. Mrs. Collins seemed to have no emotional attachment to it and said, "I tossed it on Toby's bed because his father made it for Toby and would want him to have it. If Toby is dead, the FBI can have it." Winslow had noted lots of family photos with Toby as a little boy—prekindergarten—were in the album. After that, all but two of the pictures were of Toby alone, with his father, or in groups of mainly men. Most of the latter photos were at entrances of caves. Winslow wondered who had taken those shots. He doubted Mrs. Collins was the photographer.

A face had been blacked out with a pen or a permanent marker in several of the later pictures. Winslow wondered who had blacked out the faces and why. He'd already checked and learned he could remove ballpoint pen marks with vegetable oil, black highlighter with water, and permanent laundry marker with nail polish remover. He thought Sara would want him to try but knew the process would be laborious. If he failed, the photo would be destroyed.

Winslow had also scanned several of the photos using facial recognition technology. The problem was the comparison data bases were mainly for those who had been charged with crimes, had been in military, or were employed by various federal and state agencies. Most of the individuals in the photos were not in the federal data bases. Winslow suspected Sara or Jack might recognize several in the photos now that they'd interviewed many of the cavers.

Winslow whistled as he scanned the files, he'd copied from Toby's home computer. They were a gold mine and were all well labeled and grouped logically. Thank goodness for Toby's autism.

Toby had kept detailed records on the Sandia Man Cave for the last fifteen years. His records included what had been done and who from the Sandia Grotto group had participated in the cleanup of the cave every month. Much of the removal of graffiti and litter had been done by Toby and his father. Candy Lopez's name appeared in the log at least six times during the last year.

Besides the monthly log, Toby had kept a file of correspondence with those who had worked on the cave. Two of the emails from a year before were to Joe DeLuca and Ed Sanchez. In these emails, Toby berated the men for coming late to a cleanup and doing a poor job. A second email to them was dated a month later:

> *I notified the council of the Sandia Grotto*
> *that you were verbally abusive to me. You*
> *should not have tried to punch me. You will*
> *no longer be allowed in Sandia Man Cave.*

Winslow noted several cavers had been sent copies of the email. He put this email at the top of his list to show to Sara.

Winslow was not sure of the value of the family records on Toby's home computer. They included: a copy of Jacob Collins's will and documents on the creation of the Collins Eye Associates, Inc. Surprisingly, Toby had accessed the documents several times during the last month. Toby had also scanned his birth certificate, college diploma and notarized transcript, his marriage certificate, and other documents into his computer archives.

Winslow was starting to examine Toby's personal documents when the phone rang.

Jack Drum said, "I'd like to finish my interviews with the cavers today. Have you found the names of the cavers who fought with Toby?"

"Yep, I can also send you photos of those who worked in the cave during the last ten years. You might be able to identify individuals not currently on the Sandia Grotto membership lists."

"Darn. Nothing I want less than more names that lead nowhere. Give me the names of the two who fought with Toby. Ralph Edwards couldn't remember their names."

"Joe Deluca and Ed Sanchez. I'll send you two relevant emails. Anything else?"

"No. I'm in a hurry."

Winslow ignored Jack's last comment. He was proud that he and the medical examiner had identified the victim so quickly. "The lab evidence is clear. The victim is Toby Collins. The blue suit in the cave also belonged to Toby."

"Yeah." Jack disconnected.

Winslow was disappointed. Jack Drum wasn't much different than most of the agents. He considered it a waste of time to listen to details from the lab.

***

Winslow now turned his attention to the data he collected in Candy's apartment. He had not looked at them when he returned to the lab yesterday afternoon. He was too busy cataloguing the data from Toby's apartment and the Collins home.

Candy's apartment in general and the files on her computer were the opposite of Toby's—messy and disorganized. Almost as soon as Winslow had begun looking at the piles of journal reprints, photos, and casual notes on her apartment's floor yesterday, Candy had complained that he was delaying her progress in finishing her dissertation. They had reached a compromise. Winslow would copy files and emails on her computer. He could also browse the stack of materials on her floor, table, and other flat surfaces, but he would only collect those items not related to science. He quickly realized ninety percent of the stacked materials mentioned bacteria and molds found in caves. Most of the rest were brochures or magazine articles on caves. A few notes from Dr. Levine and several photos were interspersed in the piles.

Winslow had extracted the notes and photos as quickly as he could while Jack had tried to interview Candy for over an hour. Finally, Jack had suggested Winslow give up on the paperwork and check out the bedroom and bathroom.

The search had been easy. There was one tiny closet, a chest with four drawers, and a double bed with a single pillow in the bedroom. Candy's few clothes were hung in the closet or stuffed in the chest. There were no men's clothing anywhere. Winslow doubted Toby had spent much time in Candy's apartment.

The bathroom was primitive with a shower, toilet, and a small sink with a mirrored medicine cabinet above it. The medicine cabinet was crammed with toothpaste, bandages, gauze, tape, aspirin, a thermometer, over-the-counter ointments, and a large plastic vial containing partial sheets of blister packed pills.

Winslow had been carefully documenting all the products in the medicine cabinet when Jack yelled, "Stop wasting time. You'd better go to Levine's lab and download everything from her lab computer, too, especially any emails to or from Toby."

Winslow had suspected Candy was continuing to be less than cooperative. He grabbed the vial and stepped into the main room. "Candy, do you mind if I take thus vial from your medicine cabinet?"

She had glared at him. "Why not? The FBI doesn't seem to think I have any right to privacy."

Jack had added. "Stop wasting time."

***

Winslow pitied Candy as he looked at what he'd collected from her lab computer the day before. She was scraping by on a half-time research assistantship.

The records on her lab computer contained data or were drafts of manuscripts. Most of her emails were work-related and to her boss or others, including Toby, in the lab. There were occasional emails to Toby and members of the Sandia Grotto group on caving events. Winslow hadn't taken the time to search for deleted items on Candy's lab computer because a woman lab tech had watched him the whole time and complained he was upsetting the lab routines.

The data from Candy's home computer revealed more about Candy's life. Some of the details didn't make sense. First off, her computer was new. Winslow didn't see how she had gotten the funds for a MacBook Pro. He guessed Toby had given the computer to her. Second, he found more than a dozen letters of application for postdoctoral research and for temporary teaching positions in Colorado, New Mexico, and Arizona. In each letter, she'd inquired about the possibility of a position for a friend as a lab tech. Winslow assumed the friend was Toby and guessed the letters indicated Candy thought she was in a long-term relationship. Third, she had dozens of photos on her computer, most included Toby. She had five archived photos of a young and then teenage dark-haired girl with a woman. He assumed those photos were of Candy and her mother.

As Winslow scanned the emails on Candy's home computer, he realized Candy had been disappointed a lot during the last six months. Dr. Levine had informed her the half-time research assistantship in his lab would end on the first of June. She had received ten rejection notes but had been offered a nine-month teaching spot at Colorado State *only if* she could report to work by August first with her Ph.D. completed. The department head making the offer knew of no open position for a lab technician in his department.

Candy also had an extended discussion with a physician about an apparently chronic but unnamed condition. The physician had ordered her to monitor her temperature twice daily for months. His last email, dated four months previously, said surgery might be necessary if her status didn't change.

Sara stepped inside the lab. "I've got Bug with me. Can you be ready to show me what you've got in five minutes after I settle Bug in my office? I know you've positively identified the victim as Toby Collins. Congratulations" She didn't pause. "Jack told me that he'd follow up with the two cavers who argued with Toby."

***

"Show me what you've got."

"Here are the emails Toby sent to Joe DeLuca and Ed Sanchez. Doesn't seem enough to provoke a long-term grudge."

"Agreed, but Jack may be able to use them to learn more." She frowned. "Do we know anything about Toby's emotional state? Was he on any antianxiety or antidepression drugs? I think physicians often prescribe them to children with autism, but most adults avoid those drugs because of their side effects."

Winslow rummaged through his notes. "I found only one prescription bottle marked Prozac in the medicine chest in Toby's condo. I didn't collect the bottle because it was half-full and was dated ten years ago."

"Okay."

"I checked on the web. Prozac is a selective serotonin reuptake inhibitor used to treat depression, panic attacks, and obsessive-compulsive disorder."

"Good. You saved me work. It sounds like a logical prescription for an adult with autism. I bet it produces side effects. So, Toby didn't continue to take it." She marked out a point on a list marked *To Do* at the top. "Did Toby's emails suggest emotional behavior?"

"The most emotional notes were the emails to the two cavers, but you've seen them already. They're statements of facts. I'll bet the guys who got those emails laughed and called Toby a control freak."

Sara closed her eyes. "Maybe that's why he was killed. He drove someone crazy by trying to control every detail of his and their lives. What else do you have?"

"Look at Toby's photo album—you know the one I found in the Collins house. I don't know whether Toby or his mother blacked out several of the faces. I did some checking; I think I might be able to remove the blackouts without destroying the photos."

Sara tapped her finger on one of the photos. "You're betting Toby must have been annoyed with the person if he blacked out their face. If Mrs. Collins blacked out the faces, it indicates her pettiness. Either way we need to talk to the person. I think we've got to try to uncover what's behind the blackouts." She took a sip of diet cola and began to finger another pile of photos. "What about these pictures? Where did they come from?"

"From Candy's apartment."

"Several of these looks like those in the album—shots of groups of cavers. Maybe you can determine whose face was blackened out by elimination. Not much of an idea but it might save you hours of work trying to remove the blackout ink on Toby's photos." She stood and began to pace. "Ralph thought Toby had fought with his brother last month. Evidently, Ben had showed up at the monthly clean-up at the Sandia Man Cave. Did you find any mention of the argument or who was present?"

"That's strange. I thought Toby's notes on the monthly cleanup were complete. I don't remember seeing any mention

J. L. Greger

of Ben." He pounded on the computer. A document labeled Sandia Man Cave appeared. Winslow scrolled through it until he reached the last entry. "Candy, Valeria Perez, and Gabe Marcus helped Toby clean up the cave on April seventh."

Sara ran her finger along the date. "That would have been less than a week before he is believed to have been killed. Toby described the work as removal of new graffiti and trash. Could he or someone with access to his computer removed further comments?"

"Don't know. I didn't retrieve the deleted records on Toby's home or lab computers." A photo appeared on the screen. "Toby included this photo in his report. It looks like at least three water bottles and a banana peel were left in the cave, along with some spray-painted graffiti."

"Can you enlarge the graffiti so I can read it?"

Winslow tried to enlarge the orange writing on the cave wall, but the letters were still unclear. "I'll try a few tricks later. I think one of the words is *Tob* something."

Sara nodded. "Could be Toby. If so, someone was taunting him." She stared at the enlargement. "Candy didn't mention witnessing a fight or even a problem at the cave." She grimaced. "We really haven't gotten her cooperation. Did you find anything I could use on her computers or in her apartment?"

"Maybe. Candy Lopez had financial problems, but she had a new MacBook Pro."

"You wonder how she got the computer?"

"Yep, I sent you an email a couple of minutes ago outlining other documents I found on her home computer."

Sara pulled up the memo her laptop. She said "Interesting," twice while she read the email from Winslow. "This will help me get answers from Candy. Your notes explain why she's so panicked. She'll have a hard time completing her dissertation, getting it approved by Levine, taking her oral exam, and moving to Colorado Springs by August first. Have you completed your inventory of items from Candy's apartment?"

"Yep." Winslow sorted through the pile. "Oh wait, I took a bottle of pills in the medicine cabinet. Jack didn't give me time to study it."

"Let me see them." Sara put on gloves and pulled the pills in a blister pack and then the folded medical explanation for use of the pills from the plastic vial. As she unfolded the sheet, a one-inch square card fell to the counter.

Winslow grabbed the card. "There's a phone number on the card."

Sara studied the sheet. "This makes sense. I think Candy was trying to get pregnant. You'll have to have someone in the lab analyze the pills, but the medical data sheet is for Clomid, a medication that induces ovulation and help women get pregnant. It's common for women to take their temperature daily to determine their ovulation cycle when they're trying to get pregnant. I'll bet this is the number of her gynecologist."

CHAPTER 10: Will Jack Learn New Tricks?

Jack suspected he was on thin ice. Everyone knew Carbonne's and Sara's relationship extended beyond their work roles. He didn't care. "I've been used. While I was following up on useless leads, Sara and Winslow tracked down the best ones in the Toby Collins case."

Carbonne looked up from his computer screen. "Sit down and tell me what happened."

"This morning Winslow gave me the names of the two cavers who argued with Toby. I found them at work; they're both trainers at Defined Fitness. I talked to the two men separately. They laughed about their spat with Toby a year ago. Both said Toby was a 'geek and control freak' who'd blown a 'playful shove' into something big. They claimed they joined the Sandia Grotto for adventure, 'not to be a maid for a minor cave with a phony history.'""Do you know what they meant by a 'phony history?'"

"I do now, but it's not worth discussing."

"Better put a few details in your notes. Did you believe them?"

"Yes. They also had alibis on the Tuesday, Wednesday, and Thursday of the week Toby was killed. They were in the Fort Stanton Cave."

"While you were busy with the cavers, what were Winslow and Sara doing?"

Jack felt uncomfortable. Carbonne had offered him no sympathy, but Jack answered anyway, "They sorted the junk Winslow collected yesterday. Then Sara got search warrants, so Winslow could confiscate more junk—the computers that Toby and Candy used in Levine's lab and Toby's computer from his condo It seems he forgot to extract the deleted files yesterday."

Carbonne drummed his fingers on his desk. "What are Sara and Winslow doing now?"

"Sara is looking at pictures to see if she can determine whose faces were blacked out in several photos, while Winslow wastes time trying to erase the blackouts from other photos with chemicals."

"You didn't want to help?"

"Come on, man. I'm an agent not a tech." Jack became more nervous when Carbonne smiled like a Cheshire cat.

"You think you drew the short straw because you pursued potential suspects who proved to be duds. Meanwhile, Sara attended to picky details and may now be onto something important." He pointed to his screen. "Sara has emailed me you're both interviewing Candy—your prime suspect now—today. Right?"

"We're waiting for a lawyer from the public defender's office to arrive. I brought Candy here after Sara and Winslow proved Candy lied repeatedly yesterday."

Carbonne coughed. "Sounds to me like you learned an important lesson. Take time to listen to those in the lab—even if much of what they say bores you." Carbonne stood and walked to his door. "I recorded our conversation and sent it to your phone. Listen to it. I think your own words will prove to you that Sara didn't trick you."

Jack felt like a fool, but he tried to keep his lips from quivering as he walked to the door.

"Don't be upset with yourself. You'll gain patience to attend to details with time. Although not as much as Sara has. She's anal. Learn from her and let her spoil you. The past director of this office and I enjoyed working with her because she usually supplied us with details before we knew we needed them. You might as well enjoy that luxury, too. I guarantee you'll never have another partner who anticipates the needs of fellow investigators so well."

Carbonne frowned. "Managing Sara can be hard." He shrugged. "Always hand her a diet cola at the start of a conversation. It slows her down. Accept your innate disadvantages. She can think and talk faster but also recognize your innate advantages. You can run faster, shoot better, and can flirt with women. This means you can play the 'good cop' after Sara has nagged suspects like their mothers, or you can be the 'bad—tough cop' and let her play motherly." Carbonne opened the door and pushed Jack out. "I do the latter because I'm not as handsome as you."

***

Jack handed a can of diet cola to Sara, "The public defender lawyer called and should be here in thirty minutes. Can I help you with the photos?"

Sara's lower jaw dropped. "It's tedious work, but I think I identified two photos of the same scene. To be honest, these shots of people standing in Sandia Man Cave are boring. If I'm right, it looks as if the face blacked out was Candy's."

"Mrs. Collins probably did it. She dislikes Candy."

"Or Toby could have done it. If so, it means Toby's and Candy's relationship went through a rocky patch."

"Or was over. Most men would have been annoyed if they thought their girlfriend was trying to trap them by getting pregnant."

Sara pulled the bag with the small card from a pile beside her computer. "I thought so until we found this card with Toby's handwriting and prints, but not Candy's prints, in a vial with her Clomid medication. I called the number and expected to reach her gynecologist. I didn't. I reached a lawyer."

"What did he do for Toby?"

"I don't know. The lawyer—Aaron Broder—refused to answer any questions. Attorney-client privilege. So, we must find Toby's will. Toby's heir can grant Broder permission to answer our questions. Without a will, we're at Mrs. Collins's mercy—at least if the marriage isn't valid. Why don't you go through the business records on Toby's computer. I think Winslow said Toby had copies of his birth certificate, diploma, and marriage license. Surely, he kept a copy of his will—if he had one."

***

Jack looked through a mirror into the small conference room. The public defender looked as if she was too young to have graduated from law school. Candy must have thought the same thing because she was lecturing the public defender. He might learn something important if he turned on the microphone to listen to their conversation.

Sara shook her head when he touched the switch. "We don't want a judge to dismiss evidence we gain because of her lawyer's incompetence. An experienced defender would have refused to use this conference room. They all know it's wired for sound." She picked up a pile of papers. "I'll take the lead and be the bad cop. Then you can be Prince Charming."

Sara spoke as she strode into the conference room. "Candy, there's something about your marriage that doesn't make sense to us." She shook her head. "Actually, there's a lot that doesn't make sense."

Candy groaned. "Boomer, you don't get it. It worked for us."

Sara didn't seem annoyed. Jack wondered if Sara even knew she'd been insulted as she slid two photos toward Candy. "Are you sure it worked for Toby? Why did he blackout your face on this photo?"

The young lawyer gasped. Candy rubbed the black spot. "You don't know it was my face covered."

"Yes, we do. This is a photo we got from you. Sara pushed another photo across the table. "You can see the photo is the same, but your face is showing."

Candy looked at the photos. "They could have been taken at different times. Toby's pictures of cavers at the Sandia Man Cave all look similar."

"I matched the clothing worn by you and others in the photos. They were taken on the same day." She pushed two other pictures toward Candy. "Here is another pair of photos. Your photo is undamaged. Your face is obliterated in the one from Toby's album. Why? I think Toby was angry with you."

Candy fingered her ponytail. "You don't understand what being around Toby was like. It was easy to anger him. Then he could be childish."

"What did you do to anger Toby?"

"Who knows?"

"If you answered our questions, we might sympathize with you. We've met your mother-in-law. We also know you were trying to get pregnant. That can be a frustrating experience for a woman over thirty-five."

"You had no right..."

"Cool it. We had a search warrant. We found Clomid pills in your medicine chest and your computer record of your daily temperatures."

"It's none of your business." She turned to her lawyer. "Aren't you supposed to help me?"

The lawyer whispered to Candy but said nothing Jack could hear.

Sara frowned. "Do you realize that you are currently our chief suspect in the murder of Toby Collins. It's time for you to share everything with us about Toby's mother, brother, fellow cavers, and co-workers." Sara kicked Jack under the table.

Jack guessed that was his clue to be the good cop. "Look, I can see you were under tremendous pressure. I saw the fourteen job application letters on your computer. I know Levine was ending your paltry half-time research assistantship on June first. I didn't find any evidence that Toby was trying to find a job and go with you to Colorado. Seems to me like he was being a jerk."

Candy stared at him, and tears flowed down her cheeks. "You've got it wrong. Toby loved me—or at least wanted to have a child with me, but he couldn't stand the thought of leaving his condo or the Sandia Man Cave. Those two places reminded him of his father, the one person he truly loved and trusted."

Sara gave Candy no sympathy. "Did you argue?"

"Toby didn't argue. He just stopped talking. His mother's nagging always made everything worse. Sometimes, he was silent for days after she ragged on him."

"So, did you know he'd blackened your face out of the photos?" Sara tapped the photos.

"Yes, he did it months ago. We started trying to get pregnant when his dad was ill, more than a year ago. Jacob had pointed out to Toby there was a way to break the family trust agreement. Toby was angry when I didn't become pregnant immediately. He didn't understand. When he finally understood I might be too old, he was angry. He blackened my face out of his photos. I went to a gynecologist, and he prescribed Clomid."

"Did Toby see other women then?"

"Yes. I begged him to give me a chance to see if the medication worked."

Jack leaned forward. "You must have been angry. He was treating you like..."

"A brood mare." Candy shrugged. "Look I'm thirty-five, have no family, am no beauty, and am about to earn a Ph.D. in a field with limited employment possibilities. Toby was rich—

or would be if his plans worked. I couldn't afford to be angry. Besides, I was fond of him, I guess."

Sara pulled the photos back. "When did you tell Toby you were pregnant? I'd guess a week before the wedding."

Candy shook her head. "Toby was too suspicious to accept a statement from me. He went to the gynecologist with me. When I was about five months pregnant, I had amniocentesis. It's a boy. Toby was thrilled and arranged our marriage for the next week."

"That's why you worked at home during the last month. You were starting to show. We need the name of your gynecologist."

Jack said softly. "Also, there's the matter of your lies. Yesterday, you said you didn't know if Toby had seen a lawyer. We found a card in your bottle of Clomid pills. Obviously, you knew Toby had a lawyer. Was it Aaron Broder?"

Candy flushed. "You confused me yesterday. I wasn't ready to talk about my pregnancy. I could see my life turning out like my mother's—struggling to raise a child by myself. I was confused, and you kept asking silly questions."

The public defender whispered in Candy's ear and then stated, "My client was upset and didn't understand your questions."

"Candy has a motive and has knowledge of the murder site at Sandia Man Cave. If Jack and I interpreted Jacob's will and the family trust contract correctly, she didn't need Toby once she was married and pregnant."

Candy screamed, "No!"

CHAPTER 11: Jack Finds Working with Sara Is Difficult

Thursday

Sara ran up to the door as Jack rang the buzzer at the locked front entrance of Collins Eye Associates. Jack growled, "I thought you said Ben requested we appear at his office at seven this morning."

"He did because he wanted us out before his clients and most of his staff appeared." She texted Ben Collins. "I saw a couple of cars parked behind the building. Let's check the back entrance. Maybe it's unlocked" Her phone pinged, and she read the text. "Oh."

Jack went into a fake drawl. "The Masta wants us at the back servants' door."

"Yes. I don't think this will be a pleasant interview."

"You think." Jack chuckled and trotted to the rear exit, forcing Sara to run to keep up with him."

The man at the back door wore a white lab coat. His facial features—aquiline nose, blue eyes, and receding chin—looked like those of Toby in pictures. However, this man appeared to be thirty pounds heavier than Toby and was bald.

Sara extended her hand. "Dr. Collins, thank you for making time to see us."

Ben Collins turned away. "We can talk after we're in my office."

Jack whispered in Sara's ear. "Bet the brothers didn't get along."

Ben closed the door to his office as soon as Jack and Sara entered. "My brother was a black sheep. I don't want to give the staff more to gossip about." He picked up a page from the inbox on his mammoth black desk. Jack started to sit in a chair in front of the desk.

Sara walked to a small side table. "We want a friendly conversation with you about your brother and his problems. Why don't we sit here?"

Ben snorted. "If you insist. I don't want to waste a lot of time."

Jack let Ben rush past him to the table and then gave Sara the high sign. She immediately pasted on a broad smile, but it didn't change Ben's tense expression. "What was it like having Toby as big brother? Were you pals as boys?"

"Toby wouldn't talk and threw tantrums when he didn't get what he wanted." Ben chewed his lip. "Toby was never a pal with anyone."

Jack thought, *Looks like Sara's pleasant exchange of memories failed.* He wondered what Sara would try next.

She persisted in trying to paint a rosy picture of the Collins family. "Your father spent a lot of time with Toby. He must have enjoyed Toby's company."

"My father's every action regarding Toby was due to guilt. Toby ruined my parents' marriage and turned my mother into alcoholic."

"She seemed sober when we spoke to her."

Jack nodded in agreement.

"She drinks in the evening. It's the only way she can sleep."

Sara smile faded. Jack knew she was ready to start asking hard questions. "When was the last time, you saw your bother?"

"I don't remember. Does it matter?" Ben started to stand.

"Sit down." Jack spoke firmly. "Our time is valuable too."

Ben sniffed but sat down. "Probably a couple of months ago at Mother's house"

Jack decided to bluff a bit. "Funny we have witnesses who claim they saw you at Sandia Man Cave several weeks ago."

Ben flushed. "Couldn't be. I'm here all day every weekday. It's not safe to climb up to that cave at night. I spend all my time on weekends with my wife and daughters."

"I can check with your secretary about your appointments during the last two months."

When Jack stood and strode to the door, Ben said, "That won't be necessary. I needed to talk to Toby about a month ago. Mother told me a day when Toby would be at the cave. I figured he might even talk if he was in his favorite place."

Jack returned to his seat as Sara said, "Okay, what did you talk about?"

"Not much."

Jack lolled in his chair. "Come on, man. You must remember what was important enough to force you to climb up the spiral staircase into the cave. What was it?"

"Toby needed to sign a document."

After a pause, Sara asked softly, "Did he? Did you two fight?"

Jack could see beads of sweat on Ben's forehead. Sara had Ben on the run.

"We had a disagreement. Nothing physical on my part." He paused. "I don't want to answer any more questions without a lawyer present."

Sara shrugged and handed him a sheet of paper. "We found an extremely interesting email in Candy's computer files. Let me give you a copy before we leave. It's from ben2 at comcst.net."

Jack noted Ben's lips quivered as he read the short email:

> *As we discussed, you could earn $5,000 if you*
> *leave Albuquerque _alone_ by June 1.*

Jack thought Sara showed the steel behind her sweet smile when she said, "The next time we talk, we'll want to know about this email."

Ben walked to the door and opened it.

As Jack stood, he said, "Man, you're wasting a valuable opportunity. We like Candy Lopez for Toby's murder. All we could charge you with today is damaging federal property."

"What?" Ben looked more confused than annoyed.

"When you spray-painted graffiti—I think it was *TOBY SUCKS*—on the wall of Sandia Man Cave, you damaged federal property."

Ben's eyes narrowed as he whispered. "You can't prove it."

Winslow had tried, but all he could clarify in the photo of Sandia Man Cave on the day of the last cleaning was: *TOB SU*. Jack continued his bluff. "Are you sure?" You could avoid the charge if you talked about Candy." He sauntered forward. "Come on, Sara. This man must not be as busy as he says."

***

Jack joined Sara in her car. "Did you see that dude's face when we left?"

"I think I'd better get a search warrant for his appointment and billing records for the last three months before he bribes an associate to change them." Sara sighed. "He's not Mr. Personality. I doubt anyone would alter his calendar unless he paid them." She paused. "I'd better get a search warrant for his bank accounts, too. There's apt to be several. You know what puzzles me most?" She didn't wait for Jack to answer. "The dazed look on Ben's face—no matter what I said."

Jack laughed. "I think the blank look Ben kept on his face was 'cause you reminded him of his mother. He kept sneaking peeks at you like a guilty child. I bet he learned years ago that a blank stare was his best defense when his mother was on a rampage."

"I hate to think I remind anyone of Lydia."

Jack doubted the sincerity of Sara's comment. She was too confident to care what a weasel like Ben thought. However, Jack figured he should say something to contradict Sara's statement, but he couldn't think of reply that wouldn't get him into hot water. Sara was motherly, almost sugary sweet, at times and authoritative with steely determination at others. He could understand why Ben gave her a blank stare.

Sara finally broke the silence. "You've got to cover our bluffs and talk to Valeria Perez and Gabe Marcus, the two cavers who were at the Sandia Man Cave cleanup last month. They may be able to confirm our guess that *TOB* and then *SU* was really *TOBY SUCKS*."

"What I said was consistent with the photo and Toby's notes."

"Yes, but we need a strong case for this minor offense if we're going to scare Ben enough to talk. I'll chat with cavers who participated in previous cleanup activities at Sandia Man Cave. I want to check how accurately Toby's notes reflect what

J. L. Greger

they think occurred at those events, I also want to learn their assessment of Candy and Ralph."

"Why Ralph?"

"Much of what we've done has been based on Ralph's assessment of Toby as a good man who happened to be autistic. Candy's and Ben's comments suggest Toby was more complex. Ralph may have an agenda."

Jack bit his tongue. Sara was doing it again—being bossy, nit-picking, and treating him like a child. After a long pause, he said, "I already talked to all the cavers who were at the meeting we attended."

As expected, Sara didn't get his point. "I know. You did a good job, but we have a lot more info now. Don't worry I won't make it appear as if I'm checking on you."

She'd done it again—being condescending and hiding it with a pretend compliment. "Maybe you should. It might be better than letting them think we're disorganized and don't communicate."

Sara flashed an irritatingly wide smile. "I'd forgotten how young you are. It doesn't matter if they think we're disorganized now. If we tie up this case quickly, they—if they're typical witnesses—will think highly of us and support the efforts of the FBI."

He was too tired to argue. "I guess." Ben had been smart to give Sara a blank stare.

CHAPTER 12: Sara's Two Worlds

"I guess you won't want to see my erasing efforts. Jack told me Candy admitted that Toby blacked her face out in the photos."

Sara looked down at the dozens of photos on Winslow's lab bench and the row of bottles of oils, alcohol, nail polish remover, and other solvents. Although Winslow liked working with sophisticated equipment in the FBI lab, she suspected he was enjoying this project. "Your set up looks like that in a junior chemistry set for kids."

"Yep, but I guess it was all a waste."

Sara heard the disappointment in Winslow's voice. It was obvious he'd spent a lot of time trying to remove the black splotches hiding a face in several of Toby's photos. "*Au contraire*. My bluff worked with Candy, but a good defense lawyer will say she didn't understand my question. She can afford such a lawyer now because her marriage and Toby's will appear to be valid."

Winslow still looked disappointed.

"Don't forget, you were the one who found a printed copy of Toby's will in Candy's mess of papers."

He smiled as Sara spread the photos out on the bench.

"We need to pick the best examples to use as proof that Toby methodically covered Candy's face in the photos in his album. It may be the best evidence we have to illustrate that he was angry with her."

Winslow pointed to two pictures. "You can see I could remove ballpoint ink effectively from these two." The pictures clearly show Candy's face. He pointed to four other photos. They were blurred images of an indistinguishable face with long dark hair with a lot of black and purplish-gray streaks. "I couldn't remove much of the marker ink without damaging the photo."

"But together with Candy's photos of similar scenes, they suggest that Toby was angry on more than one occasion because he used different markers." She waved her hand over the six shots. "Save all of them. They will be needed if Candy goes to trial."

Winslow looked puzzled. "I thought you had another murder suspect now."

Sara looked around the busy lab. "Would you mind coming to my office. I think better when I am sitting comfortably in a chair, not on a lab stool. Besides Bug likes the company."

***

Winslow rubbed his hands together as he entered Sara's office. "Boy, I expect to hear a dark secret now."

Sara tried not to laugh at his boyish enthusiasm and handed him a can of regular cola. "You're going to be disappointed. My partner will probably come to Albuquerque, and I may be unavailable tomorrow."

"You mean Sanders, the spy guy?"

"Don't ask too many questions." Sara winked. "You know what they say—if I answer that question, I might have to kill you."

Winslow laughed. "What's up?"

"I'm going to outline what Jack and I might need so you can schedule us among your other projects. We appreciate your coordinating the lab's support of us. Can you have one of the lab's computer specialists check Toby's and Candy's personal and lab computers for deleted files? They're...."

"Already in the evidence room."

"We're particularly interested in anything that mentions the Collins family trust. You found the empty folder with that label at the Collins house and Candy seemed to have heard of the trust. That's all we've got. Someone must have the document. Aaron Broder may have been the lawyer. His and Ben Collins names would be good search words for the technicians to use."

Winslow look disappointed "Anything for me?"

"I want to—no, I must—revisit the cave with you. The evidence doesn't add up. Levine claims there's a remote area in the cave. I have no idea where." She pointed to a picture from the sheriff's office. "This could be construed as evidence of scuffling in the cave."

"I saw that poor quality photo. The sheriff's office needs a better photographer. The scuffle marks in the dirt could also have been caused by dragging something large across the cave floor."

"Hmm. It looks like something happened in the cave—I have no idea what—but Toby got into the ravine below on his own volition. If he fallen or been pushed from the cave, he would have had multiple broken bones. I'd like to search the ravine area below the cave—it's not steep—where Toby's body was found. Maybe we missed something."

"I was thorough."

"I know. That's the problem. Last night I had a brainstorm. What if Toby struggled with someone in the cave and one of them threw something into the ravine? That something could be important."

Winslow whistled. "That's like looking for a needle in a haystack."

"I agree but play along with me. Have you ever used a small drone to search an area?"

"No, but others in the lab have."

"What if we labeled objects with some sort of electronic device detectable by a drone and threw the objects from the stairs? Then we'd use the drone to locate them. If we're lucky, we might find a missing piece of evidence nearby."

"Don't know if it'll work, but I know who in the lab to ask."

Sara was heartened by Winslow's enthusiasm for her questionable idea. "I'd probably want to throw out five pages stapled together and in a large envelope because Ben wanted Toby to sign a document. Maybe we should pitch a half-pound block for comparison."

"A real experiment."

"Email me your ideas." Sara picked up Bug and began to cuddle him. "Now, back to practical details. Tell the computer technician I'd like a list of emails or documents on Toby's and Candy's computers to or from Ralph Edwards and Irwin Levine."

"I thought they and Toby were the good guys?"

"So, did I. After listening to Candy's and Ben's description of Toby, I've come to doubt my assessment of good guys."

Winslow stood to leave.

"Oh, I've asked for a search warrant to examine Dr. Ben Collins's appointment records for the last two months. I'm looking for weekdays when he was out of the office for at least three hours. That would give him time to get to Sandia Man Cave, kill or fight with Toby, and return to his office. It could be he's covered his tracks, and the technician will have to look for changes in his schedule made after the day was past."

Winslow rubbed his hands together. "So, he's the new suspect."

"Yes. I've also requested a search warrant for Ben's bank records. I think he might have bribed a staff person at the clinic to alter his schedule to hide his disappearance from the clinic for several hours. The tech checking his financial records should look for payments to anyone working at the clinic."

***

Sara called six of the cavers and gained insights into Ralph from only one of them. That caver, an engineering student, made a strange comment. "Ralph Edwards is a lot nicer at club meetings than in the classroom. He's a real fussbudget in the class and is a picky grader." All of them said that Toby's notes on Sandia Man Cave had never been questioned when he circulated them to the membership as his monthly reports.

Discouraged, she rewarded Bug and herself with lunch at McDonalds. A cheeseburger with plenty of ketchup and fries was Bug's and probably her own favorite meal.

She considered the two-hour time difference between Albuquerque and Washington, D.C., and texted Sanders at one. She got no response and returned to her office to make calls to more cavers. Two of the calls yielded nothing new. One woman made a catty comment. "Candy has been hunting for a husband for years." The woman could supply no backup evidence, except to note she'd seen Candy with Ralph in a local bar a couple of times. Sara texted the information to Jack and hoped he was having more luck than she was in uncovering useful clues.

She got no response when she texted Sanders at two—four his time. That worried her. The longer the hearing, the more apt the senators were displeased.

She lucked out when she called the next caver, a retired faculty member from the Anthropology Department at the University of New Mexico. He was talkative and considered himself a friend of Jacob and to a lesser extent, Toby.

He reaffirmed the kind comments made by others about Jacob. Then he added, "Some thought Jacob only participated in Sandia Grotto activities to support Toby. That was only partially true. Jacob knew Frank Hibben, the archaeologist who discovered Sandia Man Cave in the 1930s. Hibben's claim about humans living in the cave before the time of the Clovis man ten thousand years ago is controversial. I doubt it myself, but Jacob was always loyal to Hibben. That was typical of Jacob. He was also loyal to his wife and sons and never spoke ill of them. Anyone who ever met Mrs. Collins knew she gave new meaning to the word shrew. Both his sons were temperamental and fought continually."

Sara tried to get specific examples of arguments between Toby and Ben. All the retired anthropology prof would say was, "I'm like Jacob. I've learned to forget negative situations, but it seems to me the situation was always tense when both boys were together."

Sara was concerned when Sanders didn't respond to her text at three. Congressional hearings usually ended long before five. She called Sanders's home phone and debated calling his boss. She quickly decided her call could make a bad situation worse.

She called two more cavers. They both mentioned that Toby was "usually difficult to talk to, but he could almost be talkative when he was at Sandia Man Cave." They also complained they'd already told "another FBI agent everything they knew about Toby."

CHAPTER 13: Is Sanders Heard?

On Wednesday evening, Sara had listened as Sanders reported on the hearing that day. It had been one of the most humiliating events of his life. One senator had said, "The incidents in Manaus last week were a low point in Brazilian-U.S. relations."

As expected, Sara had tried to be a good cheerleader and reminded him, "You did what had to be done. Now you need to think about your options."

It didn't make him feel better.

Neither did her comment, "I'd be proud to support you with my presence at the hearings."

He'd told her as he had numerous times before, "I don't want you here. There's no reason your name should be blackened, too. You don't need to prove your love for me."

He'd spent the rest of Wednesday night thinking about what might happen on Thursday and about his options afterwards. His talk with Sara had helped him focus less on random fears and more on reality.

He and Sara were almost killed while in Brazil. Now they were physically safe. Sara had emphasized that was a positive point.

He had acted under the vague direction of the Secretary of State. His direct boss the undersecretary had been kept informed of all his actions. He hadn't broken any U.S. laws. Thus, he knew he wouldn't face a criminal trial in the U.S.

He didn't fear Brazilian officials would want him tried in Brazil for his actions. The President of Brazil had sent a letter praising him for cooperating with Brazilian military forces to "expose drug leaders in Brazil, destroy their base of operation, and return U.S. citizens in the Brazilian gangs to the U.S. for trial."

However, Sanders recognized that he had led actions in Brazil that might be considered an infringement on the autonomy of Brazil. If his boss the undersecretary didn't admit her role, his career in government service was over.

Sara had pointed out to him that although his chances for advancement in the U.S. intelligence community might be over, he would be a "hot" commodity as a consultant. Sara was happier as a consultant than she'd been as professor, but he didn't think he would be.

Since childhood, he'd wanted to be a spy for the U.S. That was why he'd attended Princeton. Many of the leaders in the CIA and other intelligence gathering agencies had been trained there. In retrospect, Yale might have been a better choice.

***

As he waited on Thursday afternoon in a private office of one of the senators in the bowels of Congress, he was worried. The Senate Intelligence Committee hadn't trusted him enough to allow him to listen when employees from the U.S. Embassy in Brazil and three other U.S. citizens had testified on Wednesday afternoon and Thursday morning. He had arrested the latter three because they had worked for the Brazilian drug cabal.

However, he appreciated that one of the members of the Senate Intelligence Committee had provided him a place shielded from public view while he waited to appear again before the committee. He knew most senators had one or two of these private offices for tete-to-tete meetings and for a place to sleep during filibusters, but he'd never been inside one before.

This one was decorated like a man cave in an upscale home, with a small bar, refrigerator, microwave, and a large-screen television. He wondered whether the senator's wife or a staff person had chosen the pretentious contemporary furnishing in black and red.

The junior staffer sitting behind the kitchen island seemed to be answering emails and had ignored Sanders since he told him, "The committee will call you in around two." That had been two hours ago.

Sanders heard a key turn in the lock. A young woman entered. She looked past Sanders and said, "We're both to escort him to the hearing room."

Sanders hated the way staffers—no older than his daughter—treated visitors on the Hill. These young staffers were inordinately self-assured. He reminded himself this was not the time to think negative thoughts and followed the staffers up worn marble steps to the passageway that connected the U.S. Capitol to the Hart Senate Office Building. In the past, he'd enjoyed "people-watching" when he walked through this wide underground tunnel. Now he hoped no one was watching him. He noted his guides avoided the crowd by the elevators in the Hart Building and guided him up back stairs.

They led Sanders to a side door and pushed him toward the witness table. He saw the undersecretary had chosen a seat several rows back. He was isolated and on his own at the witness table.

The chair of the committee began, "Mr. Sanders, we learned a lot yesterday and this morning. Now we want to make several points before we ask you more questions."

Sanders couldn't understand why members of this committee wanted to make statements. No press was present. At least he hadn't noticed any reporters in the almost empty visitors section when he entered.

Two senators—one from the Republican and one from the Democratic party—read statements noting that the loss of life and the destruction of U.S. consular properties in Brazil had demonstrated he was "foolhardy."

Another senator listed a series of potential "dire consequences" of Sanders's actions.

A fourth senator said, "Mr. Sanders, you are either naïve and lucky or are smart manager. I personally think you succeeded in preventing the overthrow of the government in the state of Amazonas in Brazil by a drug cabal because you chose your associates well. They deserve credit, but you decided to come to this committee alone. That action may reflect a character flaw."

Sanders took a deep breath. He had wanted initially to invite several staff members from the U.S. Embassy in Brazil to accompany him to the hearing, but the undersecretary had negated his invitation. In the end, the Senate committee had invited them to speak at the hearing but had not allowed Sanders to hear their comments. He felt he couldn't convey this information without insulting everyone.

This would be an hour of misery.

The chairman of the committee began the questions. Sanders barely had time to answer one question before he was bombarded with another. Sanders noted a couple of the questions were above his grade level. "I don't have the authority or data to make such policy decisions."

Finally, one senator insisted Sanders name the woman scientist who caused the "Brazilian gang members to reveal more about themselves in a couple of days than you and other professionals had been able to in months."

Sanders forced himself to look the senator in the eye. "She couldn't have done it if I and the embassy staff had not laid the groundwork. She would prefer to remain anonymous."

The senator scowled. "Stop playing games. We know who she is. She consults regularly for the FBI, State Department, and other groups" He held up a thick file and snickered. "Are you afraid your lady will outshine you?"

Sanders straightened. She's not my lady or anyone's lady. She's her own boss." More softly, "That's the problem. She only agreed to come to Brazil as a scientific expert for one week. She was convinced...

"Speak up."

"She believed the problems in Brazil were so great that all I could do there—if I were lucky—was to get maimed and not killed. Then she'd be stuck nursing me for months."

Several committee members laughed. One woman senator said, "You were afraid she might insult us. How quaint."

Another senator said, "I'll make a note that your friend should not be invited to a public hearing, but we—at least three of us—would unofficially like to hear the opinion of someone with no private ambitions. It's obvious to all of us that you are ambitious. We all know a couple major administrative positions for a person with your skills will be available soon."

Several chuckled.

The chair said, "We expect to be consulted on these appointments. We hope you learned something from our comments to you. In the meantime, your boss will direct you to prepare a proposal for actions in countries with questionable trust in the U.S." He hammered his gavel to end the hearing.

Most of the senators ignored Sanders and chatted among themselves as they ambled out. The undersecretary, with her face frozen in a mask, ignored Sander's attempt to gain her attention and rushed out with an aide running behind her.

Senator Holms from New Mexico sauntered over to Sanders. "I'd like to talk with Sara Almquist. Are you planning on seeing her soon?"

Sanders blinked. "I don't know."

"We understand you often find official excuses to jump on a military flight headed for Kirtland Air Force Base in Albuquerque to *consult* with her. I'm surprised Sara Almquist puts up with such a cheap date." The senator shoved a card into Sanders's hand. "I'll fly home to Albuquerque on Friday afternoon and not leave until Monday morning. Staff in my state office on Gold Street in Albuquerque can usually locate me."

***

An hour after the hearing, the undersecretary emailed Sanders and insisted he report to her office in thirty minutes. The terseness of the message suggested she was in a bad mood and feared others might see the message.

He arrived early and was told by an aide to wait in a nearby conference room. Usually, he was told to wait in her office.

The undersecretary didn't smile as she hurried into the conference room at exactly six. She sat, flipped on her laptop, and—he assumed—turned on the recording app before she spoke. Her tone was distant—as if she had memorized her lines—as she summarized her view of the hearings.

She pointed out that he'd been lucky. Two of the senators on the committee wanted to "chastise you for your flamboyant disregard for life and Brazilian autonomy" in a public forum. But they all agreed further discussion of the events in public was *not* to the advantage of the U.S. However, they were intrigued by your ability to gain the cooperation of key individuals in the Brazilian military. They want to learn your perspective on dealing with unstable governments in South and Central America where the drug cabals arguably might he more powerful than the governments or in which the cabals are embedded in the governments."

Sanders wondered which senators had made the request. He decided it was best to nod as his boss continued her rehearsed comments. She said several times, "I had to fight for you. Don't goof up your last chance."

Sanders recognized by her pauses and tone that she wanted to use another word beside *goof*. He also thought of the Shakespeare quote: *The lady doth protest too much, methinks.* He realized his thoughts reflected Sara's attitudes. This could be dangerous because employees, who wanted to keep their jobs in the State Department, never blurted out what they thought.

The undersecretary pushed a single page document across the table to him.

As he studied the sheet, he realized he'd been right. Most of the undersecretary's comments, except the ones about her efforts to help him, were on the sheet. She had yet to say anything spontaneous or offer him sympathy for his ordeal at the hearings. He decided Sara was right. Accordingly, he requested several days of vacation to unwind and think about the new assignment.

"Fine but have the report on my desk by the end of next week. I shouldn't have to say this, but I will. The Secretary and the Senate Intelligence Committee will punish you if any details of the last three days or points in your report are revealed to anyone." She'd waved her hand as if to dismiss him and almost ran from the room.

Sanders wondered when the next military flight would leave Andrews Air Force Base in Maryland for Kirtland Air Force Base in Albuquerque. He'd packed a light suitcase this morning. His laptop would give him access to all his notes from his service in Brazil, Bolivia, and Cuba. He could get to the base in two hours.

CHAPTER 14: A Lovely Mishap

Friday

Sara thought she heard pounding. She looked around her dark bedroom. The clock said it was one-thirty. The noise resumed. She was finally awake enough to realize the original noise came from her front door. The last pounding came from her bedroom window.

She sat up debating what to do. She didn't think she'd annoyed anyone in the current case enough for them to try to attack her. Candy didn't have the energy. Ben was too confident in his lawyer's abilities. But suspects in other cases previously had stalked her and attacked her at her home.

There was another possibility. Sanders might have obtained a seat on a military jet into Kirtland Air Force Base, but he had a key to her house and wouldn't need to make a scene. She pulled back the curtain and peeked around the shade into her small back yard.

A man—about six-foot tall with brown hair—was walking toward her sunroom in the back of the house. In the darkness she couldn't see the man clearly, but it was probably Sanders. She slid open one of the windows in her bedroom. She could hear the man cursing.

It was Sanders.

"Sanders, what are you doing? Why didn't you use your key? Or call and tell me you were flying in to tonight?"

"When I got to Andrews, the last flight to Albuquerque was ready to leave. No time to call."

Sara wanted to say, "Calm down." She decided the order would only agitate him more after what must have been a ghastly day. Instead, she said, "Honey, why don't you wait at the door to the sunroom. I'll let you in."

She didn't bother to put on a robe but slid her feet into moccasins, closed the bedroom door so Bug wouldn't wander out, and padded through the kitchen into the sunroom. She unlocked the door.

Sanders staggered in and wrapped his arms around her. "Can't think straight. I couldn't sleep on the plane."

"It's all right, Honey" She kissed his cheek.

He hugged her tighter and pushed her against the glass wall of the sunroom. "I missed you. You were right."

She wondered what she was right about, but this was not the time to ask. She lifted his chin gently and began to kiss his lips. He sighed repeatedly and then separated his lips slightly at first. She pushed her tongue forward. He opened his mouth wider, and her tongue began to move. Then his hips picked up the pace.

He pulled at her T-shirt. "You don't need that ratty old thing." He pulled up the shirt enough that he could stoke her breasts. His massage became more insistent, and her nipples hardened.

Sara knew her neighbors couldn't see into her sunroom, because a wall and a steep hill backed the yard. Although the glass wall was probably sturdy enough to withstand an assault, she thought it safer to retreat inside to the sofa in the living room or the bed in the bedroom. She tried to move toward the door of the sunroom to the kitchen.

He didn't allow himself to be moved. Instead, he pulled her pajama shorts down. His fingers slid over her hips and buttocks as he stopped kissing her and looked about the room.

She felt herself being pushed onto the metal and mesh recliner. The recliner swayed but she was too excited to care as he removed his belt, dropped his slacks, and stepped out of his jockey shorts.

The pounding of his body against her was intense. The recliner creaked and swayed. She guessed the edges of the metal hinges on the lounge probably were gouging his knees. They certainly scratched her buttocks. He didn't seem to care. Neither did she.

Then it happened.

There was snapping noise. The metal and mesh recliner crashed to the floor. Sara felt a sharp pain as her tail bone hit the concrete floor first. She hoped the bone hadn't broken.

Sanders groaned and crawled off her. He sat on the floor for several seconds before he began to laugh. "That's what I get for trying to act like a young stud. I was angry about the events of the last three days and relieved that they were over. I didn't realize I didn't have your pass card until I reached the gate to your community. While I was debating what I should do, a resident arrived. I zipped in after him."

"You were lucky. They almost roll up the streets in this community after ten." She started to roll to her side so she could get on her knees and then stand. She moved slowly because her back hurt, and she didn't want to look like a beached whale as she tried to stand.

Sanders seemed not to notice her slow movements. He was instead pulling on his shorts as he spoke. "I rushed to your front door. That's when I realized I'd forgotten to bring your house key, too."

Sanders looked good as he stood before her. His abdomen was flat, and his legs and arms toned. She was surprised he'd acquired a tan on his legs, arms, and chest while in Brazil. She hadn't noticed his tan during her five-day visit there. She hadn't thought of Sanders as a sex object during those days. She was too intent on staying alive.

"Did you know your doorbell isn't working? You must have been in a deep sleep because I pounded on your front door. In desperation, I came around to the back."

She was finally on her knees. She put one hand on a steady table and stood. She hoped he didn't notice her awkwardness. He must not have or more likely he was kind enough not to mention it.

"You looked so appealing in the dim light as you slid open the door to your sunroom. Your legs looked so long. The T-shirt is so worn it leaves little to the imagination." He shook his head. "I couldn't believe I hadn't made love to you in Brazil. I..."

She put her finger on his lips. "We had a dry spell. I'm glad we broke it, but that lounge..." She pointed to the heap on the floor. "...was not supportive."

He laughed. "I've wondered several times if this sunroom would be fun place to make love. I guess we're too old for anything but a bed." He pulled her close and kissed her.

"Maybe not too old, but I need to invest in a higher quality, cushioned chaise lounge." She led him inside "Are you hungry?" When he shook his head, she said, "I brewed some ginger peach tea tonight as I repeatedly called and texted you. I also have some rosé in the refrigerator."

He opened the refrigerator and wrinkled his nose. "No one will ever accuse you of being a wine connoisseur." He put the decanter of peach tea on the counter as Sara placed two iced glasses next to it. "Is this one of the artisan teas you get from your favorite shop in Santa Fe?"

"Of course. I may not be an expert on wine, but I like good quality teas brewed carefully."

He patted her rear end. "Always practical." He ran to the back door. "I was so excited; I think I left my case and computer in your back yard."

***

Sanders smelled good after his shower as he strolled into the kitchen. "Are you sure you don't need to work on your latest case this morning?"

"I thought you'd arrive this morning and left assignments for staff. We have time to enjoy breakfast at a new bistro. Their egg mimosa with ahi tuna is fresh and satisfying. We might even stop at American Furniture Store and the shops on Furniture Row to look for a new lounge for my sunroom."

Sanders picked up Bug and sat on a stool at the kitchen counter. Bug looked up contently as Sanders stroked his back. They both watched Sara unload the dishwasher.

"I can tell you didn't expect me to arrive until mid-morning. You've been busy for the last hour cleaning up the bathrooms, running laundry, and neatening up Bug's paraphernalia. You know the only time he touches most of his toys is after you put them in his toy box. Then he only does it to show you he's the boss."

"He's training me. It's his form of playing fetch. He throws an object and I fetch it."

Sanders continued to stroke Bug. "I noticed you already put the remnants from last night in the garbage can and rolled it to the curb."

"They start collecting garbage here at seven-fifteen on Friday."

He dangled a treat in front of Bug. Bug turned his head. "He must be tired of this type of treat."

Sara glanced at Bug as she pulled clean utensils from the dishwasher. "No, he doesn't waste his efforts on silly games anymore. He'll eat the treat if you put it in front of him, but he doesn't beg unless he's in the hospital entertaining a patient."

Sanders put Bug in his bed on the sofa and placed the treat on the edge of the bed. Bug licked up the treat. "What else do you have on the docket for today?"

"I thought we could visit a national historic site a few miles away. It's called Sandia Man Cave." She pointed to a coffeemaker on the counter. "I put it out in case you needed a caffeine rush."

He nodded and pulled ground coffee out of the freezer, filled the pot with water, and tinkered with the controls. "I know I've been wrapped up in my own problems this week, but isn't the national historic site the location of the murder you're investigating?"

"Yes. I think my dislike of the cave is hampering my interpretation of the data we're collecting."

"What do you mean?"

"I can't imagine liking anyone who liked that cave. It's so gray... boring... so dark."

"You aren't into spelunking."

Sara closed the door to the empty dishwasher, pecked Sanders on the cheek, and gave the stove top and counter one last swipe. "I've learned those who tramp around in caves here prefer to be called cavers not spelunkers. Spelunking has such an irritating sound."

"I don't know the word has a musical sound."

She changed the subject. "The stores don't open until ten. We can get in an outing to the cave before we shop. Winslow has agreed to meet me at the cave at seven-thirty."

Sanders shook his head. "I think I'd rather stay here with Bug while you do your cave work. I want to start working on a new assignment anyway."

Sara laughed. "You're not into caves either."

Chapter 15: Is Sara Wasting Time?

Winslow and a tall, thin woman were watching a drone buzz around the entrance to the cave on the cliff several hundred feet above them when Sara arrived at the parking lot of Sandia Man Cave at seven-twenty. "You're early," she said as she climbed out of her car.

Winslow walked toward her. "Flor and I weren't sure our drones and tracking devices were up to this assignment. We wanted to do a test flight before you arrived." He pointed to the drone. "Flor is seeing if the drone can get close to the treetops as if flies toward us. It's a rather sharp descent from the cave for the drone."

Sara watched as Flor circled the drone in the air twice as it moved from the cave entrance to the base of the cliff, which supported the enclosed spiral metal staircase. Flor's eyes constantly moved between the drone and her control panel. She didn't break her pattern as she spoke to Sara. "Dr. Almquist, I hope you won't be disappointed with what we can do with the drone."

"I can't be disappointed. I know this a hare-brained stunt but...

Winslow interrupted, "She's desperate and knows I like challenges."

Sara watched the drone swoop along the trail leading down the hill from the base of the staircase, occasionally darting over the treetops in graceful circles. Sara didn't talk because it was obvious Flor was concentrating on the drone. Flor seemed to be telegraphing her manual commands by contorting her face. She pursed her lips when the drone was descending rapidly and smiled when the drone was circling at a more constant level. Finally, Flor landed the drone twenty feet from where they were standing in the parking lot. Flor raced over and picked up the drone as if it was a baby bird and seemed to cuddle it in her hands.

The drone looked like a gray, four-legged spider. It was only about four inches high and was just over a foot-long diagonally. The camera lens mounted on it looked like a giant eye.

"Is it heavy?" Sara asked.

"No, about two pounds." Flor proudly added, "It can stay in the air filming about thirty minutes. Then it needs recharging."

"Are we ready to start the experiment?" Sara turned to Winslow.

"Yep." Winslow removed a bag from the back of the FBI van. "I need to tell you about the limitations of this test. The test envelope alone weighed seventeen grams; the envelope with an additional five pages weighed thirty-nine grams. The smallest transmitting device we had weighed thirty grams. The best Flor and I could do to approximate your suggested model was to put a transmitter and a small magnet in each envelope without any pages. I also put a transmitter with a magnet in small plastic bags. I thought those bags might not get caught in the foliage of the trees, and the items Toby or his assailant pitched might not have been paper."

Flor sounded apologetic when she added, "We added the magnets because they may enable a drone to recover the transmitters. They're not expensive per se, but the costs add up. The lab chief ...."

Winslow finished her sentence. "Wasn't enthused about this project. She thought it was too iffy, but we convinced her it would allow us to test the capabilities of the drones."

Sara wondered if she should apologize to Flor and Winslow for involving them in this potentially useless project but decided to avoid negative thoughts. "You two certainly tried to set this up right. I thought we'd toss or drop the packets over the metal fence at the top and at least one other spot along the spiral staircase. It seems to me if two people were fighting for control of a packet, it could be thrown or accidentally dropped anywhere along the climb." She turned to Flor. "How do you want us to coordinate our drops with your drone? Will you stay here, or will you position yourself on the landing at the foot of the spiral staircase?"

"The latter."

The three hiked up the path to the foot of the metal staircase. Sara had never learned to distinguish between pines, firs, and spruce, and Winslow seemed to enjoy educating her as he pointed out various trees. "The tall trees with orange bark and long needles are ponderosa pines. They're predominant tree in the Sandia Forest."

Winslow's commentary allowed Sara to enjoy the views without tensing over the climb. However, she gulped when Winslow pushed her onto the first step of the spiral staircase. The climb was easier than before because Winslow distracted her by saying "Bang-up" repeatedly as they watched hawks circle above the trees.

When Sara and Winslow reached the cave mouth, Winslow phoned Flor. He and Flor had decided Sara would throw the first packet from the top stair on a command from Winslow once he received the okay from Flor. Sara tried to throw the envelope packet as if she was preventing someone else from getting it. She was as bad at throwing the envelope as she had been at pitching softballs in high school. The drone's camera showed the package was caught high in a nearby pine.

Winslow decided he would do the throwing while Sara manned the phone connection with Flor. Winslow lobbed an envelope from the location where Sara had stood previously. The envelope hit a tall tree and tumbled down the pine's side. Flor flew the drone closer to the pine and moved it down the pine's side, past the location where the previous envelope was balanced on a bough. Nothing looked interesting.

Winslow cast one of the plastic bags in the air. The drone recorded the bag's trajectory. The bag didn't become enmeshed in the needles of a pine and fell to the ground, where it disappeared in the dry needles and debris at the foot of the pine. Flor said, she'd use another drone to try to retrieve the packets later.

Sara and Winslow descended the steps to a second point where the spiral stairs seemed to extend out over the ravine more. Winslow stood near the outer metal fence on the stairs and slung an envelope, a plastic bag, and then another envelope over the top of the guard fence. Meanwhile Sara stood several steps above him and close to the cliff. Sara thought her panoramic view was amazing, but Winslow was convinced his view was more complete.

After the throws, Sara slid to the outer edge of the step. She looked down and realized the view through the open grate in the metal steps was awe inspiring. Then she looked out. The pointed tops of dark green pines stretched for miles with occasional accents created by shorter trees or dead gray remnants of trees. She inched back to the cliff side of the stairs and finally admitted the truth to herself. She had enjoyed scenic mountain views from high perches many times, but this was scarier. She feared the metal staircase might be—like the last mile of road to the cave—in need of repair. It was certainly rusty in spots. She hoped she was being silly.

While Sara had been distracted by the view, Flor had recorded the descent and landing places of the packets with the drone's camera. Flor told Sara. "One envelope is caught about twelve feet above the ground in a ponderosa pine. The other envelope and the bag are on the ground less than twenty feet from that pine."

Flor's voice became higher. "OMG. There's a scrap of paper caught nearby in a tree." Flor carefully determined the coordinates of the tree and then described the scrap. "It's white and maybe four inches across. I got the drone's camera close enough so I can see black smudges on the paper. It's not toilet paper. The paper is stiffer. It could be a piece from a torn manuscript."

As Flor and Winslow conferred, Sara crawled along the outer edge of the staircase and examined the outer railing. The rail didn't appear to be bent anywhere, but Sara noticed extensive scratches and rust near the location of the second throw.

When Winslow saw what Sara was doing, he yelled, "Stop. Let's do this right." He collected his gear and ran up the stairs past Sara's location. He pulled out a mirror, which looked a bit like ones used by dentists, from his gear. Then he focused the mirror on the underside of the top railing as he crawled down the stairs on his knees.

Near the scratched area that Sara had identified, he stopped. "I think I see something red. It could be rust or it could be blood. There are several red spots. No smears." He swabbed the area. He continued down the spiral but found nothing else of interest.

As Winslow collected samples, Flor plotted how they could reach the area where the throws from the second site on the stairs had landed. It would not be an impossible climb and it was only one hundred feet from where Toby's body had been found.

As soon as the three huddled at the base of the steps, all agreed on several points. It would be worthwhile to examine the area between where Toby's body was found and where the transmitters had fallen when thrown from the second location. The debris caught in the tree did look like a torn sheet of paper and should be retrieved if possible. Sara would be of no help in the retrieval process. She could view the results this afternoon in the lab.

Sara called Sanders to tell him she'd been delayed and then bumped down the rocky path from the parking lot at ten miles an hour. It hadn't improved since the last time, but she had a better attitude about Sandia Man Cave. She wondered why and decided on three possibilities. This time, she'd taken time to enjoy the breathtaking views of the Sandia Forest. Winslow was a better hiker than Chuy, and that had made her feel safer. She'd spent no time in the dark cave.

***

Sanders seemed pleased that Sara had been delayed. It had given him more time to outline his new project. She noted he hadn't told her about this project, not even who had assigned it. He also carefully closed his computer files when she arrived home.

As she changed her clothes, he stood in the bedroom door. "Do I need to go along on this shopping trip for a new chaise lounge for the sunroom?"

Sara stood with her arms akimbo and tried not to look annoyed. "I can't force you to come, but I think you need to talk to Carbonne. The wedding is tomorrow evening around sunset at Acoma. He asked you to be his best man, didn't he? I think you must have some details to discuss."

Sanders looked at her blankly.

"Like the ring or rings. Aren't they your responsibility as the best man? I assume you'll give the main toast at the fiesta

 J. L. Greger

after the ceremony. And then there's our gift to the couple. I have no ideas, and cash seems cold."

Sanders winked. "I assume you have business to do at the FBI building."

Sara kissed his cheek as she walked past him into the bathroom and looked in the mirror. She had sweat a lot at the cave site. Her hair was hopeless and too short to pull back in a ponytail. She put on a headband to pull it back from her face. "I'm supposed to participate in an interview at one-thirty. That gives us almost four hours to get to Albuquerque, shop for the lounge, and eat lunch."

"I see." He smiled. "Bug and I will wait in the car while you shop. If you follow your usual pattern, you'll zoom around one or two stores. If nothing meets your specs, you'll order it online. I don't mind missing the process. We can discuss the specs for the chaise lounge on our way to Albuquerque. My main spec is the lounge shouldn't have a metal frame with sharp edges."

CHAPTER 16: Are Jack and Sara in Sync?

Jack scanned his messages. Carbonne had been right. One thing nice about working with Sara was her attention to details made his work easier. Yesterday, she'd gotten a warrant and had a technician collect all Candy's financial records. He read the message from the technician:

> *Candy Lopez has a checking account with Wells Fargo Bank. I can't find accounts in any other bank or brokerage. The University of New Mexico directly deposits her paychecks into her checking account twice a month. A check for one thousand dollars from the Collins Family Trust was deposited in her savings account on April 12 and another check from Ben Collins for the same amount on April 26. Her expenditures are routine.*
>
> *The statement for the last month is attached.*

An email posted at five-thirty this morning was from Sara:

> *I can't attend the meeting with Aaron Broder at nine this morning. Broder should be cooperative if you show him Toby's will and Candy's signed statement as the inheritor of Toby's estate that she wanted all Toby's records released. I emailed him the first document yesterday.*
>
> *Don't forget. We need a copy of Toby's trust as well as a copy of the Collins Family Trust.*

Jack almost laughed. Sara certainly kept her personal life private. He knew her significant other was due in today because Winslow had said yesterday that he hoped Sara would bring "her big-time spy" into the building on Friday. Jack was amused how young and impressionable Winslow was, but Carbonne had been right. Winslow had been pleased when Jack stopped by the lab yesterday for an update.

***

"Mr. Broder, do not be difficult with the FBI. I have all the documents you need to share with us information on the Toby Collins estate, which includes the Collins Family Trust." Jack wondered why Toby had chosen this man as a lawyer. He was too young to have been the lawyer who drew up the trust for Jacob almost twenty years ago.

Aaron Broder stroked the reddish stubble on his face. "Mr. Collins did not want any information released until his son was born. I'd warned him it might not be possible." He fingered the documents that Jack had given him. "I see I have no choice. Toby's will and trust are simple. Candy receives half of Toby's estate as required for a spouse in New Mexico. The residue is to be placed in a trust for his son. The trust is to be administered by Dr. Ralph Edwards."

"How long has Ralph Edwards known about the provision?"

"I personally notified Mr. Edwards that he was mentioned in Toby Collins's will and trust when Mrs. Candy Collins nee Lopez notified me of her husband's death two days ago."

Jack hated to admit Sara had been right. Until now, he'd thought Edwards was a forgetful, old man. But they'd both been right on one point. Candy was incapable of telling them the whole truth. She never mentioned contacting Broder. In fact, she denied knowing him. "What do you know about the Collins Family Trust and Jacob Collins's will?"

"I didn't prepare those documents. They were drawn up twenty years ago. Toby provided me with a copy of them about two years ago when Jacob was still alive." Broder handed Jack a copy of Jacob's will and a document entitled *Collins Family*

Trust. "In essence, in these documents, Jacob left his home and personal goods to his wife, Lydia, and all the assets of the Collins Eye Associates to his wife and younger son, Benjamin. The rest of his fortune was placed in a trust with himself as the sole trustee. The funds in the trust were available to Mrs. Collins only for medical costs and expenditures had to be approved by the trustee(s). However, the funds were available to Toby at any time and for any purpose. Upon Jacob's death, Benjamin and Toby would become the trustees. Upon Toby's death, the trust would be closed, and all funds given to Benjamin."

"Sounds like Jacob and Lydia weren't on the best of terms. Couldn't she break the trust? In this state the spouse is entitled to fifty percent of the estate."

Broder smiled. "That wasn't a problem because Jacob's will made it clear that the house and business constituted more than seventy percent of his assets."

"What did Toby say when he gave you the documents?"

"Not much. He wanted to be sure he understood the provisions of the next document." Broder handed Jack a document entitled *Amendment to Collins Family Trust.* "Jacob amended the Collins Family Trust two years ago. Jacob could do that because he was the creator of the trust and the sole trustee at the time. He specified upon his death, funds in the trust were available to Toby or Toby's children but not to Lydia for any reason. He left both Toby and Ben as the trustees upon his death."

"Who helped Jacob modify the trust?"

"The attorney who drew up the trust for Jacob almost twenty years ago modified it, but he died of a long illness about two months after Jacob. Evidently, neither Jacob nor his lawyer told Lydia and Benjamin of the change in the trust. The old lawyer's partner hadn't realized the oversight and notified Ben and Lydia of the amendment only six months ago."

Jack thought Sara was missing out on the most interesting comments he'd heard so far in this case. "Toby must have asked you questions. What do you remember?"

"Funny thing. Toby's main question was: Can my illegitimate children claim this inheritance?"

Jack wanted to curse. Now he'd have to track down those children. He tried to remain calm. "Odd question. Do you think Toby had illegitimate children?"

Broder stroked the stubble on his face. "I couldn't imagine him having many girlfriends. I advised him to name all illegitimate and legitimate children in his will and trust. As was often the case with Toby, his answer was... unusual. He said, 'No kids yet, but I'm working at it. Dad wants me to marry the mother.'"

"That's it."

Broder shook his head. "I saw Toby again about five months ago. Toby was agitated because his mother and brother were contesting Jacob's amendment to the trust. I provided the documentation needed. A judge decided against Lydia and Ben four months ago."

"End of story?"

"No, you'll note Toby signed his will three weeks ago. A week before, he instructed me to prepare the will as if he and Candy were married and indicated that 'problem would be solved as soon as amniocentesis results were in.' I received a copy of the lab results from the amniocentesis tests on Candy's baby and the marriage license last week. He stated the boy was to be named Jacob Tobias Collins, but it's not binding."

"How much of these details does Candy know?"

"One of the reasons I was hesitant to speak to the FBI is I find Candy Collins nee Lopez to be almost as odd as Toby. She came to my office shortly before the wedding and asked if Toby's death would affect the inheritance rights of her son."

"Really?"

"When your partner—Sara—called, I was uncertain to whom I owed client-attorney privileges. I checked with the bar association. Officially Toby was my client. Now Candy's unborn son, not Candy, is my primary client."

Jack stood ready to leave. "One more point. How much money will this baby inherit 'cause of his father's and grandfather's trusts?"

"Over two million dollars."

Jack guessed he had gasped because Broder added, "Ophthalmology is a lucrative practice. Jacob Collins was generally considered the best ophthalmologist in New Mexico for many years."

***

Jack emailed the main points of his discussion to Sara. Sara replied immediately:

> *I don't know what Ralph gains by playing games with us. Let's scare him by both of us interviewing him in a conference room in the FBI building. I can be there by one-thirty.*

Ralph Edwards didn't seem surprised by Jack's request. He agreed to appear at the FBI building at one-thirty on condition he get a tour of the lab. Jack sighed. Ralph didn't seem like a man with a guilty conscience.

***

Jack saw Sara and a middle-aged man of average looks breeze into Carbonne's office at one-fifteen. She rolled a cart with soda and a plate of cookies into the conference room less than ten minutes later.

Ralph Edwards was already waiting in the conference room. As Jack watched from the observation room, Ralph examined the mirror at one end of the room and felt for wires under the table before Sara arrived.

Ralph laughed when Sara entered. "Dr. Almquist, are you trying to scare me. This room has one of those special mirrors. I assume Jack is watching me from behind the mirror."

"Ralph, we're not here to intimidate you. We need your help." Sara batted her eyelashes. "I guessed you were a diet lemon soda man, but I also have diet and regular cola on the cart, too. Jack is young enough to still want all the calories in regular soda."

Jack figured Sara had signaled he was to play the bad cop to her flirtatious good cop. As soon as he entered the conference room. Sara said, "Jack, I was explaining to Ralph that we need his help because he is such a *close friend to Candy.*"

Jack noticed Sara and emphasized the last four words. She was hinting Ralph and Candy were more than casual friends. It worked.

Ralph reddened slightly. "I... I had drinks with Candy several times during the last four months. Well, I had a beer. She had a soda. Someone might have seen us together and jumped to the wrong conclusion."

                                                    J. L. Greger

Sara batted her eyes. "Two of the women cavers suggested you were cozy with Candy. They seemed to be jealous of her. Do you know why? I doubt that Toby appealed to them." Jack restrained himself from smiling. Sara had exaggerated. Only one caver had mentioned spotting Ralph and Candy together several times at a bar.

"Women can be catty. I also doubt any of them knew how wealthy Toby was. I only learned the size of his inheritance two days ago when a lawyer—I can't remember his name—called. It seems Toby appointed me the trustee for his trust."

"So, you're saying Candy never talked about Toby's will or trust?"

Ralph laughed. "I helped Candy write her resume and job application letters. She was—and still is— frantic to find a job. I also edited the review of literature for her dissertation. She needed the help, and Levine was useless."

"Okay. But I never found a bar was a good place to edit a student's writing."

He shrugged. "Your students probably weren't as nervous as Candy. I was trying to get her to relax." He smiled. "In the process, I learned she was pregnant."

"How?"

"She refused to drink any alcohol and complained of being tired all the time. Her face also changed. She got dark patches on her cheeks. I noticed because my daughter experienced the same type of spots when she was pregnant."

Jack thought, *If Ralph is lying, he's a real pro.*

Sara nodded. "So, how many grandchildren do you have?"

"Three. I think they ruin your theory that Candy and I were an item. Remember I'm an old prof who has had come-ons from dozens of female students. What's more Candy's not as pretty as most." He gave a half-hearted smile. "Do you want to show me the lab facilities now?"

Sara leaned back. "How large do you think the trust you'll be administering is?"

"The lawyer didn't say, but Jacob often worried about Toby's future. He figured Levine would fire Toby if the contracts ran out. Levine's rather lackadaisical approach to Candy's career development suggest Jacob was right."

"But you thought about the size of the trust?"

"Of course. Now I remember the lawyer's name. It's Broder."

Jack stood and was surprised when Sara touched Ralph's arm. "How much would you guess?"

"Jacob was modest man, but in his day, he was one hell of an eye surgeon. Poor Ben will never live up to his father's reputation. Hmm. Lydia was a spendthrift, but Jacob kept her on an allowance for the last twenty years. I'd guess Candy and her baby will get more than a million dollars."

Sara walked to the door and then turned, "One more thing, everyone agrees that Jacob and Lydia were not happily married. Can you guess why?"

"It's no secret. Lydia wanted to institutionalize Toby when he was diagnosed with autism at four. Jacob wouldn't allow it. That boy traveled the world as Jacob, without Lydia, took him to countless specialists and provided him with endless learning opportunities. Finally, Toby showed an interest in caves and an aptitude for lab work. Neither of which interested Lydia."

Sara opened the door. "I know a young man who would love to tell you about our lab here."

As they walked down the hall, Ralph said, "Lydia is a sad case. In high school in Santa Fe, she was the belle of every social event."

Sara stopped. "I thought you met Jacob when he started caving with Toby."

"I did, but I've known Lydia since grade school. I was one of the many men who dated her when we were undergrads at UNM."

Sara looked surprised.

Jack said, "This doesn't sound like hall conversation. We'd better return to the conference room."

Sara literally pushed Ralph into the conference room, but then was distracted by a ping from her laptop.

Jack took the lead. "How long did you date Lydia?"

Ralph chuckled. "You've got it wrong. I was poor and a serious student. Lydia was a flirt and ambitious. I tutored her for a Physics for Poets class and sneaked in a couple of soda dates."

"A what?"

"Before Jack could say more, Sara said, "Physics for Poets was the nickname used at many universities for a physics class with no math prerequisites. How did Lydia do in the class?" She returned to fiddling with her laptop.

Ralph laughed. "She dropped out of school."

Jack noted Sara still seemed distracted, and he thought this topic should be explored fully. "When was this?"

Ralph shrugged. "I was studying for a test in differential equations when she called to tell me her parents were sending her to New Orleans. I guess it was in the fall of my and Lydia's sophomore year."

Sara looked up from her laptop at Jack. "Differential equations is an advanced math course." She stared at Ralph. "When did you see her again?"

Ralph seemed to tabulate his thoughts on his fingers. "At a faculty mixer about fourteen years later. She was changed." Ralph seemed to study the ceiling. "She was tipsy and held a glass of wine in one hand as she showed me a picture of her two-year-old son, Benjamin. I could see an older boy standing apart from Lydia and Ben in the photo. When I asked, she mumbled something like, 'A mistake… that can't be fixed.'"

Jack was suspicious. "Are you sure you didn't meet Jacob then?"

Ralph gulped. "I saw a man with a worried look approaching Lydia. I figured he was Lydia's husband. I didn't know what to say and left the mixer quickly."

Sara looked up from her laptop. "I'm fascinated by this pot-boiler. Tell me more."

"You sound like my wife, Anabelle." Ralph flashed a big smile suggesting he and his wife were close. "When I told Annabelle about my weird conversation at the mixer, she was intrigued." He paused. "I doubt she was jealous; she always trusted me. A couple of months later, Annabelle told me that she'd met a Lydia at an event for faculty wives. Anabelle had learned that Lydia was married to an affiliate faculty member in the med school."

Jack's curiosity was also piqued by this mini espionage story. "Did Annabelle spy on Lydia over the years?"

"You make it sound nasty. It wasn't. Annabelle served on several committees in a faculty wives' group with Lydia. Lydia was often mentioned in the social column of the newspaper."

Sara frowned at her laptop. "Can you summarize what you learned?"

"Lydia was ashamed that Toby was autistic but enjoyed being the wife of a successful, rich older man. The marriage looked happy on the surface until about twenty years ago when Lydia suddenly dropped out of the Albuquerque social scene. That's about when I met Jacob because he and Toby became active cavers."

Sara whispered into Jack's ear. "That was when Jacob created the Collins Family Trust. It was his way of limiting Lydia's spending." Sara turned toward Ralph. "Do you know what changed? What did Annabelle think?"

Ralph laughed. "I have no idea what happened. However, Annabelle always thought Jacob had threatened to divorce Lydia and restructured their financial arrangements. She said about then, Lydia started complaining that Jacob was 'cheap with her.'"

"I'd like to talk to Annabelle."

Ralph slumped. "That would be difficult. She died five years ago."

CHAPTER 17: Does Sanders Pity or Envy Carbonne?

Sanders was glad when Sara left him and Bug in Carbonne's office. The shopping trip had gone as he expected. Sara identified a two-person chaise lounge in rattan she liked at the American Furniture Store, but she disliked the cushions and the painted blue color of the rattan. She decided to check several sites on the web.

Her conversation with Carbonne before she left the men to talk had been short. "Jack and I are tired of witnesses lying in this case. This is our third run at Ralph Edwards. So, you and Sanders will have plenty of time to talk about the wedding." She left before Carbonne could speak or Bug could beg to come along.

Sanders waited until the door closed. "We had to do an emergency shopping trip this morning. I like buying furniture and art for my condo. Sara is always helpful and tactful as I savor beautiful pieces. But when she's shopping for her home, she's a whirlwind scouring for the best buy." He leaned down and settled Bug at his feet by offering a treat.

Carbone laughed and seated himself at his side table across from Sanders. "I always tell Barbara I'll love whatever she chooses when it comes to furniture. Not true, but it's never worth an argument. It's how I feel about the wedding, too."

Sanders tried not to frown, but he was concerned that Carbonne was about to make a major mistake—marry a woman because of outside pressure. "Are you having second thoughts about marrying Barbara?"

"Quite the contrary. Barbara is four months pregnant now. I never thought I'd be so eager to be a dad. If it was up to me, we'd have married a couple of weeks ago in a private ceremony." He shrugged. "I don't want anyone from my family at the wedding, but pueblo traditions are important to Barbara—or at least her mom." He shrugged. "I'm willing to try to please her mom. She's a tough and funny old broad, but she's got this thing about weddings."

Sanders was satisfied the wedding wasn't a mistake. Now he mentally reviewed the list of Sara's questions about the wedding. "All women have a thing about weddings."

Carbonne looked surprised. "Sara doesn't. She didn't want one even after you took her to India to propose."

"She wanted a commitment." Sanders saw no reason to admit again she wanted the commitment because he'd strayed with a young woman. Carbonne knew the basic information. "The rings were important to her." He slid down in his chair. "She also thinks weddings are for young, pretty women. She…" He didn't want to say more. It was too private. He straightened in his chair. "That brings me to the first question Sara thought I should ask. What about your rings? Will this be a single or double ring ceremony? As the best man, do I need to do anything special?"

Carbonne stood. "I think I'll tell my secretary I'm through for today." He pointed to a cabinet. "There are a few choices there. The whiskey is only so-so. You'll want ice. The ice is in the freezer section of my under-the-counter refrigerator." He pointed to the refrigerator, ambled to the door that connected his office with that of his secretary, and disappeared.

Carbonne looked worried when he returned. "Administration of even a small unit of the FBI, like the New Mexico region, is a pain. The egos of some agents." He laughed. "Funny, I'm telling you."

Sanders swirled his drink. "Personnel management is the worst and best part of the job. Now about my questions."

Carbonne appeared to ignore Sanders as he dug into the back of a file drawer and cursed. Finally, he pulled out a small black velvet box. He looked more relaxed after he snapped open the top. "I hate to admit it, but Sara *might* be right. It's time for me to think about the wedding. It is tomorrow. I haven't except for this." He closed the top of the box and handed it to Sanders. "I guess this is your responsibility now until you present it to me in the ceremony."

Sanders opened the box and choked. The ring was exquisite. He checked the inside of the band. It was eighteen

                                        J. L. Greger

carat white gold and engraved: *With love always*. The setting was at least a one carat diamond with turquoise insets on the sides."

Carbonne's lip quivered. "I hope Barbara likes it. Her mom helped me pick it out. I liked wider bands, but her mom said they weren't comfortable. She thought the ring should have some turquoise to reflect Barbara's heritage. We both agreed gold was better than silver. She thought the diamond was too expensive, but what the heck." He took a gulp of whiskey.

Sanders realized Carbonne's complaints about the wedding were mainly his attempt to hide how nervous he was and much he wanted to be married. Sanders closed the box. "Barbara will love it." He sipped his whiskey. "Did you insure it?"

Carbonne took another gulp of his drink. "Her mother wouldn't let me take it from the native craftsman who made it until I got insurance. That was after she argued with the artist over the price for an hour."

Sanders pitied Carbonne. Buying a wedding ring with your future mother-in-law sounded like a foolhardy task. Carbonne was rather naïve, considering he was forty. "Women who've known hard times, like Barbara's mom and Sara, know the value of money and never stop haggling over prices. I expect Barbara will too. Get used to it."

Carbonne finished the whiskey in his glass. "You asked about the ceremony. Barbara's mom said all I had to do was select a best man, bring the ring, and say, 'I do.' Then she frowned. 'Many grooms on the pueblo have such bad headaches from their stag party the night before, they can't even do that. I expect *you will not be one of them*.'"

Sanders had seen Carbonne nurse a drink for an hour at FBI events. He'd never seen Carbonne empty a double shot of whiskey in a few gulps. He suddenly recognized another of his duties. "Let me refresh your drink. I think I'd like a club soda now. It's hot today and I think I'm dehydrated. How about you?"

Carbonne looked dazed for a moment. "I don't need more whiskey either. I'd like my usual—a diet cola in the can."

Sanders wandered to the refrigerator and studied the selection. "I forgot you and Sara shared that questionable habit—drinking diet cola straight from the can. Speaking of

Sara, she wants to know what you want as a wedding present. She thought cash was *cold*. That means we probably need to ask her or Barbara for suggestions."

Carbonne popped the tab on the can and took a long swig. "Better ask Sara. She can handle an interview with a suspect while conversing on her laptop on another topic. Barbara is too nervous today to do that."

Sanders pulled out his phone.

"Sara responds better to an email because she always has her laptop on during an interview. And she complains text abbreviations and the small screen on a phone annoy her."

Sanders thought Carbonne understood Sara better than he did in some ways. "Let see." He put away his phone and pulled out his laptop:

> *I'm sitting with Carbonne. We have no ideas. What do you think would make an acceptable wedding gift?*

He was surprised how quickly Sara replied:

> *Did Barbara or her mom assign Carbonne any responsibilities for the wedding? Is there anything Barbara and he need to pick up tonight for the wedding?*

Sanders read the questions to Carbonne. "They sound like loaded questions to me. I suspect Sara has talked to Barbara."

Carbonne went to the desk and studied his computer. "Barbara says tonight we need to pick up the booze for the fiesta."

Sanders nodded and typed to Sara:

> *They need to stock the bar for the wedding dinner.*

This time Sara didn't respond immediately.

Carbonne said, "That's a good sign. They must be making progress in the interview."

Sara responded:

*We could supply all the beverages for the
wedding. I suspect Barbara doesn't want an
open bar. She told me she hates wedding
receptions where everyone is plastered. That
means we need to buy soft drinks, too. They
need champagne for a toast. What's his future
father-in-law's favorite drink?*

Sanders read the email to Carbonne.

"Finally, a question I can answer." Carbonne laughed. "Barbara's dad likes beer. Her mom buys the cheapest stuff she can find. He's always pleased when I bring him a pack of Sam Adams."

Sanders hesitated before he typed:

*Sam Adams beer is the father's favorite. We
should pick a good champagne for the toast.
Perhaps an assortment of wine and beers for
the guests.*

Carbonne and Sanders waited for a couple of minutes for a response. Carbonne was quiet at first and then said, "You know we have at least one murder in the pueblos in New Mexico every month. Almost all of them are attributable to a drunken fight at a social event. I don't want our wedding to be one of those events."

Sara's email appeared:

*When I threw parties for graduate students, I
could prevent bad behavior by only supplying
wine—no beer. Let's buy enough champagne
for the toast, plenty of soft drinks and wines,
and a limited amount of Sam Adams beer.
Should we supply plastic glasses? How many
will be at the wedding dinner?*

*To make it special, we could supply good
glasses for the wedding party for the toast.
Don't tell Carbonne the last point. It'll be our
surprise gift.*

After Carbonne listened to Sanders's selective reading of the email, he said, "We'll need plastic glasses. Barbara expects sixty will show up. If you get the booze, Barbara and I can leave tonight for Acoma. That will please Barbara and her mother."

Sanders noticed that Carbonne didn't ask questions about Brazil. Instead Carbonne checked his emails and looked furtively at his door. "You know, it's normal for a groom to be nervous. I'm glad no one I'll ever see again, except Sara, saw me in India when I proposed."

Carbonne continued to check his emails. "I wonder what the problem is. Sara should be here by now. Barbara is already headed home. She told me to thank you for the perfect wedding present."

Sanders thought he should maintain the semblance of a conversation. "I suspect Sara discovered she'd missed major points and decided she needed to ask more questions. Her mind was not exactly focused on the interview, considering all our discussion on beverages for the wedding."

Carbonne only nodded.

Bug got up and paced the room.

Sanders tried again. "You know this case is hard for Sara. She was under a lot of stress in Brazil, and she doesn't like caves."

Carbonne blinked. "She's also breaking in a new agent." He paused. "Odd that the Sandia Man Cave is spooking her. She usually enjoys challenging locations."

"Like I said, Brazil was almost too much for her. I think she lost some confidence." He didn't add that he'd lost more than a little confidence in Brazil. The hearings and his boss's coolness had also shaken him. He didn't plan to admit his problems to Carbonne and focused on Sara. "She associates caves with molds, bats which she says are the ultimate source of many viruses, and..."

There was knock on the door. Jack entered. "We finally cracked the guy. He's not the murderer. Sara took him to the lab for a tour." He seemed to suddenly notice Sanders and his eyes opened wide. "OMG. I didn't realize you were Sara's... friend. You lectured my class at the FBI Academy in Quantico."

CHAPTER 18: Wedding Ado

Sanders drove to his favorite liquor store in the Albuquerque area, while Sara calculated how much champagne, red and white wine, Sam Adams beer, and soft drinks were needed for the wedding party. In the liquor store, Sara pushed the cart while Sanders selected the wines and champagne. She couldn't help but smile inwardly because they had become quite a predictable couple. They had not discussed the choice of wines or champagne. They both knew that was his expertise. Neither had they discussed the purchase of soft drinks and glasses at the supermarket. It was her area of expertise.

As they left the liquor store, Sanders said, "Now for the hardest part: the selection of the fancy glasses for the bridal couple. Where do we go now?"

"I have an easy solution." She waited to complete her answer until she had strapped Bug in his seat in the car. "I was given twelve Waterford champagne flutes when I was married."

Sanders gasped. Sara seldom mentioned her short-lived marriage to another assistant professor over twenty years before. Her husband had only acknowledged his homosexuality after they'd been married a couple of years. He knew Sara still exchanged Christmas cards with her former husband and his male partner.

"Why don't I wrap up the crystal and give it to Carbonne and Barbara. I've never used most of the pieces. I looked at them the other day. They're in perfect condition. They're nicer than anything we'd buy."

Sanders was perplexed. "Isn't it tacky?"

"I don't think so. A friend of mine gave all her crystal to her niece when she got married last year. The young woman was thrilled. Besides using them at the wedding for her family,

Barbara might use them for other big upcoming celebrations, like the baptism of their child.”

Sara noticed Sanders was quiet for a couple of minutes. He sighed. “You’ve already bought the boxes and wrapping paper, haven’t you?”

“Okay, you’ve guessed my secret. Barbara lamented to me the other night that her wedding lacked any sparkle. She thought the plans reflected her mom’s practicality too much. I’m not much of sparkler either, but I thought...”

“You thought right.” He paused, frowning as if he was trying to be tactful. “Do you have any other ulterior motives?”

“No. You know my marriage lacked any sparks. I still like my ex-husband. The crystal flutes don’t remind me of unpleasant events.”

“That’s not what I meant. You’ve met my daughter’s boyfriend. Did she tell you something she neglected to tell me?”

“My, you’re being suspicious tonight.” She leaned over and kissed him.

“Well?”

Sara kissed him again. “They have no plans, as far as I know. She’s too intent on succeeding in her law clerkship.”

Sanders was still frowning.

Sara decided it was time to change the topic. “We must get our presents to Acoma early tomorrow. It takes about two hours to drive there from my house.”

***

Saturday

Sara and Bug sat in the old church atop the Acoma mesa. Barbara was getting dressed and preparing for the wedding feast. Sanders and Carbonne were in a nearby house pretending to be preparing for the wedding. Sara suspected they were exchanging war stories on their past experiences together in Cuba and their assignments since. After she and Sanders had delivered the beverages this morning to Barbara’s ceremonial home on the mesa, Sara realized she had no other function.

She had made excuses and wandered with Bug to San Estevan del Rey Mission Church. The church had a colorful history. It was near the location where, during the Pueblo Revolt of 1680, the residents of Acoma had thrown a priest off the 360-foot mesa to his death. Sara had listened to tour guides several times previously. Their renditions of the death of the priest had differed, but all had stressed the priest had not ministered to the natives needs but rather to his own and Spanish greed.

As Sara and Bug had ambled around the outside of the church, she had noted it sturdy adobe walls and two sawed-off towers made it look more like a fort than a church. The graveyard at the front entrance was so barren that Bug found little to sniff.

Sara had noted a drop in temperature of at least ten degrees when she entered the church. She guessed the adobe walls were at least two feet thick at their base and at least a foot thick at the roof. The walls probably kept the church warm in winter, too.

The interior walls were whitewashed with only occasional faded squares of paintings. The front façade was covered with religious scenes typical of retablo art, but the artwork was worn and not embellished with silver, gold, or ornate carvings. She felt the faded artwork in this church was a more sincere testimonial of faith than the gaudier versions in many old churches. It might also reflect this church was maintained by a Protestant congregation.

Sara had brought a towel to sit on because as she remembered the church had no pews. She hadn't needed to bother. Barbara's mother had placed ten folding chairs a respectable distance from the altar, which was covered with juniper and agave flower stalks. Judging by the number of chairs, it appeared Barbara had won the argument to limit the wedding to family even though the wedding feast was open to everyone in the pueblo.

Sara felt her nose itch, and she sneezed twice. The juniper was pretty, but its pollen irritated her sinuses. She pulled one chair to a rear corner of the church as far away from the juniper as possible, laid out the towel and a bowl of water for Bug, and opened a novel.

She'd read only one chapter when her phone pinged. She figured Sanders needed something and answered. It was Winslow.

"Sorry to bother you. We found fingerprints on the three pieces of paper we located in the branches and in the debris at the bases of the trees. All of them looked like parts of a scientific document. That's up to you and Jack to figure out. What I looked for was fingerprints and DNA. You know the usual."

"Don't drag out the story. What did you find?"

"Toby's DNA and one usable print of his. Candy's DNA and two of her smudged prints. That left one unidentified, usable print and unknown DNA."

When Sara remained silent, he continued, "I figured the attorney Broder was a good candidate. I called Jack and got

Broder to allow me to collect his DNA and prints this morning. I guessed wrong.”

“So, we have unaccounted DNA and an unknown print on a slip of paper that has been accessible to anyone for a week?” Sara thought Winslow was lonely in the lab on Saturday. This call could have waited until Monday.

“Not exactly, the unaccounted DNA and print was on the slip of paper caught in the tree. I doubt anyone had touched it because it wasn’t easy for Flor and me to retrieve.” He snickered. “Before you ask. The DNA was human not from a bird or squirrel.”

“What did Jack say?”

“Not to call him again this weekend. I said I didn’t work Monday usually. He didn’t care. I heard a woman’s voice in the background.”

“I don’t need to know about Jack’s personal life. I guess I should have asked him to collect prints and DNA from all the cavers he interviewed. They’re going to be...”

“Pissed if you have to contact them a third time.”

Sara noted Winslow enjoyed using colorful language. His voice went to a higher pitch when he used slang. “Let’s not panic. The print and DNA could be from Broder’s secretary. Before Jack contacts all the cavers, I’d like to get samples from Irwin Levine and Ralph Edwards.”

“Ralph was the old dude you brought to the lab?”

“Yes.”

“You don’t need to collect a sample from him. He tried to bring a soda can into the lab. Remember? I put it on my desk so he could retrieve it after the tour. He didn’t. I knew you’d want his prints and DNA, so I lifted them from the can.”

“You’re doing it again.”

“What?”

“Building the story.”

Winslow coughed. “Maybe, a bit. It’s worth it. Ralph’s DNA and prints on the can match those on the slip.”

“Oh dear. Jack and I thought we’d cleared him yesterday.”

“Can you do me a favor?”

Sara tensed. Winslow was a little too exuberant now. “If I can.”

"Bring your boyfriend in on Tuesday, not Monday when I might not be at work. I want to meet him."

***

After six of the ten chairs were filled, the pianist began to play. Carbonne and Sanders entered through a side door and solemnly approached the altar. Carbonne looked more ashen than he had after shootouts. Barbara's sister-in-law wearing an aqua dress entered through the main entrance by the graveyard. Finally, Barbara's parents led in Barbara clad in a long, scoop neck ivory satin dress. She was glowing.

The ceremony was short. Instead of the minister giving a lesson to the couple, Barbara's mom and dad alternately read sentences from what they called a wedding blessing based on a traditional Pueblo prayer:

> *Hold on to what is good, even if it is a handful of earth.*
>
> *Hold on to what you believe, even if it is a tree that stands by itself.*
>
> *Hold on to what you must do, even if it is a long way from here.*
>
> *Hold on to each other, even when it is easier to let go.*

Sara felt tears welling up in her eyes. When the couple kissed, she wished Sanders was nearby instead of standing behind Carbonne. She blew a kiss to Sanders.

CHAPTER 19: Sara Stands by Her Man

Sunday

Sanders was unusually silent on Sunday morning as he rushed to start back to Albuquerque. Sara couldn't decide if he was still brooding about the Brazilian situation, the hearings, something Carbonne said, the wedding, or her refusal to get married last year. She decided to whittle away at the problem, starting with the least threatening item first. "Did Carbonne have much to say yesterday?"

Sanders didn't reply but seemed to focus on his phone as Sara drove.

"You two had four hours to reminisce after we helped set up the liquid refreshment table in the Lewis house on the mesa before the wedding. Carbonne must have said something interesting."

Sanders didn't bother to look up from the small screen of his phone. "Sad how much a woman can change a man."

"What makes you say that?"

"Carbonne was one of the best undercover agents I've seen, but he's convinced it's too risky now while Barbara is pregnant. Did you know they hope to close on a house next week?"

Sara wanted to study Sanders's face to guess his emotions but decided it was mistake when driving. "Oh my, he's settling more than I realized. But he's doing a good job of slowly changing the attitudes and behaviors of agents in New Mexico. Fewer of them are acting like cowboys of a hundred years ago now when it comes to dealing with Native Americans, women, and the homeless. He's probably more valuable to the FBI in his current role as an administrator than as an undercover agent."

"Yes, but he misses the adventure."

"Are you saying that the seeds for divorce have already been planted?"

Sanders sniffed. "You're being a bit poetic this morning." He tinkered with his phone. "Not really, but Barbara is going to rule their household."

"I suspect Carbonne changed because he wants to be a father. He told me he wanted to prove to himself that men in his family were capable of being loving and nonjudgmental fathers."

"Hmm." Sanders stared out over the desert landscape.

Sara thought Carbonne's choices might have surprised Sanders, but they were not causing him to brood this morning. She decided to pursue a more dangerous topic. "In all the fuss over the wedding, you didn't have a chance to tell me much about the last day of the Senate hearing."

He kept staring straight ahead, so she continued, "You're good at analyzing your audience. How did the senators react to your comments? Isn't the senior senator from New Mexico on the Intelligence Committee? Holms usually seems reasonable."

Sanders groaned. "Do you have mental telepathy?"

Sara knew she'd hit a sensitive spot and waited.

"The hearing may not be over. Senator Holms wants us to meet him at his Albuquerque office at ten."

"Okay." Sara gulped. "Where's the office?"

"Gold Street."

"That's downtown Albuquerque. The coffeeshops in that area aren't open on Sunday. We may want to get something light beforehand since we skipped breakfast at the Sky City Hotel at the base of Acoma mesa."

"My mistake. I originally thought he wanted to meet us at nine."

"No problem." Sara gulped again. "I'm surprised he wants to see *us*." She emphasized the *us*. "I hope I wasn't a source of problems for you at the hearing."

"The senators didn't mention your name during the hearings, but they had a file on you and knew you consulted for the FBI as well as the State Department. Senator Holms mentioned your name afterwards. I think he wants to get your opinion on the situation in Brazil."

"Isn't that odd? I filed my report as a scientific consultant already."

"Yes." He tapped his fingers on his phone.

Sara had the distinct feeling Sanders knew more than he was saying. "Maybe I haven't asked you the right question. What did your boss say after the hearing?"

"It's classified."

"Okay but remember she's manipulative." She bit her tongue rather than say more about his boss. When he didn't reply, she added, "I love you and have faith in you. I'd kiss you now, but I'm not that skillful of a driver."

***

Senator Holms stood as Sara, Sanders, and Bug entered his inner office. Holms was ruggedly handsome. His rangy six-two-frame looked better in jeans and a casual shirt than in a suit as he was usually dressed in news clips.

Holms shook Sanders's and then Sara's hand. "I've heard about you, Dr. Almquist. You're the scientist who worked on the case a month or so ago when a poison was added to food served at a rally for one of the candidates vying for my job."

"Yes, and after that incident you changed your mind."

"My party's leadership was thrown off balance with the loss of that candidate. They asked me to reconsider my retirement, and I signed up for another six years if the voters are willing." He pushed a button and two staffers entered. "Dr. Almquist would you mind if Mr. Sanders and I talked alone for a few minutes? One of my staffers will escort you to our conference room."

Sara had come prepared and had brought the novel she'd started earlier and water for Bug. Sara had settled Bug at her feet and read only two chapters before an aide led Sara back to the senator's inner office. Sara was surprised. Sanders was nowhere in sight. Only a female aide sat on the sofa. Sara bucked up her guts and smiled at the senator. "I hope you didn't send Sanders to the car. I have the keys."

Holms smiled and motioned for her to sit.

Sara took her time in settling Bug before she sat. Then she tried to put a calm, blank look on her face. She figured if she acted nervous, he would be more aggressive. Politicians went for blood when they smelled fear.

"Did Sanders tell you anything about his current assignment?"

Sara took her time and even patted Bug's head before she spoke. "No, he arrived at my house around one on Friday morning. I had several appointments Friday. Then we went to a wedding yesterday. We didn't have a lot of time alone to talk. Besides, I don't ask him about his work. So much of it is classified. I wait for him to talk."

Holms shook his head. "You don't strike me as a patient woman."

Sara decided the best way to appear relaxed was to give full answers not like the terse ones given in court. She shrugged. "I suspect he was glad I was busy Friday because he wanted to work on a new assignment."

Holms nodded. "How much do you know about his assignment in Brazil?"

"That's hard to answer. He never outlined his total assignment in Brazil for me. So, I can't estimate how much I know."

The aide giggled. Holms didn't look amused.

"But I knew the scientific issues in Brazil because I was the official U.S. representative to the WHO conference in Manaus on malaria and other tropical diseases. The embassy staff provided me with a skimpy briefing document beforehand. I also knew that a scientist from the St. Louis Zoo had disappeared in the Amazon region around Manaus about a year ago. Sanders had sought my help a month or so ago in guessing what the scientist's value to the drug gangs might be." Holms looked bored, but she thought she should explain. "The scientist was an expert on rare poisonous frogs found only in the jungles of South America."

Holms leaned forward with his elbows on his thighs. "Did you know Sanders planned to rescue the scientist?"

"I knew his boss wanted him to, but I didn't know their plans." Sara shrugged. "I doubt Sanders and his boss knew what the rescue would entail until he was in the middle of the mess in Manaus."

"What do you mean?"

Sara glared at the senator. "He didn't expect his condo to be bombed or that I would be attacked by gangs at a convent school. And neither the Brazilian officials nor Sanders expected so many of Brazilian police and military officers would join the gangs in attacking the U.S. consular office in Manaus."

Her voice must have been become sharper because Bug rose and turned toward Holms. Sara settled Bug before she again focused on Holms. "I'm sure you've seen multiple reports. No one expected the drug gangs to be so confident and aggressive."

Holms shook his head. "I think you did."

"What do you mean?"

"Sanders said you refused to go to Brazil as his partner. He said you only attended the conference because he promised you'd only have to stay a week."

Sara forced a laugh. "I didn't want to go to Brazil for several reasons. I couldn't take Bug along. He too old to live in the tropics." She leaned down and petted Bug. "I've read many reports on the problems in Brazil—destruction of the Amazon jungle and indigenous people by ruthless mining and agricultural interests, the hostility of the previous administration toward scientists, less gun control than in the U.S., and powerful drug gangs."

Holms avoided looking at Sara and pulled a treat from his jeans for Bug. "I'm not looking for a stock answer."

Sara was pleased when Bug refused to take the treat. The dog always sensed her feelings toward others. "I thought it unwise for the U.S. to give Sanders or anyone the temporary appointment of chargé d' affaires instead of ambassador to Brazil. It signaled to the gangs that the U.S. was tentative in its approach to the country. Besides I'd been to Brazil before and didn't enjoy it, except Iguassu Falls. I'm not into beaches, carousing, or soccer."

"You're blunter than I expected." Holms sat back and placed his hands behind his head. "I think I can guess your answer to my next question. Would you be willing to be the ambassador to Brazil?"

"No way. At this point in my life, I prefer to work on problems that can be solved."

Holms snorted. "Are you sure you can't guess what Sanders current assignment might be?"

"That's not a fair question. He has not said anything about his assignment. I think Sanders did a great job of determining who in the hierarchy of the Brazilian government believed in goals consistent with those of the U.S. Accordingly, I assume his current assignment is to propose how to do it

                                            J. L. Greger

elsewhere in Latin America. Then his boss can take credit for his good ideas. But that's a guess."

"Are you sure he hasn't given you hints or asked for advice?"

"I'm sure. He doesn't want to hear me say, I told you so."

Holms stood. "Thank you for stopping by. Tell Mr. Sanders he'll be hearing from the committee. It would be wise not to discuss this meeting with anyone." Before he opened the door, he blinked. "Considering your relationship, why don't you call him by his first name?"

Sara wanted to say the question seemed inappropriate, but then most of them had. "Habit, and Sanders doesn't like his first name: Eric." As she led Bug out, she thought the wrinkles on Holm's face were deeper than she noticed before. She suspected he hadn't wanted to talk to her any more than she had wanted to talk to him.

CHAPTER 20: A Big Secret

Monday

Sanders continued to be reticent to talk on Sunday afternoon and evening. He seemed eager for Sara to leave for work on Monday morning. As she and Bug were leaving, he said, "Would you mind leaving Bug with me? I need to talk to someone who can't be questioned by others?"

Sara thought this was a good sign. Sanders recognized that he needed to share his thoughts with a sympathetic, wise individual. Bug fit the bill.

As soon as Sara pulled out of her garage, her thoughts turned from Sanders to work. She realized she no longer needed to stop by the FBI Building to drop off Bug. This meant she could arrive at Irwin Levine's lab at least thirty minutes earlier than her scheduled appointment with him. Ralph's and Candy's comments about Levine's unwillingness to mentor Candy had made her think. It might be interesting to talk to other members of the Levine lab. She texted Jack.

***

Sara carried a big box of donuts past Levine's darkened office and into the small office used by staff in Levine's lab. No one was there but the coffee pot was on. She stepped into the lab and announced, "Free donuts in the office."

Two guys stopped making entries on computers. A woman answered, "I'll be there in a minute."

Sara grabbed a glazed, yeast-raised donut and was chewing it when the men entered. "I'm a scientist with the FBI and I'm trying to learn more about Toby and Candy. What can you tell me?"

Both men grabbed chocolate-frosted cake donuts but ignored her question.

She tried an easier question. "Did either of you work on the contracts identifying microflora in Sandia Man Cave?"

One guy shook his head. The other said, "Yeah, Levine notified me last Friday that my job would end next month if at least one of the contracts wasn't renewed. I wasn't surprised he'd given Candy her pink slip weeks ago."

"Are you a grad student, too?"

"Nope, a tech. That's why Levine threw Candy to the wolves first. Grad students, as near the end as she is, will work without pay."

Sara thought it sounded like a callous attitude. "Don't you think he'll get the contracts renewed?"

"Nope. Toby was the brains with all the ideas." He lowered his voice. "During the last month or so, Toby and Levine never agreed."

Sara saw Jack was now standing at the door with an amused look on his face as he stared at the donuts. She winked at him and continued, "How do you know they disagreed? I was told Toby seldom argued."

"Right but when someone repeatedly slams a book on the lab bench, you know he's angry."

Sara turned to the other guy who had grabbed a second—a cherry-glazed, yeast-raised—donut. "What project are you working on? Are you a tech or grad student?"

"A grad student on the NIH grant. I can probably claim a master's for my work before the money runs out in six months." He chewed a bit. "If Levine doesn't have a hissy fit."

Sara decided to ask a hard question before Levine appeared. "So, is Levine a good boss?"

Both guys shrugged. One said, "He was okay when Toby was around to translate his rantings into viable experiments. But Toby lost interest in the lab months ago. Guess the constant arguing with Levine and his brother wore him down."

"Toby told you about his brother, Ben?"

"Didn't have to. Ben came into the lab twice screaming."

Sara heard someone clearing his throat. Sara turned It was Irwin Levine.

"Is there a reason you're questioning my lab crew?"

Before Sara could answer. Jack spoke. "Dr. Levine, this is a murder investigation. We're trying to talk to everyone with knowledge of Toby." Jack put his hand on Levine's back and seemed to guide him to his office. Sara thought she heard Jack say, "My partner is a lab geek, but I don't understand science. Can you explain to me in simple terms what your lab does?"

Sara continued to question the two guys. "Do you know what the arguments between the brothers were about?"

"All I know was Ben kept yelling about a trust and wanted Toby to sign some papers. Toby in his usual manner, put his head down and turned away."

When Sara saw Jack and Levine had left the lab, she said, "Do you know what Dr. Levine and Toby were arguing about?"

"Not really," said the graduate student.

The technician said, "Control of the contract with the forest service. Toby wanted to be the PI."

Both guys grabbed another donut and left when a woman in a lab coat said, "Dr. Levine has been under a lot of stress lately. He thought he would be named the head of the Molecular Genetics and Microbiology Department. Toby was being difficult, and the contracts may not be renewed."

Sara noted the woman's black hair appeared to have gray roots. She assumed the woman was too old to be a graduate student and then chided herself for making the assumption. She surmised this woman knew all the lab's secrets but needed to be courted. "Are you the lab manager?"

The woman straightened and smoothed her lab coat, which was embroidered on the breast pocket with the name *Geri* "In title no, but that's how I function. I've been with Dr. Levine since he was an assistant professor here."

Sara thought, *No wonder you look older than the usual tech or grad student.* She said, "Then you've seen Candy develop as a graduate student. When I talked to her, she seemed unenthusiastic about her work. However, most graduate students are depressed by the writing process, even if their significant other hasn't been killed. What do you think?"

"Dr. Levine should answer that question, but it seemed to me that Candy always struggled when writing papers."

Sara suspected jealously between the women. "What did Candy do well?"

The woman took a bite of a donut and chewed. "She was willing to collect samples in the caves. I, really several of us,

                                      J. L. Greger

hate going into the deep recesses of caves. They smell of rotting animals and bat guano. Crawling on those sharp rocks is…"

"Painful." Sara decided she could win brownie points by agreeing with Geri. "I thought Sandia Man Cave smelled musty, and I hated reaching into dark corners. I was afraid of what I might find."

The woman smiled. "Exactly"

Sara tried a bluff. "I also find squeezing through narrow passages in caves is difficult."

The woman stopped chewing and stared at Sara. "You discovered the secret passage in Sandia Man Cave to the hidden room? I'm told the room is large—the size of a living room in a home. Toby was always worried that someone outside our lab group would find it, but Dr. Levine always laughed and said few hikers were as thin as Toby and Candy." The woman frowned. "If you touched the surfaces in the hidden room, you may have destroyed Dr. Levine's experiment. He and Toby were studying the regeneration of microflora on cave surfaces that had been cleaned and then left untouched for years. Please tell me you didn't touch them."

Sara tried to keep her face blank. This woman had already told her more than Levine. Maybe, the woman would unwittingly tell her how to find the hidden room in the Sandia Man Cave. The rangers hadn't mentioned a secret passage. She and Chuy had looked at all the walls, but their examination had been cursory. They had seen sharp edges where rocks were separated by at least a foot but had not explored those crevices.

Sara continued her bluff. "We want to see the results of previous samplings of the walls in the hidden room before we collect more samples. Do you know where those records are?"

"Dr. Levine keeps those records in a coded file on his computer." She frowned. "They were also on Toby's computer."

Sara tried not smile because Toby's lab computer was sitting in the FBI evidence room. However, she had foolishly agreed to Levine's request to return the computer to Levine's lab after an FBI computer technician had downloaded potentially useful files from the computer. Levine had claimed keeping the computer in FBI storage was a waste of federal research funds.

Sara pretended that her phone had vibrated. "Oh dear, I need to take a call. I'll be right back." Sara rushed to the hall and punched a number. "Winslow, find Toby's lab computer in the evidence room. It was scheduled to be returned to Dr. Levine's lab today. Do *not* allow that to happen. Have a technician try to find a coded or protected file on it for a hidden room at the Sandia Man Cave. The file is apt to have a misleading title and may contain diagrams and photos as well as lab data." She listened. "I can't answer questions now."

She hurried back into the staff office. It was empty. Sara scanned the lab. Geri was not in sight. Sara thought about the comments from the two men and sidled by their lab benches. "Do you know where Geri went?"

Both men snickered. The lab tech said, "She's probably combing her hair before she reports to the boss. Gossiping Geri reports on everything in the lab to Levine."

"Are they close?"

The lab tech coughed violently and stopped pipetting. "You guessed right, but she's getting suspicious about his long lunch breaks."

***

Jack jabbed a finger at Sara as they left the medical school building. "Don't ever leave me in the clutches of a science professor again. I figured I had to listen to his arrogant comments while you were engaged with his crew. He claims his lab is on the brink of earth-shaking discoveries."

"The truth is he's desperate. His lab is falling apart. He's also hiding something. Did you tape his comments?"

"Sure. What did you get?"

Sara looked around the parking garage and muttered. "Sounds echo here." She then decided to make it appear that the conversation was of no consequence in case Levine or someone from his lab had followed them. "You're looking cheerful today. You must have enjoyed your weekend."

"Winslow must have heard a woman's voice when he talked to me on the phone. I'll fix him."

"No need. I don't want details, but I enjoy remembering when I looked good on Monday after a busy, fun-filled weekend. Now I just look tired after such a weekend."

Jack stopped and pulled Sara's arm so he could study her. "Girl, you must have had a boring weekend. You look good."

She resumed walking. "You lie well." She pointed to her car. "Let's talk."

As soon as the car doors were closed and the air conditioning was on, Jack said, "Talk."

"The site of Toby's and Levine's research in Sandia Man cave isn't a remote area—like Levine indicated. It's a whole hidden room. Only Toby and Candy have ever entered the room. I called Winslow to stop the return of Toby's computer to Levine's lab. There should be a coded files on Toby's computer with info on the hidden room."

"Including how to enter it?"

"I hope."

CHAPTER 21: Darkness in the Hidden Room

"Honey, how's it going?"

Sanders cleared his throat. "Bug's fine. He and I had a nice stroll. I've finally got a handle on my project."

"Good." Sara figured Sanders would say more about his assignment when he was ready. "American Furniture found a chaise lounge with the rattan painted white not blue in their warehouse. It will be delivered tomorrow."

"That's a relief. I was afraid you'd get the chaise lounge from an online location, and I'd have to assemble it."

Sara chuckled. "That's why I didn't select a cheaper lounge that was labeled as easy-to-assemble on the web. Now you have another choice. It appears that Sandia Man Cave has a hidden room. Even the local rangers haven't seen it. Do you want to see it?"

"Are you kidding?"

"I thought I'd give you the choice. If all goes well, I'll be home on time."

"By five?"

"Yes. We could go to The Range, or I can pick up groceries and cook."

"The Range. Love you." He hung up.

Sara figured he was making good progress on his assignment because he was in a good mood but didn't want to waste time talking. She doubted Carbonne and Barbara or even Jack and his date would have such a short, non-romantic conversation. If she was lucky, she might have time to pick up something pretty for tonight. Sanders thought she looked best in red. He liked silky fabrics. A new nightgown might make the evening more romantic.

***

Sara trekked up the spiral stairs to the Sandia Man Cave behind Jack and Winslow. Two forest rangers, another FBI technician carrying gear, and an FBI photographer trailed behind her. The only good thing about visiting the cave again was Winslow had driven an FBI van. Her car didn't have to suffer the assault of the unimproved road.

She stood at the oval entrance of the cave and gazed through the metal framework for the stairs to the mountains beyond. She took a big gulp of air, like a swimmer before submerging below the water. This was, of course, unnecessary. There was nothing wrong with the air in the cave, but it calmed her before she turned to watch Winslow pace about the cave as Jack studied the diagrams and photos from Toby's encrypted file.

"You should be seeing an arch with a somewhat smooth gray stone about four feet behind it," Jack said without looking up from the diagram.

"Do you mean this low arch that comes to my waist?" Winslow squatted to get a better look at the arch.

"I guess. According to the diagram, the arch is the start of a tunnel of about four feet. There's a hole in the roof of the tunnel. Do you think you can squeeze through it?"

"Are you kidding? I can't see anything."

The senior forest ranger a short, slim man of about fifty and the woman ranger had been engaged in an intense discussion ever since they arrived in the cave. Suddenly, he seemed to notice Winslow and spoke, "Feel around the inside top of the tunnel. You should find three sliding latches." However, he didn't more toward the recess to help Winslow.

Sara thought, *Turkey, if you know how to enter it, help us.* She bit her tongue.

Jack and the technician placed lamps to fully light the recess. The photographer readied her camera gear. The senior ranger stepped out of the cave onto the metal stairs to use his phone.

Sara knew she was being useless, but her guilt didn't overcome her dread of the cave. She was pleased when the local forest ranger—a woman with a gray ponytail—sidled close to her.

Winslow yelled. "I found what could be latches. Flat dark pieces of metal that fit into stone grooves and then extend outward." After thirty seconds, "I got one to move." He held up a piece of metal one inch by four inches and a quarter inch thick. A minute later, "Another one." Two minutes later, "The last one finally moved." He groaned as he pushed upward. Then he handed a gray slab to Jack.

Jack held up the slab so the photographer could take multiple shots. It looked like an oval sheet of plywood with foam painted gray and streaked with beige and black attached on one side. On the wood side were metal latches. "Toby was paranoid about hiding the entrance."

Winslow groaned. "Stop talking and help me. This may be booby trapped. I'm feeling fabric when I reach up."

Jack handed the apparent cover to the technician for processing and focused a lamp into what Winslow described as a three-foot black oval at the top of the arched recess.

Winslow pulled on the black fabric. Gravel and sand pelted down on him. After a few curse words, he wadded up the fabric and handed it to Jack. He stretched his hand upward. "I'm in."

Sara turned to the female forest ranger. "Are you sure none of you knew about this entrance?"

The woman shook her head. "I checked with my supervisor." She pointed to the senior ranger who was now standing not far from Jack. "He claimed ignorance two hours ago. Then as we were climbing up here, he admitted he'd helped Toby and his father disguise the entrance over fifteen years ago. He claimed a bigwig in the forest service had thought the research Jacob and Toby proposed was worthwhile and needed to be protected. So, Mr. Big Shot..." She pointed to the senior forest ranger. "...agreed to this ridiculous deception."

"Why didn't they close the cave to the public?"

"I asked that, too. Mr. Big Shot said it would be 'counterproductive' because cavers would notice Toby's frequent visits to the closed cave. They would try to explore it at night. Instead, the forest service arranged for Jacob and Toby Collins to oversee the maintenance of the cave when the forest service funded Jacob's and Toby's first research contract."

Sara wondered whether Ralph Edwards was in on the secret. The entrance looked like it was designed by an engineer not an ophthalmologist. She said, "Didn't you wonder what Toby was studying in the cave?"

The female ranger shrugged. "I thought it was dumb to sample microflora on the walls of the cave because Toby led a

                                                    J. L. Greger

crew from the Sandia Grotto club to remove graffiti from the walls regularly. How could they expect to find much growing on the walls? But I figured Jacob had gotten a politician to lean on the forest service to fund the worthless project." The woman said more softly, "I like my job here in the Cibola Forest but never liked this cave. It seemed to me to be merely an outlook to the forest."

"I need a little help." Winslow sounded annoyed. "Jack, you're not focusing the light right. Give me the flashlight."

Winslow's "Wow," echoed into the rest of the cave when he stood in the middle of the hole. "You won't believe this. Jack, you'll have to help me inventory everything here. Sara you'd better contact someone high up in the forest service. They're in for a surprise."

Sara choked. Before she could make a call, she had to see the hidden room and talk to the senior ranger, who had returned to the cave. "Okay. You and Jack can put on your booties and special gear while I stand in the hole and take a quick look."

After a technician had opened the encrypted files on Toby's computer this morning, Sara had studied the prescribed procedure for entering the hidden room in Sandia Man Cave. It was a modification of the standard procedure for exploring distant reaches of caves, like the Fort Stanton Cave, to minimize contamination of the deep recesses of a cave with outside dirt and microbes. However, no head protection other than a hair net was necessary in the evidently large hidden room, but polyester body suits and shoe covers were needed.

Sara had called the administrators of Toby's and Levine's contracts in the U.S. Forest Service and the U.S. Geological Survey. All agreed the procedures were necessary to maintain the integrity of the grants. Sara had difficulty convincing the administrators *not* to call Levine or anyone else at the university about the FBI's plan to enter the hidden room of the cave. The administrators had insisted a designated representative of the forest service should be present to monitor the FBI's activities.

The senior ranger was their designee. He had already shed his forest service uniform and was pulling on a polyester suit over his shorts and T-shirt and putting special booties over his shoes. Sara stepped closer to the ranger. "I assume you've been in this room before." She wanted to scream at the senior ranger, *Turkey, you're here for a reason.* She said softly, "Why didn't you help us?"

"I wanted to see how complete Toby's instructions were. If you had all his secret files, you would have known that I've entered the room once a year with Jacob and Toby—or Toby and Candy the last two years."

Sara again bit her tongue. "As you know the FBI only accessed Toby's coded files several hours ago. I immediately contacted the grants administrators for Levine's and Toby's contracts, including the one at the U.S. Forest Service. They all wanted us to proceed quickly. I used artificial intelligence, often shortened to AI, to screen the large files quickly, but AI has limits." She shrugged. "I'm not that good at using it. It missed any mention of annual inspections by forest rangers."

"I... I guess I should have trusted you, but this has been top-secret for so long."

"Is there anything else you neglected to tell us?"

"No."

"You'd better look through the hole before I do. It may be what looks strange to Winslow may look normal to you. Then the photographer can take shots before anyone climbs in."

The ranger nodded and crawled into the recess and looked through the hole. "Yikes!" There were a couple of minutes of silence as the ranger turned in the hole and used the flashlight left by Winslow.

He bent his knees, lowered himself so he could crawl out of the recess, and returned to Sara's side. "Toby must have had a breakdown. I can't believe he stored stuff not apparently related to his research here."

Sara thought of several appropriate curses but said, "What should be there?"

"It was normal for Toby and Candy to leave tape markers on the wall. It made it easier to sample the appropriate areas. They also kept two plastic stools here. It was too obvious to bring the stools with them each time. Plastic was the material least apt to contaminate the scene. But they never left many papers in the cave. There are sheets of paper all over the floor." The senior ranger unzipped his suit to get his phone. "My bosses will go berserk."

Sara decided it was time to take control. "No phone calls until we fully assess the situation. There's no need to get administrators upset and giving orders until we can answer all—well most—of their questions." She pointed to the photographer. "We need complete—360 degrees—photos of the floor and walls before we proceed. Let me take a quick peek first."

Sara crawled into the short tunnel, looked up at the lit hole above her head, assumed a squat position, and slowly stood clutching the metal rim around the hole. She understood why the U.S. Forest Service thought the hidden room was safe. No one who wasn't agile and who weighed much over a hundred-fifty pounds would fit through the hole.

The senior ranger had not overstated the mess. Someone had strewn at least a hundred pieces of paper—quarter pages—over the floor. Sara knew she could forget about buying something pretty to wear tonight or getting home by five as she promised Sanders. Now was not the time to panic. Even so, she almost fell as she lowered herself into a squat. Her thigh muscles weren't strong enough. She crawled over the rough stones to the main room of the cave.

Sara noticed the photographer was more adept at positioning herself in the hole than Sara had been. The technician sitting at the photographer's feet served as tripod for the camera.

Sara looked around at the three men in the tight polyester suits. They looked good—muscular but trim—even the ranger. She was glad she'd not opted to get a suit and explore the hidden room firsthand. She knew she would not look good in a tight suit.

As the photographer turned slowly and the camera clicked repeatedly, Sara and the rest of the crew plotted the procedures to be followed.

After a general discussion, Sara said, "The first step will be for Winslow to photograph a piece of paper on the floor. He'll start at the west and work counterclockwise. Then Jack will pick up the slip of paper, place it in a numbered evidence bag, and hand it to our senior ranger, who will stand in the hole. I'll serve as the gopher who delivers the bagged, numbered bags to the table where the photographer and technician will load data onto the computer." She pointed to the senior ranger. "That means you're in control. If any of us does something wrong or even starts to make a mistake, yell out. The local ranger will stay at the mouth of the cave and prevent anyone from entering. She'll also stay in constant communication with the ranger at the foot of the stairs. Right?"

"I'm done." The photographer handed the camera to the technician who scooted from the recess. The photographer sank to her knees and crawled from the recess. "I'll have the shots ready to guide us in a couple of minutes." She and the technician bent over a small table on which they arranged the camera and two monitors. The rest of the group notified their significant others that they'd be home late tonight.

The senior ranger gasped when the photographer and technician proudly displayed a 360-degree composite shot of the hidden room on one monitor. Everyone agreed it was complete. Sara hoped the plan for layering on the locations of each slip of paper worked. In the FBI building beforehand, she had estimated the photographer and technician would have at most twenty items to number in the photographs. There were probably a hundred pieces of paper on the floor of the hidden room.

It was time to begin. Winslow and Jack climbed into the previously hidden room. Winslow transmitted a photo to the second monitor; the technician assigned the slip a number; Jack processed the slip of paper. Sara retrieved the bagged, numbered, quarter-page slip of paper from the senior ranger. The photographer did a close-up shot of the print on the quarter page. The process was slow at first but became more fluid with practice.

As the papers were removed, the dirt underneath became visible. Grooves and ruts in the dirt suggested something had been dragged across the floor of the hidden room. The men took photos and collected soil samples, but it appeared little debris beside papers had been carried into the room. There was no sign of damage to the walls of the hidden room. Growth of mold didn't appear to have been disturbed, but Winslow collected samples as prescribed in Toby's extensive file.

***

The last man to emerge from the hole at six was the ranger. Sara greeted him. "I called the grants administrators and your boss as you requested. We've collected 111 bags of samples."

As he unzipped the suit, Winslow said, "It seemed like more. My cotton shorts and T-shirt are soaked with sweat."

Sara noticed that Jack was using a towel to wipe off his arms and legs once he pulled off his polyester suit.

The ranger stood motionless beside Sara. "What did my boss say?"

"Your boss and the research administrators understand that it will be several days before we'll have anything to share. They all agree, in the meantime the cave should be closed to everyone, even forest service and FBI personnel. We should all meet at the FBI Building tomorrow at eleven. That should give the technicians time to compile a basic list of items and a good map coordinating all the photos We can decide then when we expect to allow the cave to reopen."

"Good." He turned to Winslow and Jack. "While you two replace the Styrofoam and wood door to block off the hidden room, I'll have the other rangers bring up the boards to seal off the entrance to the main cave."

***

Sara staggered into her house at eight. Bug was napping on the sofa and Sanders was whistling as he typed on his computer.

"I guess no one missed me."

Both Sanders and Bug sauntered over to her. One licked her feet, the other kissed her lips slowly and deeply.

CHAPTER 22: Who Is Being Straight with Jack?

Tuesday

Jack couldn't believe his eyes. Using artificial intelligence, the computer had taken the shots of all the scraps of paper in the cave and assembled them into twenty-two pages.

Winslow had almost panted. "I'm not good at jigsaw puzzles. The computer did in a couple of minutes what would have taken me hours to do."

The computer technician smiled broadly and noted, "The three pieces in blue are the pieces recovered from the tree and the ground around the tree. They were from the apparent twentieth page of the document. The black area is still missing."

Jack was also amazed by Sara. She thanked the technician but seemed unimpressed by the technology.

"We seem to have two documents here." Sara pointed to the first two pages on the screen. "One is a two-page statement saying Toby agrees with the other trustee of the Collins Family Trust, i.e., his brother, that the distribution of trust funds can be changed. I see Toby didn't sign it. The torn pieces in this document seem to be smaller than the other document—maybe an eighth of a page. I think the two documents were torn up at different times. We have twenty pages of the other document, but it looks incomplete to me."

Jack stared at the reconstructed pages on the monitor. "It looks like scientific gobbledygook to me."

Sara traced her fingers along several phrases. "I think it's a draft of a proposal because I see words, like propose and hypothesize, and the use of the future tense. Unfortunately, we appear to be missing the first page with the title and the name of the author." She turned to the computer expert. "Can you take these three sentences..." She pointed to the first paragraph of the first page of the incomplete document. "...and see if these are in any other documents on Toby's computer. I want to know whether Toby, Levine, or Candy wrote it and when. It could be a shared document that reflects the efforts of several people."

The technician nodded.

Sara pointed to the page that the AI program had suggested was the last one. "It looks to me like this document is complete except for the title page, references, budget, and maybe an addendum. I suspect it's a draft of a proposal to the U.S. Forest Service or U.S. Geological Service for renewal of Levine's and Toby's current contracts."

"Candy would know," suggested Jack.

"Yes, but we agreed we'd rather not contact Candy, Levine, or any member of the lab because any one of them could be Toby's murderer."

Jack nodded. "And Candy has yet to give us a completely honest answer to any of our questions."

Sara turned to the computer technician. "Toby submitted grant proposals several years ago to the forest service and geological survey. This proposal—assembled by AI—should be a logical extension of one of those previously submitted proposals. See if you can find the previous proposal, while Winslow updates rest of us on the prints and DNA on the torn documents."

As Winslow, Jack and Sara walked toward Sara's office, Winslow, said "You aren't as enthusiastic as usual today. What's up?"

Sara shrugged. "I've got problems at home. The insurance company is giving me the runaround over getting my car's fender fixed. The Albuquerque Police reported on the news they solved the holdup and murder at Donut Mart without ever mentioning the help of the FBI or witnesses. I guess I'm being petty on that point. And this murder just keeps getting more complicated. With every clue, we're adding to our list of suspects."

Jack noted again how little Sara revealed about herself. He suspected it reflected how boring her life was as a middle-aged woman, but several agents had hinted Sara's past was colorful. He didn't have time to think about the conundrum because Bug rose and wandered over to be petted when they entered Sara's office. The one thing Jack was sure about Sara was that she loved the mutt. After Bug sniffed Winslow and Jack, he settled in his bed, Jack guessed he'd passed a crucial test.

Winslow immediately laid out his data. Ben's and Toby's prints and DNA were on the two-page legal document. No surprise. The longer scientific document had Candy's and Toby's prints and DNA. Again, no surprise. Winslow smiled. "Ralph's fingerprints and DNA were also on several pages of the scientific document."

Jack shrugged. "He could have reviewed the document earlier without being in the cave.

Winslow shrugged and laid out photos of the swirls of dirt on the floor of the hidden room and pointed to bits of blue fiber in one photo. "These match the polyester fiber in the suit left in the cave. Toby's DNA was all over the suit."

Jack could envision the scene. "My guess is Toby was dragged across the rough floor." He turned to Winslow, "As I remember, you looked for blue fibers elsewhere in the room but found none."

"Right, but you forgot I also found red fibers on the floor. They suggest a scuffle."

Sara lifted Bug to her lap. "You're both forgetting Toby was found in shorts and a T-shirt not the blue caving suit. Chuy and I found the blue suit stuffed in a crevice in the cave. Looks like, Toby was knocked to the floor and took off the suit before he left the cave." She tickled Bug's stomach. "I assume Toby removed his suit himself because I noticed you guys had difficulty pulling your suits off yesterday when you were all sweaty. I think it would have been difficult for someone else to remove the suit without tearing it."

Jack nodded. "I also think no one but Toby would have carefully sealed up the room."

"I agree Ben wouldn't, but Candy, Levine, or Ralph might have."

"What's your thing with Ralph?" Jack began to pace, and Bug jumped from Sara's lap to sniff him. "Ralph was helpful at the grotto meeting and didn't seem to hide any secrets from us on Friday."

"He was too nice. His fingerprint and DNA were on the torn document. Also, the entrance to the hidden room smacked of an engineer's attention to detail."

Jack coughed, "Toby was detail oriented, too."

"Granted, but Toby was a teen when the entrance was designed."

Jack shrugged. "Forget Ralph for now. Let's assume Toby wasn't killed, although he might have been injured, in the hidden room. We did find a bit of blood on the railing to the stairs. Was it Toby's blood?"

Winslow searched for the data on his tablet. "It was Toby's DNA, but it could have been there for months. There wasn't much blood—even allowing for it having been partially wiped away. I don't think it was from a major injury."

"Maybe, the blood and even the dirt swirls in the hidden room are irrelevant. Let's look at the autopsy report again for details we missed." Sara brought the autopsy up on her laptop screen. "For example, Toby's left arm was broken. Probably on the day he died because there were no signs of healing."

Jack nodded. "That confirms our theory there was a scuffle."

Sara traced her finger down the screen. "This is interesting. Toby's kidneys were abnormal with severe atrophy of the glomeruli."

"What does that mean?"

"He needed to begin renal dialysis soon. It could explain why he was in a hurry to complete what Candy called business activities, but you found no medications for renal disease in his condo. Right?"

Both men nodded.

Jack groaned. "Just, another complication that doesn't help us solve our case." He looked over Sara's shoulder at the screen. "Look at this. Toby's right shoulder was dislocated. It suggests the body might have been dragged by the right arm a short distance to where it was found." He turned to Winslow. "You explored the area between where you found Sara's *silly* test papers and where the body was found. Did you find anything?"

Winslow sighed. "The body had laid there for about a week before a ranger found it. The crew from the medical examiner's office trampled the area, too. The whole area was covered with pine needles, feathers, and bird droppings. But I found some unusual debris—four plastic water bottles. Thank goodness, the body was in a garbage bag. The soil I collected from the front of Toby's shorts and T-shirt matched the dirt in the area. The medical examiner also found a red thread on the back of Toby's shirt."

"So, Toby's body was dragged probably face-down a short way to his final resting place. The red thread could be from the killer's clothes." Sara tapped her fingers on her laptop. "What else do you have?"

Winslow shrugged. "That's it."

Jack returned to his chair. "Did you run DNA and print tests on the bottles?"

Winslow looked at Jack defiantly. "No, I've been busy." He turned to Sara and whispered, "I forgot."

Sara put her hand on his back. "This case isn't an example of my best work, either. Let's think positively. The red fiber is interesting. Red polyester caving suits aren't apt to be found in most people's closets. I doubt Ben or Levine would have one."

Jack groaned. "Candy had one, but I didn't recognize what the one-piece red jumpsuit in her closet was when I searched her apartment."

Sara shook her head. "You know the red thread might not be from a caving suit. It could be from the embroidered logo on a knit polo shirt or even from the shirt itself." She looked at Winslow. "Are you sure the fibers were polyester, not cotton?"

"No, I didn't analyze the red thread, for its content."

***

Jack couldn't decide if Sara was being generous or setting him up for a fall when she let him lead the meeting with the senior forest ranger. She had remained silent as he impressed the ranger with shots of the complete torn pages. He decided Sara was setting him up for a fall when she kicked him under the table after he said. "We have a promising new clue..."

Sara interrupted. "We think the secret room in the cave is our best source of clues." She pointed at the senior forest ranger. "You mentioned going into the room at least once a year. So, we need to eliminate you as we analyze more DNA samples." She pulled out a swab before Jack or the ranger could protest.

　　　　　　　　　　　　　　　　　J. L. Greger

After Sara performed a cheek swab for DNA analysis on the ranger, he quickly decided he had pressing assignments. As soon as he had closed the door, Jack turned to Sara, "Why did you kick me?"

Sara smiled. "I studied the ranger as you were talking and suddenly remembered he had a red embroidered emblem on his black caving suit. That embroidery could be the source of the red thread. I had to stop you from telling him the importance of the red thread. You know he's been awfully secretive about what he knew."

Jack couldn't believe his ears. Sara had added another potential suspect to the list.

CHAPTER 23: Sanders Searches for Quiet

Sanders was glad when Sara and Bug left at seven on Tuesday. He anticipated a good day of writing with long blocks of time without interruptions. He had already outlined and written two pages of the white paper for his boss that he tentatively titled, *Strategic Utilization of Human Resources in Latin America.*

At seven-thirty, American Furniture called and announced the chaise lounge would be delivered between eight and ten.

Senator Holms called a little before eight with questions about the events in Brazil. The questions were so detailed, Sanders had to look at his daily appointment log during his almost four-month tenure as the chargé d' affaires in Brazil. Sanders had saved all these records but had to retrieve them from a badly organized archive in the cloud.

At nine, the doorbell rang. The delivery men from American Furniture had already pulled the chaise lounge off the truck. Sanders apologized to Senator Holms for the interruption and expected the senator to say he'd call me back in ten minutes.

Instead, the senator said. "I'm disappointed we can't chat more. Don't tell anyone I called." The senator hung up before Sanders could apologize again.

Sanders thought Holm's questions could hardly be called a chat but had no time to ponder his conversation because the delivery men were trying to bring the double chaise lounge through the front door. It looked as if the men would scrape the paint in the hallway as they scrambled to turn the lounge on end.

Sanders suggested they bring the bulky piece of furniture around the outside of the house and carry it directly into the sunroom. As the men struggled to position the chaise lounge in the sunroom, Sanders feared Sara had made a mistake in her measurements.

Eventually the lounge was placed in the room. Sanders thanked the men and lay down on the lounge. With the back in its most upright position, the lounge was a perfect place to work and worry.

He had worked for only a half-hour when his boss called. She was more talkative than she'd been during the past week and rattled on about trivia, even asking how he'd spent his weekend. She wasn't typically interested in his life. She ended their conversation by saying, "I don't want you to misunderstand my request last week."

He didn't interrupt to say what he thought. *It was no request. It was an order. No, it was a threat.*

She continued, "I wanted your thoughts quickly because I'm sure there will be questions. I didn't want senators to speak to you directly without the secretary's knowledge."

Sanders knew he shouldn't lie to his boss. He decided a sin of omission was better than a sin of commission and didn't answer her unspoken question. "I'll have the report to you by Friday as you requested."

Afterward, Sanders wished Sara was there to listen to his problems. He felt as if he was a mouse caught in a battle among three cats—the undersecretary, perhaps her boss the Secretary of State, and the Senate Intelligence Committee. He knew Sara would give him sympathy but would suggest that his boss might not have told her boss—the U. S. Secretary of State—all the pertinent details. He decided he'd rather be with Bug now than Sara. Bug understood the angst of being controlled by a woman.

During the next thirty minutes, he made steady progress on his report. Then the phone rang. Sara was eager to know if he liked the lounge. Then she got to the real purpose of her call. "I'm stymied. Although we've uncovered more clues, they haven't helped us eliminate any of the suspects. Unless the lab performs a miracle, I think Toby's murder might remain a mystery for a long while. I'm hoping you need a break from writing." She didn't wait for him to respond. "Why don't Bug and I meet you at Tamaya for a late lunch?"

Sanders knew he should say no, but he was hungry. He increasingly noticed large meals after seven in the evening produced heartburn and interfered with a good night's rest. He guessed it was the price of age and stress. "Yes, I can be there in an hour. I'll get us a table on the patio by the screen, so Bug has a good view of courtyard."

***

The Tamaya Resort was on the Santa Ana Pueblo only a few miles from Sara's home. The luxurious resort had three outdoor swimming pools, a spa, a golf course, a stable of horses, riding and walking trails, and several levels of restaurants.

Sanders admired the large bronze statues of actual pueblo residents in traditional garb in front of the main entrance to the hotel as he strolled from the parking lot. On a whim, he browsed the resort's main shop. Sara had commented several times that the store featured "pretty" women's clothes. He'd describe their women's wear as chic southwestern-themed clothes. He saw a pink and aqua jacket, which would look good on Sara, but he didn't buy the jacket. His ex-wife and daughter had taught him that women preferred to select their own clothes.

He wandered to the upper patio with its panoramic view of the cottonwoods along the Rio Grande River with the Sandia Mountains towering in the background. Then he strolled to the Santa Ana Café on the lower level of the hotel.

He chose a table at the edge of the restaurant. There Bug could look through the mesh floor-to-ceiling screen at a courtyard with an adobe *horno* where a woman was baking traditional pueblo bread. He breathed in the aroma of browned bread and heard children screaming—thankfully in the distance—in the adobe-enclosed pool behind the courtyard. He ordered a glass of white wine and began to work on his laptop.

He was so engrossed he didn't notice Sara until she aligned Bug's cart between the mesh screen and the table. The little dog preferred sitting in his own cart to sitting on a chair in restaurants. It pleased restaurant staff, too.

"I think it's a good sign that you're so absorbed by your work. Is the report developing well?" Sara tried to smile, but her lips only quivered.

Sanders knew she was worried about him but was polite enough not to ask for details about his project.

"Your writing is always clear and concise. I'm sure you can produce a document that will make your boss look good, even though she may not admit it." She waved to the waiter and

                    J. L. Greger

sat across from Sanders. "The parking lot is full. They must be having a large conference here today with a catered lunch because this restaurant isn't very full."

Sanders laid his hand on hers. "I'm not as fragile as you seem to think. I know I have options if my employment in the State Department is ended, which seems likely. Both Holms and my boss called this morning."

"Interesting. You might be in a good negotiation position. Think about it. Do they have reason to think you know more than you admitted? I know they both told you not to talk to anyone—which means me." She flashed a smile at the waiter when he placed the menus on the table. "I'd like a quinoa salad with chicken."

Sanders fumbled with the menu. "She knows the menu better than I do." He perused his choices. "I'll have the pueblo fish and chips." He wanted to keep the conversation light. "It's rare that a restaurant offers trout in a fish and chips combo."

Sara seemed to take his cue. "I think the Santa Ana Pueblo supplies some of the meat, fish, and vegetables served in the restaurant. I'll bet they caught the trout in the Rio Grande." She paused for only a couple of seconds. "It would be interesting to know more about the business arrangements between the Santa Ana Pueblo and the Hyatt Corporation for this resort. I'd bet it's complex. The pueblo owns the adjacent casino and the land. The mayor of Mercado said the deal the Santa Ana Pueblo struck with Tesla for a car showroom on their property was masterful. It seems Tesla made a multi-million-dollar contribution to local schools as part of the deal. I wonder what Hyatt had to pay to construct their resort here."

Sanders appreciated Sara's efforts not to be nosy about his business but had no idea of how to answer her question. He was thankful when their food arrived. She promptly cut up much of the chicken on her salad and placed it in a bowl for Bug. Sanders was not pleased when Sara's phone buzzed.

"Oh, hello Chuy." As she listened, she pulled a pen and paper from her purse. "I don't understand. Why didn't anyone notice a car left at the side of their street for almost three weeks?"

Sanders picked at his fish and listened to Sara's conversation.

"Sounds like a good plan. Thanks for not letting any of your deputies touch the car. I can meet you in a half-hour."

After she hung up, he waited for an explanation from Sara. None came. He finally asked, "What was that about?"

"I've not been organized in this investigation. I wondered how Toby got to the cave because his car wasn't in the parking lot on the first day of the investigation. But Candy said he often left his car at a friend's house and hiked to the cave. Considering the roughness of the road, it made sense at the time. Then I forgot about the car."

Sanders stroked Sara hand. "I'm not the only one stressed out by Brazil. By the way, who is Candy?"

"The murder victim's pregnant girlfriend—I guess wife—and caving partner. She's also a suspect." Sara rapidly shoveled salad into her mouth.

"Where are you meeting Chuy?'

"Only a few miles from here. Chuy thinks I should see Toby's vehicle before its moved. A couple in Placitas called the sheriff's office this morning to complain. They said Toby Collins often left his SUV near their house for several days at a time. They were worried because Toby's SUV had been parked by their house now for almost three weeks."

Sanders was saddened that Sara would rush away and he'd have no chance to show her the attractive jacket. They needed time alone together without deadlines or the problems of others. The drive to and from Acoma had been the only time since he arrived when they really talked, and the trip had been marred by worries over the wedding and the meeting with Senator Holms. In the evenings, they'd been too tired for much conversation. "Why don't you leave Bug with me? We'll take our time finishing our meal before we return home. We men need to talk."

Sara flushed. "I'm sorry. I'll try to be home by five."

Sanders looked around the restaurant after Sara rushed out. It wasn't busy. There was only the soft clatter of plates as the busboy cleared tables. He pulled out his laptop. "Bug, why don't you nap. This is a perfect place for me to write."

CHAPTER 24: Putrid Answers

Sara couldn't believe her nose. Chuy and one of his deputies were standing by a dusty, red Land Rover SUV. Its hatch door was open. The rancid odor emanating from the vehicle smelled like rotting flesh.

Chuy greeted her. "Look inside the car."

Sara held her breath and peered through a side window rather than the hatch to avoid the brunt of the stench. She expected to see a body but instead saw two coolers, an open box filled with papers, and a tub of empty water bottles. "Have you taken fingerprints or samples for DNA analyses?"

"No, the couple in this house..." He pointed to the home across from the vehicle. "...are sure the car belongs to Toby Collins."

Sara noted the nearby home looked as if the original structure had been a trailer and rooms had been added as needed. One addition had a sloped shingled roof. Two others had flat roofs. Sara figured the original owners had been hippies, and the current owners hadn't wasted money on trying to make their home and yard appealing. It wasn't uncommon in Placitas. The unincorporated village was a weird combination of millionaire mansions with panoramic views and ramshackle remnants of a hippie community.

Chuy continued speaking as Sara studied the house. "Evidently, Toby paid them a hundred dollars a month in return for the parking space. As I told you when I called, they claimed he often left this vehicle here for several days at a time. We opened the vehicle because they complained of the stink. We lifted the lids on both coolers and didn't see any body parts only two rotisserie roasted chickens in trays and rotting berries. I thought the FBI could handle all analyses."

As Sara backed away from the car, the deputy asked, "Don't you want to examine the items in the car?"

Sara winked at him. "I'll leave that pleasure for the lab crew. They should be arriving soon." She turned again to Chuy. "Did the neighbors say when they first saw the car?"

Chuy pointed to the deputy, who checked his phone. "They said the car was parked here before eight a.m.—when they first looked out—on the Wednesday they left on vacation almost three weeks ago. It was in the same spot when they returned home last Thursday. They finally called today because of the smell."

Sara counted on her fingers. "That coincides with the medical examiners estimate of Toby's time of death. He thought Toby was killed one to two weeks before the rangers found the body on April twenty-first. We now know Toby was alive early Wednesday morning—that's April twelfth—when he left the car here. We've found no evidence that he used his computer and phone after April twelfth. So, he probably was killed on April twelfth."

"Sounds logical."

Sara held her breath and leaned in to look at the box of papers. The top sheet was a cover page of a grant proposal to the U.S. Forest Survey dated two years before. She guessed it might be a copy of the grant proposal that was the basis of the torn proposal in the cave. She quickly backed away from the car and said, "Thanks, Chuy for calling me. I'd like to say we're almost through with this investigation, but the clues keep leading us in circles. We have at least four valid suspects."

Chuy nodded. "It's like that sometimes. You know it was logical for Toby to park the Land Rover here. It's an expensive car and would attract attention in the parking lot for the Sandia Man Cave. It was safer here." He turned to walk away and then turned again. "Don't forget to cite the cooperation of the sheriff's office in any FBI press releases. I need good publicity if I'm going to win the election. Adios."

Sara watched sadly as Chuy walked with a slight limp to his car. She missed the eager, young detective, he'd been before his fall and a couple of bad choices. "Good luck," she whispered.

***

The deputy stayed with the car while Sara questioned the husband and wife living in the nearby house. They explained that Toby generally hiked the mile and half from their home to the cave with a backpack. The woman said, "He claimed he

                                    J. L. Greger

didn't want the car vandalized but I always thought he didn't want people to know he was there." She paused. "He was bit strange."

The husband shook his head. "Hell, he was a zombie who refused to talk most of the time, but his money was good."

Winslow tooted the horn of the FBI van when he arrived. By then, Sara was convinced that Toby had spent many nights and days in the cave. She remembered seeing not only two plastic stools in the hidden room, but also a bed roll. The hidden room must have been Toby's sanctuary. Many autistic individuals were hypersensitive to loud and shrill noises. The walls of the cave would have muffled sounds. Candy and perhaps Ralph, would have known Toby's secrets. *Why were they so reluctant to share them?*

Winslow had already peered into the car by the time Sara had thanked the neighbors for their cooperation. "Cool vehicle. Too bad I can't take it for a spin."

Sara shook her head, and he stopped smiling.

"It looks like it was packed for a couple of day of camping. I'll take prints and samples from all surfaces as I inventory the contents. If you don't mind, I'll start with the coolers. If it's only food, I'll dispose of the rotten mess, so I don't gag."

"Whatever you think best, but don't be tempted to drive the SUV back to the FBI building. Call a tow truck. I think we should keep this vehicle in the FBI's locked parking area until I get some answers."

***

"I'm tired of misleading, incomplete answers. Candy, do you realize we could charge you with Toby's murder?" Sara stared at the disheveled woman who had only moaned when Jack had pulled her red polyester caving suit from her closet and told her the FBI had found red fibers in the cave at a site of a potential fight in the hidden room.

The lawyer from the public defender's office whispered in Candy's ear. She shook her head repeatedly and finally said, "You've got it wrong. Toby often—well occasionally—invited me to his inner sanctum. He preferred to write and even live there. He found it a soothing place to escape loud noises and glaring lights. I thought it was spooky when he closed the trap door."

Sara thought it was time to offer some genuine sympathy. "I would have wanted to scream if he had dropped that door in the hole and I was inside the room."

"I did scream the first time, but I learned to control what Toby called my 'silly' fears."

"Weren't you afraid someone could lock you inside the hidden, dark, almost soundproof room?"

"Not really. Jacob had that concern. He had an engineer help him design the cover. The metal wedges looked like they slid into cracks in the rock, but they actually slid into a metal hoop. Inside the hidden room the hoop was obvious." She stared at Sara. "Didn't you notice the latches on the back of the wooden door? We collected the metal wedges before we entered the room and attached the latches on the back of the trap door to the hoop when we were inside."

Sara didn't want to admit she'd seen the latches but had not thought about their use. She also remembered a metal rim around the hole. That must be the hoop Candy was describing. Candy's comments had reconfirmed her guess that Ralph Edwards had designed the entrance to the hidden room. It meant Ralph Edwards had lied or at least misled her earlier.

Sara decided this was a good time to try to build rapport with Candy. She could worry about Ralph Edwards later. She saw Candy's lawyer smiled slightly. This was probably a good sign. "How did you overcome your fear of caves? The hidden room gives me the willies."

Candy lifted her head and stared at Sara. "I thought I was the only one afraid of caves. I got used to the darkness, but reverberating echoes inside deep caves still scare me."

Sara thought this could be a turning point if she didn't push too hard. Candy had uttered what seemed like honest statements. Jack had bet her on the way to Candy's apartment that this interrogation would result in more lies and little progress. She had bet him a drink at McDonalds that she'd finally get Candy to talk but had believed he was right. Now she had hope of winning a free drink. Sara saw Candy had returned to her previous position with shoulder sagging and her head almost hitting the table.

Sara reached across the table and touched the tips of Candy's fingers. "If you're afraid of caves, why are you studying microbes from caves? Why are you an active caver?

"You don't understand what's it's like to have no options. You're successful and confident."

Sara remembered Candy considered herself plain and too old to still be single. "What do you mean you have no options? You're obviously bright. I read your published papers. Your work is thorough and worthwhile." She moved her left hand to cover one of Candy's. "Ralph told me Levine wasn't a good mentor. I agree with Ralph. With good writing and analytic skills and your unique caving experiences, you have lots of options when you finish your degree."

"Yeah, to be hack in a lab the rest of my life. I'll be a postdoc and then a research associate, dependent on the funding of the next grant forever. Work in a lab for me is leg cramps from standing all day and headaches from tedious attention to endless details. And getting grant and contract renewals is always hard. The worry gives me heartburn."

Sara thought she was getting to know the real Candy. Then Jack leaned over Sara's shoulder and flashed by her face a photo he'd evidently just found. It surprised Sara so much, she lost her concentration. "Where was I? Oh yes. So, you don't like lab work. Do you like collecting samples in caves?"

Candy looked up. "The microorganisms that survive in caves are so brave."

Sara suppressed a gasp. "What do you mean? How are the microorganisms brave?"

Candy lifted her head and wiped tears from her cheeks. "Brave might not be the right word. The microorganisms have adapted to the darkness... and limited water and nutrients. They not only survive but grow and produce amazing chemicals to protect themselves. When I'm busy collecting samples—with plenty of light focused on my work— I can ignore the emptiness around me... and in me."

"So, you like certain aspects of the science?"

"Yes, and I like working around men more than women." Candy lowered her head again.

Sara thought this was a chance to explore the relationship between Candy and Toby—to see if anger or jealousy could have driven Candy to kill him. The photo Jack had shown her would make most women angry. "Was Toby easy to work with? Did you like working with him?"

"He listened to my ideas. So did Jacob." She raised her head and bit her lip. "Jacob always said I was good for Toby. He encouraged us to spend time together in the hidden room. We not only collected samples, but we wrote there... together."

Sara thought of the food in Toby's car and the bed roll in the hidden room. "Did you do anything else? We found Toby's car today. There was a lot of food in a cooler."

Candy and her lawyer looked confused. Candy answered, "Cavers always bring food and water along. He must have forgotten he had food in the car."

Sara decided not to follow up on that lead and instead motioned to Jack to sit down. He had been listening through his earbuds to Sara's and Candy's conversation as he wandered about Candy's apartment pulling drawers out and checking their underside, sliding a metal ruler into cracks and pushing out debris, and occasionally putting something into a plastic bag.

"Did you sometimes sleep in the cave?"

"What do you mean?"

Sara pointed to the backside of the photo Jack pushed toward Candy. "I think this was taken in the hidden room."

Jack tapped the edge of the photo. "It was taped to the underside of a drawer in the chest in your bedroom." He turned the photo over.

Candy lay spread eagle on the floor of the cave in her red caving suit. The suit was unzipped all the way from her neck to her crotch. She had nothing on underneath the suit.

The lawyer gasped.

Candy screamed. "Toby wanted a baby, but... he could only perform in the cave. That's why we spent so much time there."

Sara tried not to stare at the photo. It provided a logical explanation for the swirled dirt on the floor of the hidden room and the bits of red and blue fibers. She also thought a jury might understand Candy's frustration and eventual anger with Toby if they saw this photo. "Did having sex in the cave turn you on?"

Candy turned red as she straightened in her chair. "No. The floor was hard. The sharp edges on the rocks hurt my back and knees. But Toby convinced me if I had his baby, I'd always have an income. His trust would provide money." She put her hand over the photo. "It was degrading, but I had no choice."

"Did it make you angry?"

"Not really."

Sara doubted the answer. "When was the last time you visited the cave?"

Candy lowered her head and whispered to her lawyer before she spoke. "This will look bad. It was on Wednesday morning almost three weeks ago."

"So, that was April twelfth?"

"I guess."

Sara decided to bluff "Did you work on a manuscript with Toby?"

"No, we worked on another proposal. This one was to be sent to the National Science Foundation eventually. We didn't make much progress, but Toby was frantic to get enough funds to cover my salary."

"Did you work on the proposal before or after you had sex?"

Candy emitted a squeak like a mouse. "Toby always wanted to work first. After we had sex on the twelfth, he said that he didn't want me to visit the cave anymore. He said it wasn't necessary, I was pregnant." Candy jerked her head up and her eyes seemed brighter than usual. "Can you imagine how I felt? I was so angry. I tore up the proposal and threw the pieces around the room. Then I lifted the door and left."

Sara thought about the torn pages in the cave. "Did you rip all the pages, or did you save a couple?"

Candy looked down again. "I saved the title page because Toby had listed me as a Co-PI. It was the kindest thing he'd ever done for me."

Sara guessed a psychologist would say Toby was trying to show Candy, he loved her or at least appreciated her. She knew this wasn't the time to play psychologist. "Did you accidentally pick up another page or two?"

"How did you know? I picked up not only the title page but also the last page too, but I didn't notice until I was going down the stairs. I tore up the last page and threw it out over the trees. It was my goodbye to the cave."

Jack had bounced in his seat ever since Candy had admitted anger. "I can't believe you didn't hit Toby. All the women I know would have bashed me if I talked like he did. Did you at least slap him?"

"No."

Jack leaned forward. "Candy, did you follow him when he left the cave later, sneak up behind him, and hit him? He deserved it."

Candy straightened. "I didn't kill him. Why would I? He and this baby are my ticket out of endless work with little to show for my efforts. He never hit me. Much of the time, he was kind. I thought he was my best option."

Sara stared at Candy in disbelief. In one sense, Candy's marriage sounded like legalized prostitution. Candy had never said she loved Toby or that Toby loved her. On the other hand, Sara pitied this woman driven by fear of an uncertain and destitute future.

"I agree with you. It would have been a foolish emotional outburst for you to kill Toby. And I don't think you're prone to spontaneous outbursts of emotions. But I'm no expert. I think you need to talk to a psychologist for two reasons. One, a psychologist might be able to help you understand that Toby loved you but because of his autism couldn't express his love in ways you could appreciate." Sara hoped this statement was true but recognized it might not be. "Two, both the FBI and your defense will need the testimony of a psychologist on your mental state if we go to trial. Let's start with an evaluation by a psychologist under contract with the FBI."

Her lawyer nodded in agreement, but Candy cried hysterically.

***

Sara called a psychologist with whom she had worked with before on FBI cases. He was busy and referred Sara to a young man who had recently completed his training as a psychologist—Paul Brimley.

Sara called Brimley, who agreed to meet Candy at the FBI Building, where he was consulting on another case.

Sara consulted with Candy's lawyer and Jack and then said to Candy, "The psychologist will see you in an hour. Why don't we first stop at a McDonalds and get something to drink? Maybe a sandwich if you're hungry. It will be Jack's treat."

Jack groaned. "I should have known better than to bet against you."

CHAPTER 25: Is Jack in Charge?

After they had settled Candy with the psychologist, Sara handed Jack a list. "We have a lot of loose ends."

"Like what?"

She pointed at the handwritten list. "One, computer techs were supposed to check Ben's schedule during the last two months and see if changes had made in Ben's supposed calendar after the day was over. Two, the lab should have analyzed the plastic bottles found near Toby's body for prints and DNA. Three, Winslow may have found something useful in Toby's Land Rover. Four, by now, the computer techs should have tracked the revisions of the grant proposal to determine Candy's and Levine's input. It also dawned on me it was unlikely Toby could connect with the internet when in the cave."

Jack rolled his eyes as Sara spoke. "I get the picture. I also think we should have the lab check for semen on Candy's caving suit. It would tend to authenticate her story. I'll talk to Winslow about your first three points. Point four dealing with the scientific papers is all yours." He smiled. "Then there's another little problem. We haven't identified the murder weapon. I'm sure it's not in Candy's apartment. I even checked for loose floorboards."

Sara's phone pinged and she studied the screen for thirty seconds. "I need to get home early today."

Jack was surprised by Sara's direct statement with no explanation. He waited for more.

"Please. I'll cover for you sometime." She seemed earnest.

"Okay. I'll try to pull together all our evidence on Ben. The fact that his two pages were scattered with the bits from the research proposal makes me think Ben could have been in the cave before or after Candy. It's weak but..."

"Great." Sara rushed off.

Less than twenty minutes later, the psychologist summoned Sara and Jack with an email:

> *I want a copy of the tapes of your interviews with Candy.*
>
> *You were right. Toby didn't mean to be abusive, but you forget about Levine. He called Candy a "slut" and said he "pitied poor innocent Toby getting stuck with her." How did you miss Levine's abusive behavior?*
>
> *We need to talk now. She has threatened to kill Levine. It's your fault.*

***

Brimley's red face returned to its normal pale color as Jack explained the situation. "We read Candy her rights each time we saw her and had a new search warrant each time. A lawyer from the public defender's office was with her the last two times. We caught her in several lies. You should listen to our tapes before you make accusations."

Sara, in her usual overly detailed manner, added that she had tried to explore the relationship between Levine and Candy. She consulted her notes and cited comments from her interviews with Levine, Ralph Edwards, and the technicians and graduate student in Levine's lab. "All but one disliked Levine, but no one mentioned a sexual overtone in Levine's remarks to Candy."

Brimley finally sighed. "Candy told me you tried to help her. Perhaps, your comments in the last interview made Candy admit her real problems to me. Still Sara, I'm surprised as a woman scientist you didn't recognize the profound effect sexual harassment can have on a woman."

Sara bit her lip. "I'm sorry. This case has been a nightmare and Candy is...'

Jack decided to defend Sara. "Candy keeps playing games. Are you sure you've determined her real nature?"

Brimley shrugged. "You'd better arrange for police to monitor her tonight in some sort of shelter. In her current state, she might try to escape the shelter and kill Levine."

Jack suppressed the urge to scream and only muttered "Darn," repeatedly.

Sara straightened. "I think we need to listen to the tape of *your* interview with Candy. What did you do to turn Candy's depression into potentially aggressive behavior?"

"I don't know."

Sara continued, but her voice was softened. "Or are you suggesting Candy has been acting depressed to hide her underlying anger. If so, she could have killed Toby. After our last interview, Jack and I were ready to cross her off our list of suspects for Toby's murder because we thought she was suffering from understandable depression. I mean she's a graduate student trying to finish her Ph.D., is pregnant, has been told her financial support ends shortly, and has just learned of the death of her husband."

Brimley closed his eyes and sighed. "I don't know. Perhaps, I shouldn't have mentioned Freud's theories to her and explored her sexuality so much."

Sara's face turned pale as she stood. "Dr Brimley, do you understand your role as a psychological consultant for the FBI?"

***

Jack didn't ask Sara what she was going to do when she rushed from the room. He guessed she'd first inform the ranking agent in the building that a difficult but non-dangerous suspect had been turned into a potentially dangerous one requiring continuous oversight. He wondered if she would call Carbonne and interrupt his honeymoon. Sara and Carbonne behaved more like siblings than worker and boss. Anything was possible, but he doubted Sara would call Carbonne. He guessed she'd seek advice from the psychologist who had referred Brimley to her. In any case, Jack was sure Brimley would learn a lot in the next twenty-four hours.

After Jack talked to Brimley a bit more, he was convinced Candy could be destructive in the group home setting the psychologist had suggested. Jack arranged for Candy to stay in an FBI safehouse with two guards. As luck would have it, space was available in a safehouse with an endangered witness from another case. They would be kept in separate areas of the house.

Jack left Brimley to listen to the tapes of the previous interviews with Candy and almost ran down the hallway to the lab. Winslow's hard evidence and can-do personality were a joy after dealing with Brimley.

***

Winslow's smile faded when the door to the lab closed behind Jack. "Isn't Sara coming? Isn't her boyfriend here today?"

"Sorry man, you get me. Sara has her own problems. What have you got from the car?"

"In the goo inside the so-called cooler was a grocery receipt." Winslow shook his head. "I'm surprised the mix didn't dissolve the ink, but I was able to see that the groceries had been purchased on April twelfth at seven in the morning at a local Walmart."

"Good. It confirms all the other estimates of the time of the murder. Anything else?"

"There were two identical cave axes at the bottom of the box of papers. One was engraved with TC—Toby's initials— and had only his fingerprints. The other was engraved with JC—Jacob's initials—and had Candy's and Toby's fingerprints. I checked with the medical examiner. There's little doubt. He was killed with a similar cave axe."

"Guess that's why I couldn't find a cave axe in Candy's apartment. Logical and tends to suggest Candy had no way to kill Toby. What else?"

"Checked with the rangers. Internet coverage is spotty in the Cibola Forest and not possible in the cave. One agent said she'd seen Toby sitting with his laptop on the stairs to the cave many times. She guessed internet access was available there."

"Bet we both know the spot."

"Yep, but it means the blood spots at that point on the stairs are useless in regard to this murder investigation." Winslow shook his head. "A lot of wasted work, but the water bottles near where Toby was found are interesting, well sorta. Lots of unknown DNA and prints on the bottles. However, two of the bottles had Toby's prints and DNA. One had Ben's prints and DNA, also."

"We got him."

                                    J. L. Greger

"Doubt it. Both bottles have glove prints that partially destroyed many of the other prints. I think someone wearing gloves handled the bottles after Toby and Ben."

"It could be anyone, but those prints might be enough to scare Ben into being honest, if presented right. Guess I'll talk to the computer tech next about Ben's appointments." As Jack walked away, he thought Sara and Carbonne were right—a good lab tech like Winslow could be an agent's best friend.

***

The computer technician sniffed when Jack approached her desk. "What do you want?"

"I'm checking on the searches done in regard to Ben Collins's schedule and his financial and computer records."

"I'm sorry to say I've found some irregularities. Ben did the surgery on my mother for cataracts. I'd trust him to do mine when the time comes."

"Is that why you didn't forward your finds to Sara or me?" Jack sat in the chair by her desk.

"Young man, I don't think you realize how many searches I do for arcane data. I never get a positive response from the agents." As she spoke the woman was pulling up files on her computer.

Jack remembered Carbonne's advice to make lab staff feel appreciated. "This will be different. I'll tell you how I'll use the data."

The middle-aged woman stopped spluttering. "I'm sorry to be so hostile but one of the agents exploded at me this morning." She turned the screen so Jack could see it better. "I tracked changes in Dr. Collin's calendar over the last two months. It wasn't easy. His calendar was changed almost hourly on some days, *but* there were only four times that the appointments were changed after the appointments supposedly occurred. One time was about a month ago on April seventh."

Jack did a double take. "I think that's the day Ben argued with Toby while the Sandia Grotto group was cleaning graffiti from the walls of the Sandia Man Cave. I'll have to check. Can you print out the calendar as it appeared that day and as it was altered later?"

"Of course."

Jack peered at the screen. "Can you tell who made the changes?"

"Not really." The tech traced her finger along a side column. "It was done on Dr. Collins's computer. I assume several staff members had access to the computer on his desk."

"How about the other times his calendar was changed after the appointments were supposed to have occurred?"

The tech scrolled down the screen. "Three weeks ago, the calendars for Tuesday, April eleventh and Wednesday, April twelfth were altered by someone on Dr. Collins's computer." She printed out the before and after schedules before Jack could make the request.

Jack scanned the sheets. "Do you realize one of those days is the day of Toby's murder?"

"Oh dear, I had hoped these data would clear Ben of suspicion." She scrolled rapidly down the screen. "I also found post-event changes on the calendar for last Thursday, April twenty-seventh, between one and three."

Jack sighed. "Sara and I must have spooked him when we talked to him last Thursday morning." He flashed a wide grin at the woman. "You've been helpful, but I have more questions. Did you have a chance to check whether Ben had written personal checks to any of the employees in Collins Eye Associates?"

"Yes, I checked. His checks were all to businesses. However, he appears to withdraw five hundred dollars about twice a month through an ATM." She pulled up a page on her screen. "Oh, last Wednesday he withdrew an additional thousand dollars."

"He must like paying in cash."

"Seems so. He and his wife appear to use different cards, and she pays all the household bills. I did find one surprising purchase about three weeks ago. He bought a cave axe from REI on the same Tuesday that was altered on his schedule."

"Print that." Jack studied the screen. The purchase had been made during the time Ben was out of the office—or at least had altered his schedule. "You may have given me what it will take to get honest answers from Ben Collins. I appreciate your help."

The woman's lips quivered as she gave a thin smile. "It's a pleasure to help agents when they cooperate."

                                          J. L. Greger

Jack whistled as he started to walk away and then turned back. "I forgot. Were you able to gain any info about Ben's email to Candy?"

The woman blinked. "What are you talking about?"

He pulled out his phone, frantically searched his files, and showed her Ben's email:

As we discussed, you could earn $5,000 if you leave Albuquerque <u>alone</u> by June 1.

CHAPTER 26: Sanders Decides

During the drive from the FBI building, Sara had pondered what had prompted Sanders's text:

I need to talk to you before five today.

She still had no idea when she walked into her home at five minutes to four. Sanders was sitting on the sofa petting Bug. Sara sat next to him and put her right arm around his shoulders. "What happened?"

"Bug and I stayed at Tamaya after you left. I was making good progress on my project. The Secretary of State called. He asked me a few questions about my project. Then he asked whether I wanted my boss's position as undersecretary. When, I asked what happened to her, he said it was 'irrelevant' and wanted my answer by five."

"Oh, my. Can he offer you a position? I thought an undersecretary position had to be approved by the Senate after a hearing before a Senate committee."

"Of course. He offered me an acting temporary position while personnel staff in the State Department reviewed my credentials, prepped me for the hearing, and prepared the papers for my nomination."

Sara had a bad feeling. "Isn't it unusual to give the candidate the position on an acting basis while getting ready for the hearing?"

He frowned. "Probably but the secretary seemed eager to make changes."

"Okay." Sara wanted to make Sanders think about his rather unusual situation. "Are you comfortable with the rush? It could put you at a disadvantage in a hearing because your actions during the interim period could be challenged. As you well know, it's hard to get your footing in high level positions at first."

Sanders stared at her.

She thought he looked like a woebegone, wet dog and decided he needed encouragement from her now, not questions. "First off, I should say I'm impressed. The offer is a real honor. You've always wanted a high-level position in Washington. But is this the position you wanted?"

"As you know I wanted to lead the Bureau of Intelligence and Research of the State Department. Or I guess, a leadership role at the CIA or FBI. I want to use my expertise is in obtaining and analyzing data—intelligence. I don't want to determine policy and spend much of my time at Congressional hearings. It's what my boss does."

She kissed Sanders's cheek. "Did you tell the secretary what you thought your strengths are? And what you wanted?"

"I did. He said it wasn't on the table now."

"I guess you must decide how important a title is to you. Is the title more important than the work?" She decided it was time to address his secret assignment, even though it might upset him. "Look, I don't know what your boss and the Senate Intelligence Committee asked you to do, *but* I can guess. It was basically to write a policy piece on how to use espionage more effectively."

Sanders pulled away from her. "Not really."

"Okay, but it was related to your ability to use data gained through espionage to win the cooperation of leaders or potential future leaders in Brazil and previously in Bolivia and Cuba."

Sanders groaned. "Do I talk in my sleep?"

"Sometimes, but not coherently."

He pulled a treat from his slacks and gave it to Bug. "You bluff well."

Sara snorted. "My so-called bluffs are based on educated guesses about data and people." She got up and pulled two cans of soda from the refrigerator and a glass from a cabinet. She handed the glass and a can to Sanders. "As you know, I haven't trusted—That's the wrong word but I don't know the right one—your boss for a long time. She has an impossible job and seems insecure."

"She's cautious because she doesn't want to destabilize hard-won alliances."

Sara silently practiced what she would say next. "She knows what policies and alliances she wants and expects you— and any of her staff who care—to make her wishes happen." Sara didn't add that several staffers in the State Department had told Sara that they were looking for new jobs because they'd given up trying to please the undersecretary.

Sanders sipped his soda. "It's not that simple."

"Let me finish. I think—and you usually agree—that policies must be based on reality, not wishes. You're good at recognizing reality and modifying your wishes to reach an acceptable compromise with others. She always expects to get her way."

Sanders stood and began to pace. "Politicians make promises and then must deliver. My boss is a good politician." He continued to pace.

"The question is: Are you?" After a minute of silence, Sara added, "I should have accompanied you to Brazil, but Bug couldn't survive a move to another country, especially a hot jungle. He also would have been miserable if I left him with someone else. It would be like killing him either way."

Sanders snorted.

Sara thought she'd better continue rapidly before Sanders said something about Bug that they'd both regret. "I will go to Washington with you. Well, I won't sell this house, but Bug and I will spend almost half of our time in Washington. I can get occasional assignments there. That way, I won't poke into your business too much but will be supportive. You know we've functioned well as a couple because we've allowed each other enough space to be ourselves."

Sanders continued to pace.

"Bug and I will take a walk while you make your decision and call the Secretary of State."

***

Sara and Bug took a short walk and then sat in the shaded seats at the bocce courts. One of things she liked about her home was the variety of activities available in the adults-only community. She and Bug watched six men and two women playing bocce ball on the two courts. All of them knew Bug and greeted him by name. She doubted most of them knew her

J. L. Greger

name. It was okay. She didn't know most of their names, but they all shared a sense of camaraderie.

She doubted she'd build casual, comfortable relationships easily in Washington. Sanders's condo was almost on Capitol Hill. Everyone there was always rushing to work or events and seldom took time to chat, but she did have a secret weapon. She'd found walking a dog regularly in a neighborhood was a good way to meet friendly people.

Her phone pinged. Jack had been busy.

> *Winslow found two cave axes in Toby's car. Candy appears to have used Jacob's old cave axe. Neither of those axes had blood stains but the medical examiner confirmed a similar axe was used to kill Toby. These are from REI.*
>
> *Ben was busy on April 11. He bought a cave axe at REI, pulled $1,000 from an ATM, sent the email bribe to Candy, and altered his calendar. Candy deposited a thousand dollars in her checking account at two-thirty the next day—April 12.*
>
> *Ben's alibis are bogus. His calendar was changed for April 7, 11, and 12. I think we should interview him together at his office tomorrow at 8. I checked. His first appointment is at 8:30.*

Sara's response was rapid:

> *I'll be there at 7:45 tomorrow.*

Sara knew she next logical task for her was to review Toby's grant proposal. She pondered how to retrieve her laptop from her house without disturbing Sanders. The idea of reviewing Toby's grant proposal on the small screen of her phone was unthinkable. Then she felt someone's hands on her shoulders. It was Sanders.

"I made my decision."

"Oh." Sara waited as Sanders walked around the covered bench and sat by her.

"I'm not taking my boss's job. Funny... The secretary wasn't surprised. He even said. 'That's smart on your part."

"Did he say anything else? What about your secret project?"

Sanders lowered his voice and leaned closer. "Let's not talk here."

Sara let Bug take the lead and she circled one arm around Sander's waist as they walked back to her house. When they reached her drive, Sanders said, "The secretary told me to take Senator Holms's advice. I must have acted surprised because he laughed and said, 'You didn't think the senator would have talked to you without telling me. We are in the same party.' The secretary also told me I could talk to you about the project. He said, 'Holms tells me you have the perfect partner for a politician. A woman smart enough to give good advice but wise enough to know you may not take it.'"

Sara opened the door. "Let's celebrate tonight with a good bottle of wine. I've got a casserole of chicken parmesan in the freezer and plenty of salad ingredients in the refrigerator."

"What are we celebrating?"

"Surviving a hard day."

CHAPTER 27: An Excessive Response

Wednesday

Sara pulled into a parking space at the back of Collins Eye Associates at fifteen to eight. Jack's car was already there, but he wasn't in sight. Another man appeared to be snoozing in the passenger side of the front seat of Jack's car. Sara walked to the front of the building and found Jack monitoring the main entrance.

"I wanted eyes on the two main entrances. The other agent—Doug—spotted Ben entering the building at seven-thirty. Neither of us have seen him leave."

"Are you anticipating problems?"

"Yes. The evidence against Ben may not be enough to convict him of murder but he is acting guilty. I got a search warrant as you suggested. On a whim last night, I checked whether he'd scheduled any flights recently. Last Thursday after we talked to him, Ben booked a business class ticket to fly from Denver to Mexico City on Delta for yesterday and another business class ticket to fly from Denver to San Juan, Costa Rica for tomorrow. I called Delta. They said they would allow Ben to board another flight if seats were available 'cause he'd called and said he'd not be on the flight yesterday. Did you know there were open-ended flights?"

Sara laughed. "You're showing your youth. When I first flew, bigwigs often booked open-ended return flights on international assignments. I figured the real purpose of business class was it allowed flyers with extra money to in essence book open-ended flights, *but* I never knew the details. Good job. Now what?"

"We go in. Doug stays in the car and watches the back exit." Sara donned a headset with a mouthpiece and ear buds per Jack's instructions. Jack led the way to Ben's private office, where Jack and Sara had talked to Ben the previous week.

Sara knocked and then pushed the door open when no one answered. She saw a balding man of about Ben's height pull a black object from his desk and run to a side door. "Stop. FBI. We have a search warrant. Put the gun down."

Jack didn't wait for Sara to finish. He said one loud "Darn," and ran down the hall.

Sara notified Doug to expect Ben to run out the back door and to summon help. She heard in her in-ear monitor a slurred, "Yes," a car door slamming, and heavy breathing.

Jack yelled, "Stop FBI. We just want to talk." Sara guessed Jack had seen Ben moving down the cross corridor because Jack ran there.

Sara ran into Ben's office and then through the open side doorway into a small office. A woman with her eyes opened wide screamed, "You've no right."

"We're FBI. Those who help Ben Collins escape this building will be arrested for abetting the escape of a criminal. Where did Ben go?"

The woman seemed to deflate and moaned, "Don't know. Not his secretary."

"Is there an intercom system in the building? Can you access it?"

The woman shaking badly pushed three numbers on her phone and handed it to Sara. "Speak into it. Everyone will hear."

Sara grabbed the phone and said, "FBI emergency. Ben Collins, stop running and turn yourself in. Everyone in the building is advised to stay where they are. Do not try to help or hinder Ben. He may be armed and dangerous." Sara turned to the woman. "Where are exits to the building besides the main back and front doors?"

Sara repeated the woman's words into her mouthpiece so only Jack and Doug could hear. "Three exits on the back; only one is unlocked to allow easy entrance from the outside. Each is at the end of a cross corridor. One locked exit on each side."

She turned to the woman. "Is there a second floor or basement to this building? How do I get to them."

J. L. Greger

"The basement contains our records and can only be entered with a pass card. There are surgical suites on the second floor. You can use this cross corridor to get to stairs to the basement or the second floor."

"Does Ben have a pass card?"

The woman opened the top desk draw and pulled out a card. "No. This is the one he'd use."

Sara took the pass card and transmitted the new info to Doug and Jack. "How soon will other agents get here?"

"They should be here in one minute," said Doug. "I've not heard from Jack."

She hadn't heard from Jack either and was worried. The good news was she hadn't heard a shot either. That changed as a shot reverberated from below. Then there was another shot.

Sara handed a card with the FBI's alert line number to the woman. "Call this number. Stay on the phone and take instructions. If you need to reach me, use your intercom system." Sara grabbed a big book from the shelf and whispered into her mouthpiece as she ran, "Heard shots. I think from the basement. Proceeding down same corridor as Ben and Jack."

Sara wedged the big book into the external exit door at the end of the corridor. She could hear sirens in the distance. She spoke into her mouthpiece, "Wedged open back exit where Jack and suspect last seen. Am exploring the stairs to the basement."

She heard heavy breathing and a muted "Yes," in her ear bud. Doug continued, "First place I'll send arriving agents."

What should she do? She couldn't rescue Jack, but she could get the basic layout of the situation for agents, *if* she was careful.

She descended the stairs slowly and wished she had a gun. *Too late now*. There was a door with a window at the bottom of the stairs. She crawled down the last steps so no one could see her through the window.

She peeked through the window. All she saw at first was a blank wall. She heard a moan and looked to her left. A door with a keycard entry system was at the end of a short hall.

Ben lay on the floor in front of the door with his hands and feet handcuffed. Dribbles of blood were on Ben and the floor. Jack sat nearby. The hole in Jack's slacks and the blood stains on them suggested he was the one injured, but the moans came from Ben.

Sara yelled into her mike, "Officer down! We're in the basement at rear entrance with door open."

She opened the door at the bottom of the stairs and sighed with relief. The amounts of blood on the floor and on the leg of Jack's slacks were not large. "Jack, how bad is it?"

Jack glared at her. "Bad enough. Darn fool shot at me when you blasted over the intercom system. I shot at his legs to scare him, but the bullet ricocheted off the concrete floor and hit my calf. By then Ben was shaking and dropped his gun. I made him put cuffs around his own ankles and wrists. Then I waited for you." He growled. "You took your time."

"I'm not a real agent and I'm afraid it shows. I left the exit door open to this stairwell. Help should be here…"

Three agents thundered down the stairs. Two of them created a chair with their arms and carried Ben up the stairs because he couldn't walk with the cuffs around his ankles. The moment they reached the top of the stairs, Sara heard Ben scream, "Lawyer."

Meanwhile EMTs moved a gurney into the small hall, hooked Jack up to monitoring systems, and placed him on the gurney. Before they carried Jack away, Sara said, "Why didn't you report on what you were doing?"

"I was busy, and you were talking enough for all of us."

***

Jack was back from the hospital before Doug and Sara could question Ben in the presence of his lawyer. It seemed the bullet had passed through the skin and a bit of muscle in Jack's calf. Sara recognized that although the wound was minor, Jack was in shock because he'd never been shot before. She urged him to go home to rest, but he ignored her and a physician's advice. He kept insisting, "I want to nail the twit."

Sara started the interview by reading the list of potential new charges against Ben because of his escape attempt. Sara chuckled as she read the list and saw Jack smile. Ben had turned what could have been a simple interview into a major event by trying to run. As expected, Ben refused to answer any questions about his flight reservations or his actions during the morning.

Jack didn't act like an injured agent and asked the next question. "You bought a cave axe at REI Tuesday, April eleventh. Where is it?"

Sara provided details, including a copy of the receipt.

Ben seemed dumbfounded and whispered to his lawyer, who nodded. "It was a birthday gift for my oldest daughter. She wanted to go caving with her uncle. Just what I need another whacko in the family."

Jack repeated, "Where is it now?"

"In my daughter's room."

Doug stood. "Ben, do I have your permission to retrieve it. We can get a search warrant."

The lawyer whispered to Ben before Ben said, "Sure."

Doug disappeared.

Sara detailed the evidence *proving* Ben had visited Sandia Man Cave on April twelfth. Sara felt confident enough to use the word *proving* because the psychologist had learned that Candy had almost backed into Ben's car as she left in fury on that Wednesday around noon.

Ben's lawyer listened to the points more carefully than Ben and encouraged Ben to speak.

Ben said, "Sure I was there. I found Toby sitting under a tree working on his computer. He gave me a bottle of water. I asked whether he signed the agreement. The weirdo smiled and pretended to tear up a piece of paper. We argued. I might have shoved him, but not that hard. He fell and moaned about his left arm. I ran away before he slugged me."

The lawyer said, "I doubt you can trace Toby's death to a head injury caused by a fall. You've been strangely silent about the autopsy report, even though you forced us to listen to your comments on the body's decomposition when found. I suspect your case will fall apart when the cave axe found in Ben's daughter's bedroom is analyzed."

Sara didn't allow the muscles in her face to move. "We'll see. Now, let's examine other sets of charges against Ben." She proceeded to list the vandalism charges stemming from Ben's painted slander of Toby on the cave's wall the month before. She noted Toby and members of the Sandia Grotto group had been removing the graffiti when Ben arrived on April seventh. "Two members of this group claimed Ben admitted spray-painting the slur."

The lawyer laughed. "Vandalism is a misdemeanor."

"Ben also threatened Candy and bribed her." Sara pushed a copy of the emailed blackmail note across the table.

The lawyer laughed. "This is only May. The note's deadline is June first."

"Ben broke his usual banking pattern and pulled an extra thousand dollars from his account on. April eleventh. The next day Candy deposited a thousand dollars into her checking account." She sorted through a pile of papers and found records of Ben's ATM withdrawal and Candy's ATM deposit.

"It doesn't prove anything."

Sara decided to bluff. "Candy was pleased with the cash payment but was distressed by the photo."

Ben squirmed in his chair. "What photo?"

The lawyer stopped Ben from saying more and held his hand up to hide his lips as he whispered to Ben. He withdrew his hand. "I think we should postpone any more discussion until the cave axe is found and analyzed in a lab. My client is exhausted and should return home."

Jack slapped the table. "Are you kidding? He's a flight risk. He's got at least two open-ended flight tickets. Even New Mexico judges will insist he be held until his arraignment..." Jack grinned. "...and this case will be arraigned in federal court by the U.S. Attorney."

The lawyer whispered to his client. Ben burst into tears.

CHAPTER 28: Who Is Ruthless?

Thursday

Jack sat with his leg propped up on a chair. Bug had sniffed Jack's leg when Jack limped into the conference room and then lain down by Jack's other foot. Even though Jack's feet were immobile his upper body wasn't. He thumped on the table as he read the lab report. "I can't believe that twit ran from me. He knew that cave axe had never been used. Let alone sunk into Toby's head."

Doug shook his head. "I was sure, too. Innocent men don't run like Ben did."

"I guess this incident shows Ben may not be autistic, like Toby, but he's not a rational adult either." Sara shrugged. "Moreover, Ben knew he'd been at the cave near the time of Toby's murder. He also knew he was a suspect because of his past behavior at the cave. It's not surprising that he didn't think anyone would believe his story." She sat down. "At least Ben and Candy have nailed down the time of the murder. Both saw Toby on Wednesday around noon. No one—that we know of—saw or heard from Toby on or after Wednesday afternoon. Toby sent his last email on Wednesday around eleven. Those details fit with the medical examiner's estimates. Most likely, Toby was killed between noon and sunset on Wednesday, April twelfth."

"Agreed, but I thought we'd solved the case as I lay on the floor at Collins Eye Associates." Jack rubbed his leg. "Ben had a motive." Jack added on his fingers. "Toby's refusal to allow the trust to be changed and Candy's pregnancy cost Ben at least a million dollars."

"But he is innocent." Doug added, "Three staff members at the eye clinic are willing to testify that Ben returned by one to his office on Wednesday, April twelfth. They remembered because he was jittery. He dropped surgical utensils on the floor twice during the eye surgery he performed at one-thirty. He was so slow, they had to reschedule several patients. None of the staff could leave until after six."

Sara sighed. "Poor Ben. Here are the charges against him: Vandalism of federal property from a month ago and threatening and bribing Candy from three weeks ago. Today we're charging him with resisting arrest and endangering the life of a federal agent."

Jack shook his head. "I hope the federal judge doesn't snicker at the arraignment. What did the U.S. Attorney say?"

Sara had spent an hour on the phone with two lawyers from the U.S. Attorney's office. She saw no reason to report both lawyers had snickered throughout most of the discussions. "They want to settle out of court. They doubt Ben will go on another crime spree. They plan to offer Ben a deal after they explain to Ben that he could receive twenty years for shooting at a federal agent."

"What's the final offer?"

Sara read the notes on her laptop. "Three months in jail and a year's probation afterward. Ben would have to do a thousand hours of prescribed community service. The U.S. attorney will require Ben to complete his community service by doing cataract and other eye surgeries on prisoners in the federal prisons, particularly ones in Florence, Colorado. One of the lawyers talking to me thought walking into the supermax facilities in Florence would make Ben—and I quote—'urinate in his pants.'"

Jack sighed. "I guess that will be my revenge—thinking about Ben working in the clinic of a high security prison. I've never seen it, but I hear the supermax in Florence gives you the willies when you enter it."

Sara looked up from her laptop. "I've interviewed a prisoner there."

Both Jack and Doug stopped what they were doing and stared at Sara. "You?"

"It wasn't pleasant, but the prisoner I was seeing was scarier. I thought of the supermax as my protection." She wrinkled her nose. "There is one strange feature to the attorneys' decision. To make this decision viable, they'll have to arrange for Ben not to lose his medical licenses."

Jack rubbed his leg. "Is that unusual?"

"Yes, I wonder if someone in the U.S. Attorney's Office is Ben's patient and owes him a favor. Or if they have a prisoner in the supermax or elsewhere in the federal prison system that they think can coax to tell them something important if he gets surgery done on his eyes by an experienced ophthalmologist, not a physician finishing his residency in ophthalmology." Sara didn't add the prisoner she knew in the supermax was about the age to need cataract surgery. He also had the temperament to demand the best medical care and probably knew secrets that would be useful to the FBI. *It was from a lifetime ago.* She thought a second and realized it was only two years since she'd seen him.

"Talk about being cynical. Sara, do you think the U.S. Attorney would withhold medical treatment to get info from a prisoner?" Jack rubbed his leg. "We could find out if we tried."

Jack had jarred Sara from her musings. "Your leg must not hurt much if you're frisky enough to try to trip up the lawyers in the U.S. Attorney's Office. It could be dangerous." She played with her laptop for a minute. "I also talked to FBI bureaucrats in Washington. Your wound will be handled as if you were shot by an escaping prisoner, not as a self-induced wound, in terms of insurance claims." She smiled. "But you will not receive a citation as most agents do when shot during the apprehension of a suspect. You will be allowed two days leave for medical reasons."

Jack groaned.

"Sorry, it's the best I could negotiate for you."

"That will only cover the time I have to take off to see doctors." He gulped. "Please say I won't have to see Dr. Brimley."

Sara straightened. "Dr. Brimley and the FBI have agreed mutually to end his contract. You will be seeing a psychologist I've worked with on other cases. He's seen many local agents, including Carbonne, after they were shot or after they killed someone in the line of duty. He's... helpful." Sara checked her notes. "Your appointment is tomorrow afternoon at one."

Jack leaned back. "I see you've taken care of everything. How are you going to save this investigation? As I see it, we've cleared Ben. His testimony provides Candy with a partial alibi. Toby was alive when she left Sandia Man Cave around noon. They were our two best suspects."

Sara closed her laptop. "Nonsense. Candy could have come back later and killed Toby—although I doubt it. We also have two likely suspects—Irwin Levine and Ralph Edwards. Both are ruthless enough to murder."

"Edwards doesn't have a motive and isn't ruthless."

"Perhaps ruthless isn't the right word. Ralph is like me. He could kill someone if he thought it necessary."

Jack's mouth gaped. "What would make it necessary?"

"If I knew the answer, we'd have solved the case by now. I think he's protective of underdogs, like Candy."

"No way."

Sara laughed. "Well then there are also dozens of cavers, a supervising forest ranger, and other staff in Levine's lab with potential gripes against Toby."

"Yeah, we're almost back where we started." He stood. "Hey, wait. What happened to the computer Toby was using when Ben saw him?"

***

The aroma of curry spices greeted Sara when she opened her car door in the garage. Sanders was a great cook when he was in the mood. He usually got in the mood when he completed a large task and was ready to relax. She took another sniff. She thought she smelled braised beef not chicken. Although he'd never had an assignment in India, Sanders had worked on the border of Pakistan and Afghanistan for a short while early in his career. Although he refused to talk about the assignment, several times he had prepared a beef curry based on what he'd learned in that region of Afghanistan.

Her mouth was watering when she opened her back door, expecting to see Sanders at work in the kitchen. Instead, she saw Sanders sprawled out on her sofa with Bug lying in his bed nearby. Neither of them stirred. She feared the worst and rushed forward trying to keep her voice calm. "I'm home."

Bug jumped up and ran to her wagging his tail. Sanders sat up. "I finished my report. Do you want to read it?"

"I thought you were forbidden to talk to me about it."

"I wasn't told not to show it to you. Besides it's a moot point because I emailed it to the Secretary of State and Senator Holms."

Sara leaned down and tickled Bug's tummy. "Did you send your boss a copy?"

"Yes. They told me not to tell her I'd shared it with anyone else."

Sara noted the vague term of *they*. "So, does she still have her job as an undersecretary?"

Sanders rose and gave Sara a peck on the cheek. "It does. Makes me wonder about my conversations with the secretary and Holms. I wonder if they are trying to trap her or me." Sanders hurried to the kitchen before Sara could respond.

She followed him. "What do you think they're testing you or her about?"

"I don't know. I decided to stop thinking about Washington intrigue and went shopping for curries. You didn't have anything fresh on hand. I found all the spices I needed at Talin World Market in Albuquerque. I'd like to visit it again. Your spice shelf needs help." He lifted the lid on Sara's largest pot and the aroma of blended ginger, turmeric, peppers, and coconut flooded the room. He forked the meat. "It will be ready to eat in a half-hour."

"Do you want help in the kitchen, or should I read the report?"

Sanders handed her a printed copy of the ten-page document.

CHAPTER 29: The World of Academics

Friday

Sara knew she should talk to Levine again, but she was afraid he might try to bolt like Ben. She'd already proven she wasn't up to chasing a suspect. Now Jack wasn't either. More realistically, she realized she couldn't talk to Levine again without Levine realizing he was a suspect. He was smart enough to clam up and insist on a lawyer's presence. She had no choice but to slog through the details of Toby's grant proposals. She used artificial intelligence to compare the daily revisions of Toby's latest proposal.

Sara quickly discovered Toby had written two proposals in the last six months. The one to the U.S. Geological Survey had been submitted four months before. Sara focused her attention on the second one to the U.S. Forest Service. There was no doubt that Toby, not Levine, had written the proposal. Candy had edited—mainly to improve clarity of the document—multiple times.

Toby had sent an electronic copy of the proposal to Levine in late March. Levine had sat on the draft proposal for a week and then sent a revision to Toby on April third.

Levine changed the title page so that he, not Toby, was the PI. Obviously, Levine wanted all the credit as the principal investigator.

Sara noted the budget page in Toby's version of the proposal allowed Toby to claim fifty percent, Levine ten percent, and Candy twenty percent of their salaries from the grant, if funded. Levine had eliminated Candy from the list of budgeted personnel and increased his salary commitment on the grant by two percent. This demonstrated how low Candy's salary was.

Levine made no changes in the text, but he wanted Toby to include information on the patent being sought through UNM Rainforest Innovations—the main patent commercialization arm of the University of New Mexico. Toby's work had shown the strain of *Paenibacillus* found in Fort Stanton Cave had antibacterial capabilities.

That's when things got interesting.

The next version of the proposal listed Toby as the PI with Candy as the Co-PI. Toby had removed Levine's salary from the budget completely and doubled the percentage of Candy's salary covered. Toby had also added five percent of the salary of Dr. Elmore Edwards to the budget. Sara guessed Levine's greed had angered Toby, but *who was Elmore Edwards?*

Toby had taken Levine's suggestion and reported the patent application through UNM Rainforest Innovations in this version of the proposal. He also had added another paragraph citing a patent application based on the plant growth-promoting effect of the *Paenibacillus* found in Sandia Man Cave

Sara was thunderstruck.

Toby had applied for a second patent with Dr. Elmore Edwards. Elmore and Toby had shown the bacteria in Sandia Man Cave increased the production of green chiles by plants grown in the agricultural plots of New Mexico State University. The patent application, and commercialization of it, was being done by Arrowhead Center, Inc.—the main patent commercialization arm of New Mexico State University. She thought that was a lot of work to have hidden from Levine.

Sara read the new paragraphs twice. She was no expert on patents and wondered whether Toby had created a patenting nightmare for the University of New Mexico and New Mexico State University. Lawyers would have to determine the interdependence of these two sets of patents and two strain of *Paenibacillus*.

She thought some more. Toby hadn't broken any laws in pursuing this second patent for the use of varieties of *Paenibacillus* with another investigator besides Levine. She checked. Elmore Edwards was an agronomy professor at New Mexico State University. He was a logical co-investigator for

Toby when pursuing agricultural uses of *Paenibacillus. But* Sara had several questions.

How did Toby find this agronomist? Toby's verbal communications skills would make it hard, but he wrote well, judging by the proposal. *Curious his last name was Edwards.*

What version of the proposal was submitted to the U.S. Forest Service? That question was easy to answer. Toby had scanned into his computer's files the title page of last version of the proposal with Toby as the PI and Candy as a Co-PI. This title page was time stamped by someone in the Office of the VP for Research at the University of New Mexico. This proved Toby had given the grant proposal to the university to be submitted to the granting agency on Thursday, April sixth. This version of the grant proposal also matched the one Candy had torn up.

Did Toby inform Levine? He should have.

Sara found a copy of a second time-stamped page in Toby's computer files. It was a signed addendum by Levine which said he supported the application even though he was not the PI. Sara figured the University of New Mexico didn't allow any staff but professors to submit grant applications unless they were endorsed by a faculty member. It was a standard guarantee that the university had the space and equipment needed to do the investigations proposed. Although Levine had signed it, she doubted he'd read what he'd signed.

Perhaps Toby or Candy had forged Levine's signature. She'd have a writing expert look at the page.

She could understand that Levine would have been angry when he discovered what Toby had done. She doubted it was a motive for murder.

Sara called a research administration officer in the VP of Research Offices and asked random questions without identifying herself. She learned when a grant proposal left the office, the PI was notified by email that the proposal had been formally submitted. This was usually two weeks after the proposal was submitted by the investigator to the university's research administration. Sara asked, "What if the proposal is by a post doc or research associate in the lab of a faculty member?" She was informed the supporting faculty member would be notified that the proposal had been formally submitted to a granting agency at the same time as the principal investigator.

Sara checked a calendar. Levine probably learned of Toby's deceit after Toby's wedding and her first conversation with Levine. This might explain why he hadn't displayed any animosity toward Toby when she first talked to him but was irritated when Jack spoke to him six days later. As a former major professor, she knew she would have been annoyed with Toby. Then she realized she wouldn't have forced Toby into such an untenable position.

She played the tape of her first interview with Levine. He'd been friendly—maybe too friendly—and forthcoming about Toby's bad relationship with his brother Ben. She played Jack's tape with Levine. Levine was surly and kept emphasizing Toby's arguments with his brother and Candy. Sara mused Levine had made Candy and Ben look guilty both times. It hadn't been hard. She and Jack at that time considered Candy and Ben the prime suspects. Now Ben had an airtight alibi.

She played a section of the tape from yesterday with Ben. He admitted he might not have been the only one to have seen Candy leave the parking lot at Sandia Man Cave on the day of Toby's murder. A man had been snoozing in another car with a big Stetson over his face. Ben had said the other car was still in the parking lot when he ran to his car after he hit Toby, but the man was nowhere in sight. *Could the man with the Stetson be Levine?* She regretted she hadn't questioned Ben more about the man.

She hadn't noticed a Stetson or a cave axe in Levine's office. This proved nothing. The question was: how should Levine be approached? They had no real evidence against him.

Sara looked at her checklist. She'd forgotten one key point: where was the computer Toby was using on the Wednesday he was killed?

She talked to an FBI computer technician. The technician believed Toby had networked his laptop with his home computer so that all records were shared. However, any work Toby did on his laptop when he was out of range of his internet provider would not be shared with his office computer until he returned to an area with service. Perhaps, Toby's final work on his laptop might not be on his home computer—now in the FBI lab. Sara wondered whether Toby's murderer would know that detail. *Was it important?*

Sara paced the hall outside her office with Bug trailing. It was time to act. Ralph Edwards was easier to talk to than Irwin Levine. And she had questions. Was Elmore Edwards related to Ralph? Had Ralph designed the entrance to the hidden room in Sandia Man Cave? How had Ralph's thumbprint and DNA gotten on the piece of the grant proposal found in a tree near where Toby died.

Jack was available until his appointment with the psychologist at one.

They left immediately to question Ralph Edwards.

***

As they walked into the mechanical engineering building, Jack said, "At least we know this one can't outrun us. He walks with a slight limp."

Ralph Edwards stood when they entered his office. "I wondered when you'd get back to me."

Sara had no intention of letting Ralph Edwards charm her this time. "You know lying to federal agents is a crime. Several of your comments may not have been lies per se, but they were intentionally misleading."

Edwards winked.

"We have questions. Let's start with something easy. Are you related to a professor in the ag school at New Mexico State University. His name is..."

"Elmore Edwards. He's my nephew." Ralph smiled. "I wondered when you'd learn about him."

"Did you introduce Toby to Elmore?"

"Of course. Toby needed a more creative research partner than Levine. I assume you saw their patent application to use *Paenibacillus* from Sandia Man Cave as an additive to plant fertilizers. I believe it is a stronger application than the earlier patent application with Levine because Levine didn't allow Toby to fully explore the anti-bacterial properties of the *Paenibacillus* strain from Fort Stanton Caves. He was in too much of a hurry to file the patent."

Sara knew her past perceptions of Ralph had been faulty, but she couldn't help but like Ralph. "Do you think the strains could be interchangeable?"

Ralph smiled. "I'm glad you still think like a scientist not a bureaucrat. They might be, but I advised Toby and Elmore to base their research together and patent application on only

Paenibacillus from Sandia Man Cave. I figured Levine would find it more difficult to make claims on any of their findings."

"Okay. Next question. Did you see Toby's latest grant proposal?"

"No."

Sara thought Ralph sounded hesitant. "How about part of it?"

Ralph looked nervous for the first time. "Toby stopped by my office and asked how to cite patent applications and where to include the information in a grant proposal."

Sara thought it might explain how Ralph's thumbprint got on the last page of the torn proposal. She couldn't think of a good question without revealing her thoughts to Ralph. "Next question. Did you design the entrance to the hidden room in Sandia Man Cave about fifteen years ago?"

"What makes you think that?"

Sara thought *I'm asking the question, not you.* She decided not to play games with Ralph. "The entrance looks like it was designed by an engineer. Candy admitted Jacob had sought the help of an engineer to design it."

"Yes."

"Have you been in Sandia Man Cave since?"

"Several times when Toby had trouble getting enough help to clean the cave."

Sara decided she should not give Ralph wiggle room when she asked her next question. "Have you been in or looked into the hidden room in Sandia Man Cave?"

"Only when I designed and then installed the hoop and trap door years ago."

Sara hoped to throw Ralph off guard by jumping to a different type of question. "Where you were Wednesday, April twelfth?"

"I'm surprised you didn't ask that question sooner." He fiddled with his desk computer and then turned the screen so Sara and Jack could see it. "We had a faculty meeting that day at nine. They usually take two hours. Then I had lunch with several of my colleagues."

Sara pointed at the blank space from twelve to three. "What about those three hours?"

He shrugged and moved his finger to a later time slot. "I had a zoom meeting with my nephew from three to five. Toby was supposed to join us. We called him around three-fifteen, as I remember, but he didn't answer."

"Name the colleagues you ate with." Jack pointed to the eleven to twelve space on Ralph's calendar. "I also need your nephew's email address and phone number." Jack motioned to Sara and led her from the office. "I want to do these checks now before he can contact them. You're recording everything anyway."

Sara had left the door open and watched Ralph as she talked to Jack. Ralph had confidently leaned back in his chair as if he was sleeping.

She stepped back into Ralph's office. "We've found individuals changed their calendars to create alibis in this case. We'll have to confiscate your computer and notify the VP of Research and your department head of our investigation."

Ralph winked at Sara. "I guess I'm not the only sneaky suspect?"

Sara tried to keep your face motionless. "Ralph, I know you can be clever and charming. Cut the games." She looked at a checklist. "Do you now or did you ever have a key to Toby's condo?"

"No. I know Toby kept extra keys at Lydia's house and Candy's apartment."

Sara felt a headache coming on. Had she allowed the U.S. Attorney's Office to negotiate a settlement with Ben too quickly? Ben easily could have used the key left at Lydia's house. *But how would Ben have used the key?* Besides they'd not found a key at the Collins home.

It was logical that Candy would have a key to Toby's apartment, but Jack hadn't found such a key when he did a thorough search. She thought Candy had mentioned a key in a missing pharmaceutical vial, but that never made sense.

She saw Ralph was staring at her. She couldn't think about these new wrinkles in the case now. "I want to see all your cave axes."

"They're at home."

"Do we need to get a warrant to search your house.?"

"Not if you allow me to go with you and show you where I keep them."

"Do you own a Stetson?"

"It's at home, too."

"Do you have copies of Toby's latest proposals?"

He snapped, "I already told you no." His tone changed to a more congenial one. "Your questions are more defined than before. I guess you finally sat down and read Toby's proposals. He was an amazing young researcher." He rocked backward in his chair. "I knew you wouldn't solve this case until you appreciated how clever Toby could be. Levine would never have made tenure if Jacob and Toby hadn't bucked up his research."

"Why didn't you tell me this last week?"

"I thought Candy had killed Toby. She was frantic after Toby gave one of those awful pictures of her spread eagled with her caving suit unzipped to Levine."

"Why?"

"Why what? If you mean why did Toby do it? I guess Jacob failed to educate Toby on proper—uh—sexual behavior. Toby gave out the photos as mementos at his wedding. Toby said Candy looked 'beautiful' in the picture. He didn't realize everyone who saw the picture was laughing at him."

"Why did you think Candy killed Toby?"

"She was angry when Toby handed out the pictures at the wedding and then disappeared the next day." Ralph grabbed Sara's hand. "Be honest. Any woman would be. She was still angry when she showed up at my office for the zoom meeting. She had trouble focusing on the discussion."

Sara pulled her hand away. "What made you change your mind?"

"My belief that Candy, under her rough and cracked shell, is a good person."

"You have no evidence to prove her innocence?"

"No, and I didn't want to implicate her."

Sara decided to try to make Ralph feel guilty. "If you'd told the whole story sooner, you might have decreased Candy's stress. Ben said Toby was alive at noon when he saw Candy tear out of the Sandia Man Cave parking lot. It's unlikely Candy would have arrived in your office by three if she had gone back and killed Toby." She didn't add Candy had used an ATM at two-thirty in the Student Union at the university.

Ralph seemed unfazed by Sara's insinuation. He stood and grabbed Sara's arm. "Good. Candy only needs to explain where she was between twelve and three."

Sara thought, *You must explain where you were during that period, too.* She said, "Don't forget, we have to retrieve a few items at your home." She removed Ralph's hand from clasping her elbow. "I'll also have to tell you about my significant other."

Ralph moved a step away.

                                                      J. L. Greger

CHAPTER 30: What's Next for Sanders?

It had all started last night when he gave Sara a copy of his white paper document. Sanders delayed serving the beef curry because he wanted to give Sara plenty of time to read the document. She had scanned it, making pencil notations in the margins, and then returned to the marked pages. After almost an hour she said, "It's insightful and concise, but it may not get you where you want to go." She studied him for what seemed like an hour but was only a minute. "What do you want to do with the rest of your life?"

The question made him nervous. "You know what I want. I'd like to head information gathering and analyses in a federal agency."

"No, I mean what do you want to do with your life if your dream job doesn't materialize? What will you do when the paid month-long vacation from the State Department ends?"

He'd been disappointed. She was doubting his abilities. His disappointment must have shown on his face. She rose and pulled him to the table and forced him to sit. She sat on the other side and reached for his hands.

"We both know many bright capable men and women advance to the lieutenant colonel level in the military, but most don't advance to be a general. They retire after twenty or so years of service. Many of those who didn't advance were as capable as those who did, but no appropriate positions were available for them at the time they need to advance."

He hadn't liked what she was trying to say. "Many of them were weeded out for a reason. They'd made a mistake—perhaps accidental. It didn't matter."

"Please, don't take a negative view. Many of those retiring start a second career. Military men hate to admit war—and the military in general—is hell."

Then she made a comment that bothered him because it was his biggest fear. "Similarly, those who gather information for security purposes don't like to admit... that info gathering is for the young."

He'd said, "But they need experienced leadership."

She'd patted his hand but otherwise ignored his comment. "Many of the colonels who leave the military find their second career more satisfying than their career in the military. Moreover, many generals are too old or worn out when they retire to develop a satisfying life."

He stared at her trying to force her to say something precise. Something he could argue with her. She didn't.

Instead, she said, "I think you have a wonderful opportunity now. Do you remember trying to decide what you wanted to do next when you were in high school and college? It was exhilarating and scary. You now have the same opportunity. Take your time and think. I'm eager to be your sounding board and will support any decision you make."

He'd been disappointed and a little annoyed when she added, "Your beef curry smells wonderful. You know you've never told me about your experiences on the border of Afghanistan and Pakistan. It was more than twenty years ago. Surely you can share more about your experiences there than just this recipe."

***

He'd had trouble sleeping the previous night because he kept thinking about Sara's questions. When she cuddled next to him, he'd ignored her. He didn't feel like being sexual. It was one way this so-called opportunity to be young again was different than his experiences in high school and college.

This morning Sara had mentioned it might be fun to take a four-day weekend trip. She mentioned Arches National Park in Utah or Frank Lloyd Wright's Taliesin West in Arizona. When he hadn't responded, she'd added, "We could check into La Fonda in Santa Fe and go to museums and concerts. I think the Santa Fe Opera is offering a pre-season recital with several singers who will be featured in operas this summer. Give me a call if you want to do something. I should warn them at work if I won't be in next Monday and Tuesday."

He hadn't felt like planning a trip. Nothing on television was appealing.

     J. L. Greger

He thumbed through the two issues of *Science* that sat by Sara's recliner in her main room. The scientific articles were too technical.

He wandered into Sara's office and scanned her bookshelves. There were only a few books on science or textbooks. That was fine. He didn't want to do heavy reading. Sara had told him she could find the references she needed faster on the internet than in her old journals and books. Accordingly, she'd donated almost all her texts, journals, and scientific tomes to a used bookstore several years before she met him. He remembered she had complained her books weren't in good enough condition or rare enough to interest libraires.

He was surprised by the sparseness of her collection of fiction because Sara always carried a novel with her, in case she had a spare moment. A few of the novels she kept were classics he'd read already. The rest were mysteries and thrillers. Most of the police and FBI agents he knew hated television crime shows and mystery novels because they weren't realistic. Sara didn't seem to mind the inaccuracies in the media and often commented that she enjoyed the way mysteries were always solved and villains usually punished in fiction. He was like most police officers and agents. He didn't like spy thrillers or crime novels.

After a moment's thought, he remembered Sara had proudly told him once, "I keep only my favorite novels in one bookcase in my office. A new favorite means an old favorite must be donated to a charity because I don't want those books to sprawl to other locations in the house." He noted another bookcase was devoted to photo albums, mainly with photos of Bug, art books, and histories predominantly related to Lincoln. Sanders guessed it made sense. Sara had been raised on a farm in Illinois.

Although he and Sara had been together for several years, he had never explored her home. He now wandered around the house. Bug must have been suspicious and followed Sanders from room to room.

The spaces were tastefully decorated. The furnishings were not cheap, but not high-end either. The old chest, table, and chairs in the guest bedroom were not valuable antiques and he guessed they were the only items in the house from her family. Sara had amassed a good collection of fibers arts—including rugs, wall hangings, and pillow shams—during her travels. Framed photos of her family and him were grouped in her bedroom along with four childhood dolls. Other family mementoes and travel tchotchkes were scattered throughout the house, but the main decorations were Bug's toys scattered over the floor and sofa.

He'd never thought about it before, but his condo and Sara's house were poles apart. He'd decorated his condo with valuable inherited antiques and pieces acquired at the best shops. Sara had accompanied him on several of his shopping forays. She had a good eye and caught flaws or indications that the objects were less valuable than the salespeople claimed.

However, she had not bought the best items for her home, even though she always appeared to have plenty of cash. He wondered whether Sara's ability to buy anything she wanted reflected not wealth per se but a personal choice. Perhaps, she'd learned years ago to limit her wants to what she could afford. That was not his style of living. He'd be unhappy living modestly in New Mexico. He suddenly realized Sara must sometimes be amused by his luxurious condo in Washington and jet setting lifestyle.

Her compromise of living half the time in Washington was the best they could do. Which wasn't bad for two intellectuals who were too independent to change their lifestyles—much.

This realization brought him back to Sara's question: What did he really want?

He had no hobbies—well except for antiquing. Like, Sara he didn't enjoy attending sporting events. He didn't golf or play tennis. He worked out in a gym regularly for fitness, not pleasure. Sara liked to sew and make quilts for charities. He'd never developed any hand skills, such as wood working. They both liked to cook, but neither wanted to gain more weight. He liked music, especially jazz, but didn't have the talent or determination to play in a group. In other words, he had no idea what he would do in retirement.

Sara had commented once that she thought men were less happy in retirement than the women because they hadn't developed any leisure skills. Being typical didn't make him feel

                                    J. L. Greger

better, but it forced him to accept he needed to build a second career—not retire to a life of leisure.

He knew he probably would end up as a free-lance consultant. Sara had asked an interesting question last night. What standards would he set when consulting? Would he consult for foreign countries and companies based overseas? What about large multinational corporations? She thought they all might seek his services, but what were his ethical limits? She was right he needed to chart his plans for a consulting business. It would be harder than writing a white paper.

He was relieved when his phone rang. It gave him an excuse to stop thinking about his future.

Carbonne and Barbara had come back early from a resort in Sedona. Carbonne explained, "Barbara's afraid, we won't have a room ready for the baby in time. She wanted to talk to our realtor. And I'd gotten two frantic emails from the agent subbing for me this week. I'm calling because we need your advice. The realtor wants to show us two fixer-uppers today. I know nothing about renovating a house. You've done two major renovations in your condo."

"All I know is how to hire a good contractor."

"That's more than I do. We can pick you up in thirty minutes."

***

The first house was described as a "charming, historic home with adobe walls." Sanders told Carbone and Barbara, "There will be plumbing, wiring, and pest problems." After peeking at the outmoded bathroom and kitchen, Barbara headed for the door.

The next house was a brick two-story built in the seventies. Barbara took one look at the warren of small rooms and again found the exit quickly.

The realtor suggested Carbonne had budgeted too little to find much of a house. Sanders snorted when he heard Carbonne's desired price range. "Look, your salary is good. Save yourself a lot of unhappiness. Up your budget by a hundred thousand." Carbonne admitted his banker had already given him the same advice. Suddenly the realtor found several possible homes.

Sanders accompanied Barbara and Carbonne to three more homes, which Barbara carefully inspected. Barbara looked at Carbonne as they left the third house. "I don't think we can manage any fix-it-up activities harder than painting. This last house is fifteen years old and has an open floor plan, central refrigerant cooling, and a garage. The kitchen and bathrooms are decent and can be renovated in a couple of years. We should make an offer."

Carbonne spluttered, "I didn't notice anything wrong with the kitchen or bathrooms." Barbara ignored his comment and walked over to the realtor before she could drive away.

Sanders pitied Carbonne. Barbara was going to be the boss in their household. Then he noticed how pleased Carbonne was to make a bid on the home. Carbonne was ready for a child, home ownership, the whole family thing. He envied him a bit because Carbonne was pursuing the future he wanted.

While Barbara picked up a few items at Walmart, Sanders and Carbonne waited in the car. Carbonne said, "One reason I came back early was the agent covering for me emailed me about a crisis concerning a new consulting psychologist. The guy tried to tell Sara what sexual harassment could do to a female scientist."

Sanders mentally reviewed his conversations with Sara during the last week. He doubted Sara had even mentioned a problem with a psychologist. "Is the guy still alive? Sara took a real beating from her department head at Michigan State about the time she was up for tenure."

"Was she hurt badly?"

"Figurative beating. She indicated he'd be sorry if he tried again. After that he was passive aggressive but didn't try to touch her. I suspect it was the basis of much of her unhappiness at Michigan State. But you know Sara, she doesn't talk about unhappy times much."

Carbonne looked at messages on his phone. "I knew when I left for the wedding, I would have to fire this new psychologist but dreaded all the paperwork. Three agents had complained about him but none of them completed the necessary paperwork. Once this young psychologist goofed up on Sara's case, she talked to our personnel officer, wrote up a detailed account of his mistakes, and helped the other three agents write their complaints. The agent subbing for me said the file was so complete, he approved it and forwarded it to personnel. Yesterday he and the personnel rep convinced the young psychologist to resign."

Sanders wondered what Carbonne was trying to say. He'd admitted he hadn't needed to cut his honeymoon short because of work. "So, why did you come back early from your honeymoon?"

"I was bored. I agreed with Barbara. It was time to get our 'house problem' solved."

Sanders saw Barbara pushing a cart toward the car. Before he got out to help her, he said, "I'm learning vacation time is not always fun, too."

CHAPTER 31: The Time Gap

Ralph's brick ranch home in the foothills of the Sandia Mountains had been built in the eighties. The landscaping was typical of most of the homes in Albuquerque. Plants were selected for low water use and gravel replaced grass. What was unusual about this landscape was the bushes were particularly well trimmed. From the outside, the house looked like it was ready to be put on the market the next day.

The inside was also immaculate—Sara thought pathologically neat. The recliner in front of the TV was covered with a sheet to prevent wear. Two journals were piled on the nearby coffee table. Otherwise, there were no papers, books, or knickknacks on any of the open spaces in the living room, dining room, or kitchen. There were only a couple family pictures on the walls.

"Do you spend much time at home?"

Ralph must have guessed her thoughts. "I gave my daughters most of my wife's stuff after she died. It was depressing to see dust accumulate on her treasures. I've learned it's easier to clean if I leave nothing out."

"So, where do you keep your caving gear."

Ralph led Jack and Sara to a spare bedroom and pointed to a chest. Sara noted this room was also devoid of any small, non-essential items but looked like it had once been one of his daughter's bedrooms because it was painted a rose shade. Jack pulled open one drawer after another in the chest. He placed two cave axes in evidence bags while Sara checked the dresser. She found two black caving suits with yellow embroidery, lots of black crew socks, several T-shirts, and several pairs of black gloves. She decided nothing was worth collecting. None of this gear would shed red or blue lint, like that found in the cave.

In the closet she found two pairs of hiking boots, a pair of cross-country skis, a couple of old back packs, a folded-up ping pong table, and a box of ping pong balls. Jack checked the boxes on the upper shelf. All were empty.

Ralph said nothing until Jack had opened the last box. "I like to keep empty packing boxes around. You never know when you might need them. I kept the ping pong table because my grandkids like to play when they visit."

Jack had already paced into a second spare bedroom before Sara asked, "Where's the Stetson?"

"Not in the room your partner entered. It's in my office." He glanced into the empty yellow room where Jack stood. "I gave the bedroom set from this room to my oldest daughter. Her daughter liked the white, girly furniture." Jack opened the closet. It was empty, except for a blowup mattress, a set of yellow sheets, and a pillow.

Ralph opened the door to his office. It bore no resemblance to the rest of the house. The walls were covered with photos of family and apparently past students. A Stetson hung on a peg above a group of pictures of two girls on horses and a bunch of ribbons. Ralph pointed to the Stetson. "My girls were into horses and rodeos. They were pretty good at barrel racing. I haven't worn the Stetson since the youngest one's last rodeo. She won that red ribbon at the Texas State Fair."

Sara wanted to distract Ralph. "Do you still ride?

It worked. He closed his eyes and seemed to be think, probably remembering. She leaned closer to look at the hat. It didn't look like a hat that had been worn much. She turned her attention to a photo as he began to speak.

"Not much. My wife and I sold the horses when the youngest girl married. You know riding and rodeos are expensive hobbies. Once a week, I volunteer at a horse rehabilitation center that provides services for veterans and individuals with disabilities. Several of the boys who frequent the facility are autistic."

"Did Toby ride?" She and Ralph watched Jack struggle to put the Stetson in an evidence bag.

Ralph answered after Jack completed the task, "Jacob brought Toby to several stables when Toby was a preteen, but he said Toby didn't take to horses or dogs. Toby preferred the quiet, predictable darkness of caves. It was too bad because I've seen a couple autistic lads develop deep bonds with horses." He patted his hip. I took a fall six years ago. "Riding is less relaxing than it used to be now." He smiled ruefully. "None of the grandkids are interested in riding. They prefer soccer. So, I go to lots of soccer games."

Sara questioned Ralph more as Jack searched the other rooms. Jack had confirmed the faculty meeting on the April twelfth, but he'd learned that it had ended by ten. Furthermore, Jack had been unable to reach the two friends who supposedly had lunch with Ralph afterward. In response to Sara's prompts, Ralph claimed he'd worked on manuscript in his office after lunch. The excuse while not giving him an alibi sounded plausible, but somehow Sara doubted it.

Although Sara doubted Ralph could be described as clinically depressed, he seemed lonely. His work, caving, volunteer activities, and his family didn't seem to be occupying his time sufficiently. Perhaps, it was why he had become so involved in Toby's and Candy's lives.

***

Sara dropped Jack with all the collected evidence at the FBI building an hour before his appointment with the psychologist and went to the federal courthouse in downtown Albuquerque to be present at Ben's arraignment. As expected, Ben pled guilty. The judge set the date for the sentencing hearing for the following week.

Sara thought the speed with which Ben's case was being processed was amazing. After all, he had threatened a federal agent and the agent had been wounded. She'd also never seen staff from the U.S. Attorney's office be so cooperative. They suggested Sara could question Toby at the courthouse after his arraignment, rather than having to go to the jail to question him.

A lawyer from the U.S. Attorney's office and Ben's lawyer listened as Sara questioned Ben about the individual, he'd seen wearing the Stetson over his face on the day of Toby's murder at Sandia Man Cave. Ben wasn't sure about much concerning the individual under the hat. He assumed it was a man because the individual had short hair—at least none strayed from under the hat—and large hands. He described the hat as gray.

The discussion improved when Sara showed Ben a picture of the Stetson she and Jack had retrieved from Ralph's home. Ben immediately said, "The Stetson I saw had a red hatband."

                                                                J. L. Greger

Ralph's hat had no hat band. The rest of Sara's questions demonstrated Ben's testimony would not be useful in court. He'd been too upset to observe much about the man in the car.

"Well, if you remember anything more, I'm easy to reach at the FBI building." She noticed Ben was shaking. He no longer appeared to be the arrogant man she'd met the week before. "Good luck during your stay at FCI Florence Camp. I understand it's a good minimum-security prison."

He licked his lips. "As part of my plea agreement I'll examine patients in the ophthalmologic clinic in the next-door supermax. I may even have to do eye surgery on one of the inmates there."

Sara knew it was inappropriate, but she put her hand on Ben's shoulder. "I had to question a prisoner in the supermax once. It's important you listen to the jailers and do the best job you can. The prisoner I dealt with appreciated physicians if they practiced medicine well."

Ben and his lawyer looked perplexed. The attorney from the U.S. Attorney's Office stood and pulled Sara toward the door. Once they were outside the room, he closed the door. "Ben will be in more danger if he knows the name and background of the main patient, we want him to treat." The lawyer rushed back into the conference room.

Sara knew she had guessed correctly. She knew the identity at least one of the patients whom Ben would treat. If Ben was a good eye surgeon, he had nothing to fear.

***

It was hard to describe Jack's gait when he entered Sara's office. It was a limp with a gleeful bounce, almost a skip. "This psychologist wasn't like Brimley. He didn't even smirk when he told me I wasn't a klutz." Jack instantly straightened and resumed his usual strut. "Course I knew I wasn't a klutz. He said what I already knew. I'm fine."

"Good." Sara knew she should be more enthusiastic, but she was in a funk. A suspicion was growing in her mind, and she didn't like it. "Winslow says the technicians in the lab have done a preliminary analysis of the samples we brought in from Ralph's home. They won't get to his computer until next week. However, a writing expert determined Levine's signature on the addendum to Toby's last grant application was forged. Let's hope Winslow has some good surprises for us."

They walked down the hall slowly because Jack's leg still hurt. He seemed to want to talk, but he couldn't seem to spit out what he wanted to say. Instead, he talked about the nice weather. Finally, he said, "Tell me about the prisoner you interviewed in the supermax in Florence. Did you help put him away? Would he come after you if he ever got out?"

"Yes and no."

"Come on."

"He was one of the smartest... most determined... and most meticulous men I've ever met."

"You know others that bad?"

"Bad is a subjective term. Being smart, determined, and meticulous isn't bad."

"Come on. Who else do you know with those characteristics?"

Sara thought about her days in Brazil. "My significant other—Sanders—would fit the description."

"Oh." He was silent for a moment. "You know your Sanders lectured to my FBI class at Quantico. He was tough... really tough and distant. I wondered."

Sara was glad they'd reached the lab. She didn't want to answer questions about Sanders. "Winslow, what did you find?"

Winslow pointed to the cave axes on his bench. "Ralph was a real fussbudget. There was no blood on the axes. Hell, there was no dirt in the crevices of the axes. I wonder if he's that picky with his students. He'd be...

Sara knew Winslow wanted to talk but she wanted to accomplish one more task today. "Could they be the murder weapons?"

"One was old, probably made in the 1950s. The claw wouldn't fit the hole in Toby's head. The other was the same model as Toby's two axes. It could be the murder weapon."

Sara started to leave.

Winslow said, "Candy didn't lie. Toby's semen was on her caving suit."

***

"Exactly what do you think we'll gain by talking to Candy again?"

"I want to see whether Ralph's comments will jar Candy into telling us a bit more of what she knows. Who knows maybe

                                              J. L. Greger

the fact we've cleared Ben may scare her into talking. Besides her lawyer from the public defender's office said she was busy Monday, but because of a cancellation could meet with us in ten minutes at the safe house."

Jack turned the key in the ignition and gunned the car out of the FBI lot. "I agree Candy is still hiding something big. She's so screwed up; anything is possible. Then too, she has no alibi from noon until two-thirty on the day Toby was killed." He was distracted as he merged onto I-25. "She had a motive."

"And that's why we're questioning Candy again."

"I think you don't want to face Levine on a Friday afternoon."

"That, too. Why don't you talk less as you drive so I can write my request for a search warrant for Levine's car, office, and home, which we can use on Monday. Funny thing, judges won't accept the phrase 'Levine smells.' I'm afraid a judge will give us a warrant for Levine's office but not his home and car."

***

"Candy." Sara decided her next comment would be more effective if she lowered her voice. "Do you have a death wish? Please stop withholding info. You make yourself look guilty."

Candy slouched in a chair, looked at her belly, and sighed. Her lawyer from the public defender's office whispered in her ear.

"You said you left the cave at noon on the day Toby was killed. Ben's testimony has confirmed your story. He said you almost hit his car when you roared out of the parking lot. Do you remember almost hitting another car?"

"No."

"You told the psychologist you remembered." Sara waited as the lawyer again whispered to Candy.

"I just remember wanting to get as far away from Toby as possible." Candy frowned. "I guess... I might have. The guy in the other car certainly honked."

Sara decided not to ask if Candy recognized the other driver. It was odd—but probably not important—that Candy didn't recognize Ben or his car.

"We also know you arrived at Ralph's office at three for a zoom meeting but were so upset you couldn't participate effectively in the discussion." Sara kicked Jack under the table because she didn't want him to correct her next statement.

"That means you have no alibi for your activities during the three hours between noon and three."

Candy continued to stare at her belly, which did have a baby bulge.

"We find it strange that you didn't mention meeting with Ralph and Elmore when you needed to explain where you were on the Wednesday when Toby was killed."

"I didn't want to drag anyone else into my mess."

"Well, you'd better. Let's start with something easy. Why were you so upset when you arrived at Ralph's office?"

"I told you. Toby made it clear he didn't want me anymore, except as a research partner. I..."

Jack interrupted. "Where were you before you went to Ralph's office?"

"In the Student Union eating an ice cream cone."

Jack sighed. "Did you use the ATM in the Student Union?"

Candy continued to study her belly. Her lawyer must have sensed the importance of the question. "Candy, try to remember."

Candy frowned. "I guess I did make a deposit."

Her lawyer whispered in her ear. Candy shook her head repeatedly. After the lawyer whispered again, Candy said, "All right. Ben gave me some cash the day before. I used the ATM to deposit it in my checking account."

Jack smiled. "See that wasn't hard, and it provides you an alibi from two-thirty to three. Now let's see if you can extend that alibi. How did you get to the union?"

"I walked from Dr. Levine's office. I was hungry. I hadn't eaten all day,"

Sara smiled. "That's helpful. Why had you gone to Levine's office?"

"To beg him..."

Sara hoped she could speed up this discussion a bit; she wanted to be home by five. "For what? What did he say?'

"He wasn't there, but he'd left the photo of me taped on his door. I took it." Candy looked up and bit her lip. "It was the one you found hidden in my apartment earlier."

"Did anyone see you?"

"Yeah, both guys in the lab whistled when I walked in. They told me Gossiping Geri and Levine had left around ten and hadn't returned."

Sara was suddenly hopeful. The timing was right. "When do you think you talked to the two guys in the lab?"

Candy shrugged. "About one."

Candy had finally done it. She had provided herself with an alibi. Ben's testimony indicated he had seen Toby alive at twelve after Candy raced from the cave's parking lot. The trip from the cave to Albuquerque took an hour. Candy could not have killed Toby. She had also strengthened a potential case against Levine. He could have been the man with the Stetson at the cave.

"I have a few more question. Do you have a key to Toby's condo?"

Candy and her lawyer whispered back and forth. Candy said, "I did, but I don't now."

Her lawyer nudged her.

"Okay, it was in one of the two vials missing from my medicine chest."

Sara racked her brain to understand. She remembered Winslow had taken one vial. *When?*

Jack said, "Was it in the vial in which Toby placed the number of the lawyer who prepared the Collins Family Trust? Winslow took it almost two weeks ago."

"The other one." Candy's hand seemed to tremble a bit as she pulled her hair from her face.

Sara decided Candy was reaching the end of her endurance. "Ralph said he was helping you revise or at least edit the review of literature for your dissertation. Is it done?"

"Yes." Candy's whole body seemed to tremble.

"How about the summation chapter?"

Candy burst into tears.

Sara touched Candy's hand. "Have you eaten today?"

"I don' know."

One of the agents monitoring the safe house had listened silently as Jack and, Sara questioned Candy. He now spoke. "She was frantically typing much of last night. And she hasn't eaten. I tried to encourage her to try some eggs this morning, but she claimed their smell made her want to retch. The psychologist, Brimley, never showed yesterday. She needs help."

Sara stood and led Jack and Candy's lawyer out of the room. Jack shook his head. "She's innocent."

Sara nodded. "She's also depressed and confused There's a good chance the *missing* vial with the key is in her apartment, but she missed it when she looked." She looked at her watch. "Keep her busy while I get a psychologist here."

"The one I saw."

"Yes. I shouldn't have assumed Brimley had helped Candy."

CHAPTER 32: Weekend with Sanders

Sara blew into the house like a cyclone on Friday at five. "I forgot I agreed to bring a casserole to an event tonight. So, I bought groceries on the way home from work."

Sanders observed Bug seemed as interested as he was as she unpacked items. He turned to Bug who was pacing at a safe distance from Sara's rapidly moving feet. "I think we're having chicken with pineapple and peppers."

"Yes, I'm making Sweet and Sour Chicken for the potluck at the clubhouse. If I hurry, I can have it ready by six when the event begins."

"Do you want help?"

"No. This kitchen is designed for one, but I'd like to hear about your day."

Sanders sat on a stool. "Will I be bored at this event? You know I've never gone to a social gathering here. I realized today that I'd never stayed here more than a couple of days before. We usually travel when I'm in the Southwest."

Sara had already cut the chicken breasts into pieces and was dipping them into an egg batter before she fried them. "I was worried that you'd run out of thing to do today because you'd finished your report yesterday."

"I guessed that. You called four times." He rose and went into the bedroom. He returned with two bags. "I was in such a hurry when I left Washington, I forgot how hot it can be in April and May in Albuquerque. I went shopping." He held up a pair of khaki shorts and a short-sleeved, blue shirt.

"Oh dear, Albuquerque doesn't have the best selection of clothes."

"I know. Bug and I drove up to Santa Fe. The selection of practical clothes was less, but they did have shirts that would give my wardrobe a new twist."

Sara gasped as he opened the next bag. She stared as he held up a long-sleeved shirt with horizontal orange and denim blue Southwestern style stripes. "Won't it be hot?"

"I'm used to rolling up my sleeves in Washington. The clerk said this sunset color is the rage." He pulled another shirt from the bag. It was short-sleeved with vertical stripes in sunset and navy on a beige background.

He noticed Sara busied herself in frying the chicken before she commented. "You know you don't have to dress in clothes with a Southwestern motif here. I don't." She stirred together the ingredients for a sweet and sour sauce and added the chopped green peppers and pineapple. "If you wear those spiffy clothes, I'll have to try to look more stylish than my usual khaki slacks and knit top tonight."

He was pleased. When he'd studied her furnishings today, he had also scanned her clothes. He saw the suits and dressy clothes she wore in Washington or when consulting outside of Albuquerque in one closet. In a second closet, he found the slacks, shorts, and tops that she wore in Albuquerque. He noted there was only one skirt—a long, pleated, beige one—in the second closet. He remembered she'd worn the skirt last week at the wedding with a beige top and her turquoise jewelry. He hoped he could convince her to purchase or let him buy a stylish outfit for her. "Why don't you wear the long beige skirt you wore at the wedding? You looked pretty in it."

"No one here will recognize me in a skirt. But it might be fun. There will be a band playing country songs tonight after the meal."

***

As the residents gossiped about their neighbors and ate as if this was the first time they'd eaten today, Sanders sampled a tablespoon or two of most of the dishes. He thought Sara's sweet and sour chicken with rice was a refreshing change from the other casseroles at the potluck. Most of the casseroles were heavy—baked beans, macaroni and cheese with a meat added, lasagna, or chili. The salads were good except for the ones in which the cook had floated baby marshmallows in brightly colored gelatin. *Ugh.* He noted Sara avoided the salads with marshmallows, too. The desserts appeared to reflect the work of a nearby bakery.

J. L. Greger

Sanders now knew why Sara had never brought him to a potluck at the clubhouse. He thought if he lived here these meals would be acceptable occasionally.

Sara led him around the patio and introduced him to several of her neighbors, who made vague attempts at conversation. A couple of the men spoke of international assignment they'd taken for an oil company or the military. It wasn't surprising. Sara had introduced him as a State Department official who had recently returned from an international assignment.

He was ready to leave when the band began to play. It was better than expected. He tapped his toe to the music and watched others dance the Texas two-step. He didn't ask Sara to dance because her face had frozen into an unsmiling mask as soon as others began to dance. He didn't know the details, but as a teenager she had developed an aversion to dancing. When the lead singer began to sing "I Will Always Love you," he pulled her onto the floor. "Relax and sway to the music."

She did.

They stayed for one more song and then held hands as they walked about the quiet community. Sanders realized he should spend more weekends here with Sara, but not too many. Weekends with Sara in Washington were better.

***

Saturday

Sanders and Sara were enjoying each other's company in bed when his phone rang on Saturday morning. "Dear, did you forget the two hours time difference between New York City and Albuquerque." Sanders covered the phone with his hand. "It's my daughter."

He watched Sara rise and go to the shower as he listened to his daughter. She and her boyfriend were skipping their graduation ceremony from law school and moving their belongings to an apartment in New York City before graduation. His daughter explained, "We won't have time to do much around our new apartment once our clerkships begin. The apartment needs work."

Sanders agreed with her and hung up. He walked into the bathroom and eyed Sara as she dressed after her shower. "My daughter just ruined my plans for next weekend. She's not going to walk in the Georgetown graduation ceremony. I'd planned to give her grandmother's diploma from Georgetown in an antique silver frame as a graduation gift to her."

Sara coughed and almost fell as she stepped into her slacks.

"I guess you don't think that's the right graduation present."

Sara gave him a peck on the cheek.

Sanders wasn't surprised by Sara's lack of sympathy. She had told him several times that she promised her graduate students a meal in any restaurant they chose in East Lansing, if they didn't walk through graduation at Michigan State. As their Ph.D. advisor, she had to walk across the stage with them if they chose to participate in graduation. He was surprised by what she said next.

"I'll bet she's frantic to find furniture for her new apartment. Why don't you let her select a piece or two of furniture from your condo in Washington?" She smiled. "And a thousand dollars to smooth her move. I already sent my graduation present to her: a check and a pair of pillowcases my grandmother embroidered fifty years ago. They're lovely, and I'd never used them."

***

The three of them—Sara, Bug, and Sanders—were walking in the Bosque near Sara's home, when the FBI psychologist called Sara. He thought Candy would benefit from a visit by Sara and Bug. He had moved Candy to a halfway house for battered women and their children in the foothills of the Sandia Mountains on the east side of Albuquerque. The psychologist had thought Candy would brood less about her problems in a group environment than when almost alone in the safe house. Besides, she was no longer a suspect or considered dangerous.

They'd not walked much further when Carbonne called Sanders. Carbonne sounded more nervous than Sanders remembered ever seeing him on a case. "They accepted our bid pending an inspection, which is happening today. Barbara is ecstatic but would like Sara to walk through the house with her at eleven. She wants to discuss decorating ideas. I'm afraid to ask what that means."

After the call, Sanders said, "I'd hoped we could shop for you today."

Sara blinked. "Why?'

"As a thank you."

She put one arm around his shoulder and kissed him. "After our errands, we can decide if we're in the mood to shop."

***

Sanders couldn't believe how Bug paraded toward the halfway house. The dog walked by Sara's side and didn't pull on the lead as he did when Sanders walked him. Bug slowed as he approached two children playing in front of the house and waited to be petted. Usually, Bug ignored children and almost everyone when he walked with Sara around the community where they lived. Now he understood what Sara meant when she said, "Bug is a different dog when he's working as a pet therapy dog."

Sanders had been glad when Sara suggested a man might not be a welcome guest in a shelter for battered women. Once Sara and Bug entered the house, Sanders relaxed in the car and read Sandberg's account of the life of Lincoln. It had been the most interesting book he'd found on Sara's bookshelves yesterday.

Sara and Bug reappeared after thirty minutes. He detected a change in Bug's behavior as the dog neared the car. Bug was pulling on the lead. As Sara scooped the grateful dog up and locked him in his seat, Sanders said, "Bug seemed happy to escape this visit."

"Bug worked overtime today. Candy liked Bug, but she's not a good petter. She kept trying to lift him up and hug him. Today, she had this insane idea that if her major advisor Levine went to jail, she could never get her Ph.D. She kept saying, 'I must protect Levine.' I explained that universities have mechanisms for handling the death or removal of a professor to protect graduate students' rights."

"Did it sink in?"

"I hope so. I called the psychologist and said I'd talk to graduate school officials on Monday." She sighed and fastened her seatbelt. "Now I get to play interior decorator."

Sanders told Sara about his trip to five houses with Barbara and Carbonne the day before. "This one is the best, but

Barbara has reason to be concerned. I'd have the bathrooms redone before I moved in."

***

Barbara had a determined pinched look on her face as she clutched Sara's hand and led her into the house before Carbonne had the chance to say anything.

Sanders grabbed Carbonne's arm. "Don't be a fool. Stay here in the sunlight. You'll be upset if you hear their conversation."

Carbonne turned pale.

"Don't worry. Sara is no spendthrift. Let's sit with Bug on your future back patio."

When Barbara emerged from the house, her lips were no longer pinched. "I feel better now. Sara has convinced me we could have the second bathroom redone by one of those firms that promises they can remodel a bathroom in three days or less. With the right sink counter, it could be the perfect place to bathe the baby. Sara suggested that we live in the house for a year and know our preferences before we remodeled the master bathroom."

"Is that all we need to do?" Color was returning to Carbonne's face.

"No, the second point on my list is we need to have at least two rooms painted before we move in: our bedroom and the baby's bedroom. I can pick the shades of aqua tomorrow. Maybe Mother can drive here to help me."

Sara spoke before Carbonne asked the predictable question: *Is that it?* "You could have the whole house painted before you move in. An off white would be good for rooms not in aqua, and usually it's cheaper usually to have multiple rooms done all at once."

Carbonne moaned, "That will cost thousands."

Barbara ignored him and looked at her list. "The third point is the house inspector suggested the wiring should be upgraded. I think we should take his advice. I'd feel safer."

Carbonne put his arm around Barbara. "Of course. The electrical firm we use at work also does homes. I'll call them on Monday."

Sanders stood and grabbed Sara's arm. "We've got other errands. Bye."

 J. L. Greger

Once they were in the car, Sanders said, "You were right. I don't want to shop until I've relaxed over a couple of drinks."

Sara drove away quickly. "Shopping is fun when it happens easily. Planned shopping expeditions, like young couples do when decorating a house, aren't for me anymore."

Sara had answered a question that had been buzzing in his head. Should he and Sara buy a house together and meld their households? He recognized neither he nor Sara wanted to put *that* type of work into their relationship.

Sara must have sensed his sadness. "I know what you can buy me. You can make arrangement with Molly Maids or some other service to clean my house once a week. Then Bug and I will have more time for fun with you."

CHAPTER 33: A Final Secret

"What did you do?"

Jack's yelling caused Sara to pull the phone away from her ear. "I'm not deaf. Can you explain what is upsetting you?"

"The psychologist called me 'cause your phone was turned off. He claimed Candy was muttering about 'a man hiding a hat and an axe.' He seemed to think we needed to talk to her immediately."

Sara thought Jack seemed calmer now. His voice was in his usual baritone not in a counter tenor range.

Sara decided to goad him a bit. "I guess you and your girlfriend had better get dressed. Sanders and I are finishing lunch at a restaurant near the halfway house. We can pick up Candy and bring her to the FBI building by two. You'd better tell the psychologist to meet us. Looks like our friends will have a chance to get to know each other because I doubt, we'll pull much out of Candy quickly."

Sanders had already motioned to the waiter for the bill as Sara concluded her conversation with Jack. "Is Jack's friend pretty?"

"No idea. I've never met her. Jack would never admit it, but I suspect he picks women who are bright. I'd guess she's a law student."

***

"I saw him. He was burying a hat and an axe in his back yard."

Jack wagged his finger at the psychologist behind the mirror in the observation room.

Sara agreed with Jack. The psychologist had misjudged Candy's willingness—perhaps ability was the right word—to talk. Jack leaned forward. "Candy, you've said that at least twenty times. Who is he?"

Candy ignored him and again in a soft voice repeated, "I saw him bury a hat and an axe."

Sara decided to try a different approach. "When did this happen?"

Candy gave her a blank stare.

"Did this happen yesterday?"

Candy shook her head.

"We first talked to you almost two weeks ago. That was about two weeks after your wedding. Do you remember?"

"I'm not stupid. I remember."

Sara thought Candy's annoyance was a good sign. At least part of her brain was still working. "Okay did you see the man bury the axe before or after we first visited you?"

Candy stopped massaging her belly and seemed to count on her fingers. "Before. The day before."

"You said the man was burying an axe and a hat in his back yard. Why did you go to the man's house?"

"To talk to him."

"About what?"

"Finishing my dissertation. I needed help."

Jack texted Sara and the psychologist and then pointed to Sara's phone.

Do you want me to amend the search warrant you got to search Levine's office, house, and car? We need to add the back yard. A judge will be more cooperative if we contact him now instead of at eight tonight.

Sara looked at her phone but seemed to ignore it. "What type of help did you need?"

Candy continued to massage her belly. "My nerves... I couldn't concentrate enough to write. He helped me." She began to sob.

Sara put one hand on one of Candy's hands but stared toward the psychologist behind the mirror. "I think we need a psychologist's help in here pronto."

Candy clawed Sara's hand away and returned to massaging her belly with both hands.

The psychologist looked ashen as he rushed in. "I didn't realize how deeply she suppressed what she saw. When I called you, I thought she was ready to talk."

Jack shook his head. "I guess she saw her major advisor as some sort of father figure. She sure is trying to protect him."

The psychologist ignored Jack and tried to calm Candy.

Sara rushed out and then returned with several cans of soda. "Sorry, I didn't have any cookies in my office. Jack, why don't you hit the vending machines in the basement." She opened a can of regular cola and pushed it toward Candy. "Try this. It might make you feel better."

Candy took a sip. "I saw him..."

Sara said, "I know you saw Ralph Edwards. You trusted him. So did Toby. He betrayed you."

Candy looked up. "You understand. I'm sleepy now."

***

The psychologist paced into the observation room. "The ambulance should be here soon. I think Candy will sleep for hours now that she had revealed her secret."

He stared at Sara. "How did you know?"

Jack spoke first. "She always had a funny feeling about Ralph Edwards. Kept saying he was devious. I kept thinking it was Levine."

Sara nodded. "I don't think there is any doubt—Irwin Levine is a jerk. But he always does what is best for himself. Killing Toby—even if Toby was trying to leave his lab—was not in Levine's best interest. Toby was the brains behind the grant proposals and patent applications. I suspect Levine was convinced he could talk Toby into cooperating eventually. Besides, I figured he and Geri were having a tryst on the day of Toby's murder."

Jack slapped his thigh. "I'd forgotten the last point."

"So, that left Ralph Edwards or another member of Levine's lab. No one in the lab, except maybe Geri, seemed emotional about their work. They didn't care enough to become violent."

"And Geri was with Levine."

The psychologist kept studying Candy through the mirror to the conference room. "Candy seems comfortable lying on the table." He looked at his watch. "Except for eliminating everyone else, why did you suspect Ralph?"

                                   J. L. Greger

"First off, we caught him in several half-truths. Bystanders don't lie unless they have a reason."

"That's not enough."

"Second, one of the cavers who'd been in Ralph's classes noted he was grouchy. All the other cavers called him a sweet, old man. I wanted to learn about his apparent two sides. So, I talked to his department head who admitted he'd forced Ralph to retire as of the end of the current semester. It seems Ralph gave no As to students in his classes during the last two semesters." Sara shook her head. "Do you realize how many complaints that would generate for a department head?"

Jack snickered.

The psychologist said, "Okay, Ralph was cranky, but not in a murderous rage."

Jack smiled. "Ralph had no alibi for a four-hour gap on the day Toby was killed."

Sara nodded. "When Ralph led me around his house yesterday. It was sad. He had everything so... so cleaned up. It was like he had closed the door on almost every aspect of his life. Weird."

"He was depressed. What else?" The psychologist glanced at his watch again.

"The Stetson hanging on the peg in his office looked new, not a well-worn memento. That's why I made Jack collect it. Winslow emailed me this morning. He found no traces of sweat stains on the interior of the hat. I doubted Ralph would pitch his old hat because it reminded him of happy times with his daughters and wife at rodeos, but I knew it wasn't in his house. Somewhere after the tenth time Candy said, 'I saw him bury a hat and an axe in the back yard,' I knew the truth."

"Darn. Why didn't you end my misery and not force me to listen to Candy for another half-hour."

"I knew the truth in my heart, but my mind wasn't sure."

Jack stood and opened the door. "We'd better hurry. Ralph might try to escape. The judge was quick in giving us a search warrant for the back yard."

"I doubt we need to hurry. Ralph has been two steps ahead of me during the whole case." She turned to the psychologist, "Are you sure the hospital is the best place for Candy? I always think hospital are depressing. You can assure her that she'll get her Ph.D."

"She can't take any more unmet promises. Are you sure?"

"If I judged Ralph and Levine right, I am."

CHAPTER 34: Into the darkness

No one answered the doorbell. The front door was unlocked. Sara wasn't surprised and ambled into Ralph's office. There was a stack of papers on the desk. *SARA* was hand printed on a folded page at the top of the pile.

It could wait. She proceeded to the master bedroom. Ralph was stretched out on the bed. She felt for a pulse. There was none. She turned to Jack. "I'll call the medical examiner. I'm pretty sure this is a suicide, but we need to treat the investigation as if it was a murder. The body feels cold. Ralph has probably been dead since last night sometime. You'd better notify the Albuquerque Police."

"First, I'll get the crew digging in the yard first. My girlfriend and I don't plan to be stuck here on a Saturday night."

"Send Winslow in here to help me." Tears were streaming down her face. "As soon as Winslow checks out the note on the desk, I'll read it aloud to my friend Ralph."

Jack snorted. "Friend? Ralph was playing you."

"No, he was a lonely man who felt there was no purpose left to his life. I was his last challenge."

Jack sighed. "This case is making you hallucinate."

***

"You can have the note now. The rapid DNA test showed only Ralph's DNA was present. Of course, I'll have to do the standard DNA test if this goes to court." Winslow looked at Sara. "Don't you think I should stay here as you read it? I may have to check every page in that stack."

"I doubt it. The medical examiner will want your help in finding the poison Ralph used, and Jack will need your help if his dig in the back yard yields anything." She took the page. "I'm going to read it to Ralph. I think it's what he would have wanted."

Winslow shook his head and followed Sara to Ralph's bedroom where the medical examiner was at work.

Sara sat in an upholstered armchair beside the bed and began to read the typed note aloud:

Sara,

I'm sure you've figured out the details, but I suspect Jack will need this verification. Here goes.

Toby was aging badly. Jacob put me in contact with Toby's physician two years ago. You'll find Toby's medical records in the stack of papers I left for you on my desk. Toby's kidneys were failing. Most autistic patients die early because of accidents, suicide, or congenital conditions. Toby's congenital problem—renal disease—was unusual.

Jacob told me before he died that he didn't think Toby could endure being hooked up to a noisy renal dialysis unit for hours every week when his kidneys failed. Toby's physician speculated a month ago that Toby would need to begin dialysis soon. Toby didn't want anyone else, including Candy, to know about his failing kidneys.

Toby's social skills were also deteriorating. Once Candy was pregnant, he viewed her only as hands for his research ideas and as the mother of Jacob's grandchild.

I planned to talk to Toby, not kill him, on that Wednesday. After Candy ran from the cave, I saw Toby descend the stairs as if nothing had happened. He didn't seem to notice the honks when Candy almost hit Ben's car in the parking lot. Instead, Toby settled on a small mound a hundred feet from the trail and worked on his laptop. Toby was annoyed when Ben found him. Their argument became violent. I think Toby broke his arm when he fell. That's when I decided Toby had become dangerous to himself and others. You know the rest.

Maybe you missed several details. I worked daily with Candy at her apartment or my house to finish her dissertation. She just texted me that she'd finished adding my last corrections to her dissertation. Don't allow Dr. Levine or the folks in the Graduate School to say it wasn't her work. I only did what Levine should have done as a major professor.

After I met you at the Sandia Grotto meeting, I knew you would act quickly. I needed to slow you down because Candy and I needed time to finish her dissertation. Thus, I took a vial from Candy' medicine cabinet—the one with her fertility pills and the key to Toby's condo. I wanted to remove his renal medications and his medical records, which were hidden in a box of old clothes marked, FOR GOODWILL.

Please explain to my daughters I loved them, but I had to complete my life's tasks. Tell Candy, I want her to leave the dark caves in her life and enjoy the sunshine with her son. You know people in government agencies. Help her find a position in the U.S. Geological Survey or the U.S. Forest Service.

It's been a pleasure keeping a step ahead of you as you investigated Toby's death. Now I must go into the darkness.

Ralph

Sara stopped reading and sobbed.

The medical examiner wiped his eyes and placed a hand on Sara's shoulder. "Jack, Winslow, and I can finish everything that needs to be done here. You should be the one to explain the story to Candy."

"I think I'd better check in on Jack before I leave."

Sara found Jack standing under an old cottonwood staring into a pit. In front of him Winslow was kneeling and pulling items—an old Stetson hat with a red hatband, a bloodied cave axe, a brown plastic vial with a blister pack of medicine and a key, a torn red plaid shirt, and a laptop—out of a large plastic bag.

Sara put her hand on Jack's shoulder. "The note we found explains everything. Make sure Ralph's daughters get the hat when you're through with the case."

CHAPTER 35: Out of the Darkness

Two weeks later

Jack placed a diet cola on Sara's desk and petted Bug before he sat by Sara's desk. "How's my long-lost partner?"

Sara looked away from her computer screen. "I was glad to come into work after two weeks of so-called vacation. Sanders's daughter convinced Sanders it would be easy to paint her seven hundred square-foot apartment in Manhattan."

Jack slapped the desk. "Man, even I could do that. I've helped my momma paint rooms that big."

"You didn't have to lug paint cans on the subway and up three floors to a rent-stabilized flat. And the colors Sanders's daughter chose drove Sanders up the wall. She and her boyfriend now have a purple main room, a purple and ivory striped hallway and kitchen, and a lavender bedroom and bathroom."

Jack doubled over laughing. "I doubt your man is into purple."

"He's not. He thinks walls should be ivory or beige. I wasn't surprised when his daughter called him stodgy." Sara took a swig of her diet cola. "But I got him out of New York City before either he or his daughter said anything unforgiveable. It helped that Senator Holms called and asked if we could meet with him in Washington." Without taking a breath, Sara said, "So, what's up with you and your girlfriend?'

"We broke up."

Sara patted Jack's hand. "You two seemed good together."

"I thought so, but..."

Sara waited but Jack said nothing. "But what?"

He looked at the ceiling. "She said we would be like you and Sanders in ten years, and she didn't want that."

Sara was at a loss for words. "We... we are..."

"Happy and live independent lives joined by frequent vacations and shared interests. She wants kids."

Sara patted his hands. "She forgot the age difference. Did you tell her you wanted children?"

"Don't worry about it. I talked to Carbonne. He said when I found the right woman, I'd be, like him, glad to change my goals and lifestyle." He paused a second. "Let's get to work." He handed Sara several documents with the University of New Mexico's letterhead on top.

Sara thumbed through the pages. "The university administration is processing the charges against Irwin Levine. Before he died, Ralph filed documents proving Levine lied in his grant and patent applications. Seems the psychologist convinced Candy to charge Levine with sexual harassment." She traced her finger along several lines at the end of one letter. "I need to talk to them anyway to fulfill a promise I made to Candy."

"Good. Carbonne said you'd handle everything with the university."

"What else?"

"The Sandoval County Sheriff—I think his name is Chuy Bargas—wants a report on the case. Carbonne wanted me to remind you that as a federal employee you can't endorse anyone's candidacy for public office."

"No problem. I'll call a local reporter and brag about the help Chuy gave the FBI in solving Toby's murder. The resulting article should help Chuy in his election campaign."

"You are good at covering your...." He grinned.

***

Six weeks later

It was a hot day in late June. Sara found Winslow talking to Jack in his office. She smiled as she announced, "Candy passed her oral exam."

Jack leaned back on his chair "I thought the final oral exam for a Ph.D. were supposed to be tough." He stared at Sara. "I also thought they were clandestine. Why did they allow you to attend?"

Sara fluttered her eyes in mock surprise. "Some of us are special."

                                                    J. L. Greger

Both men made crude remarks under their breaths.

Sara pretended not to hear the comments. "Remember all the paperwork I had to do to clear this case. Well, the VP for Research at UNM thought I should attend Candy's exam and see that the university was being responsible."

"What does that mean?"

"The university returned all unspent money in Levine's accounts to federal agencies and adjusted patent documents to reflect the actual work of Levine, Toby, and Candy. Levine lost his university appointment as of today after Candy's exam."

Jack shook his head. "Sounds too slick."

Sara smiled. "You're right. The university appointed a faculty committee to review the cases against Levine. They shaped the punishments meted out by the university on Levine."

"Faculty committees don't work that fast."

Sara fluttered her eyelashes. "I gave them technical advice to speed their progress during the last five weeks."

Winslow looked confused. "What about Candy? She may have a Ph.D., but she's destitute."

"Aaron Broder got funds released from the Collins Family Trust. He thinks Toby's patents are apt to become lucrative in the future." Sara pulled a can of diet cola from her purse and plunked down in a free chair. "Candy has been offered a position with the U.S. Forest Service. It will begin after she delivers Jacob Tobias Collins in a month and takes the time to adjust to motherhood, which the psychologist thinks she'll need. Candy seemed normal today at her exam. I think she's escaped the darkness of the Sandia Man Cave."

Jack slid forward in his chair. "I'm glad we can close this case. Winslow was showing me some evidence on a new case. Can I count on your support? Or are you off to a foreign location with Sanders?"

"I'll be commuting to Washington. Sanders has been appointed as a special aide to the Senate Intelligence Committee. He's hoping it's a temporary position until something better comes along."

THE END

SCIENCE AND HISTORY BEHIND THE STORY

The details on caves and spelunking (the exploration of caves) in this novel are accurate with one big exception. The hidden room in Sandia Man Cave described in this novel is fictional.

Sandia Man Cave

Sandia Man Cave is a national historic landmark in the Sandia Mountains of Cibola National Forest not far from Placitas, New Mexico. The cave was excavated in the 1930s by Frank Hibben (1).

Hibben claimed his discovery of Folsom and Sandia (pre-Clovis) point hunting tools and the remains of extinct Pleistocene mammals, including mammoths and mastodons, demonstrated humans were in the area 25,000 years ago. His claim is debatable.

Currently anthropologists believe humans first occupied the cave about 11,000 years ago (2). However, recent research (footprints dating from 22,000 years ago in White Sands National Park) suggests humans were in New Mexico at the time Hibben estimated (3)

The cave has been in the news twice during the last fifty years. The Sandia Grotto, a caving club, cleaned the cave in 2015 to remove graffiti and reveal ancient petroglyphs (4). The murder of a woman in a parking lot by Sandia Man Cave in 1999 was never solved (5).

Life in Caves

Caves shelter a variety of animals and microorganisms from the weather. Many of these microorganisms can be destroyed or changed by careless caving. Hence, the importance of a commonly cited caver's motto:

Scientists have discovered several of the bacteria and molds in caves have interesting properties—antibiotic resistance and the ability to recycle nitrogen (6,7). *Paenibacillus* is the genus of bacteria receiving the most attention as a source of antibiotics, biofertilizers, and biopesticides (8).

Two of the caves found to be rich sources of potentially useful microorganisms are in New Mexico: Lechuguilla Cave in the Carlsbad National Park and Fort Stanton Cave in Lincoln County. These caves are also two of the longest known caves in the world. It is doubtful large populations of *Paenibacillus* would be found in the hidden room (if it existed) of Sandia Man Cave because generally these bacteria are found in deep recesses of caves.

Over a thousand species of fungi, yeast, and slime molds, have been identified in caves worldwide (9). One of the most notorious is the fungus, *Pseudogymnoascus destructans*. The fungus causes white-nose syndrome in hibernating bats and has killed as many 90% of the bats at some sites (10). Although the bats in Carlsbad Cavern are famous, bats are not common in Sandia Man Cave. Hence, bats did not dramatically greet Sara at the mouth of the cave in this novel.

Autism Spectrum Disorder

Toby Collins in this novel has autism spectrum disorder. He is typical of individuals with a mild form of this syndrome.

This developmental disability is characterized by difficulties in communicating and interacting with others. Often individuals with this disability are prone to repetitive behaviors and limited interests. The symptoms and their severity vary greatly. Mild forms of autism are sometimes called Asperger Syndrome (11).

There are no definitive medical tests for autism. Scientists have reported changes in the brains of patients with autism, but several of the observations are debatable (12). The causes of the syndrome are unknown, and there is no cure. Generally, early educational interventions are helpful in reducing problematic behavior patterns. There is no medicine for autism specifically, but anti-anxiety drug, known as serotonin reuptake inhibitors (SSRIs) such as Prozac, are sometimes helpful, especially in children (13).

Recent surveys suggest autistic individuals have a shortened average life expectancy (14). Potential causes include chronic diseases, epilepsy, accidents, and poorer health care access. Obviously, autism is a medical mystery at this point.

Ralph Edwards had psychological problems, but their diagnosis is beyond the scope of this novel.

References

1. Hibben FC. 1937. Association of man with Pleistocene mammals in the Sandia Mountains of New Mexico. *American Antiquity* **2**:260-3.

2. USDA/Forest Service. Sandia Man Cave, Trailhead & Trail 72. https://www.fs.usda.gov/recarea/cibola/recarea/?recid=71221

3. Madsen DB, Davis LG, Oviatt CG. 2022. Comment on "Evidence of humans in North America during the Las Glacial Maximum." Science 14Jan2022. **375** (6577) DOI: 10.1126/science.abm 6987.

4. KRQE. Photos: Sandia Man Cave Cleanup. July 8, 2015. https://www.krqe.com/news/photos-sandia-man-cave-cleanup/

5. New Mexico Survivors of Homicide. Inc. Wanted! The murderer(s) of Carla Salinas Simmons. http://www.nmsoh.org/simmons_carla_salinas_us.htm.

6. Pawlowski AC, Wang W, Koteva K, Barton HA, McArthur AG, and Wright GD. 2016. A diverse intrinsic antibiotic resistome from a cave bacterium. *Nature Comm* **7**: 13803

7. Kimble JC, Winter AS, Spilde MN, Sinsabaugh RL, Northup DE. 2018. A potential role of *Thaumarchaeota* in N-cycling in a semiarid environment, Fort Stanton Cave, Snowy

River passage, New Mexico, USA. *FEMS Microbiol Ecol* **94** (11)173 DOI: 10.1093/femsec/fiy173.

8. Grady EN, MacDonald J, Liu L, Richman A, Yuan ZC. 2016. Current knowledge and perspectives of *Paenibacillus*: a review. *Microb Cell Fact* **15**, 203. https://doi.org/10.1186/s12934-016-0603-7

9. Vanderwolf KJ, Malloch D, McAlpine DF, Forbes GJ. 2013. A world review of fungi, yeasts, and slime molds in caves. *Int J Speleology* **42**: 77-96. DOI: http://dx.doi.org/10.5038/1827-806X.42.1.9

10. White-nose Syndrome Response Team. What is White-nose Syndrome? https://www.whitenosesyndrome.org/static-page/what-is-white-nose-syndrome

11.National Institute of Mental Health. Autism Spectrum Disorder. https://www.nimh.nih.gov/health/topics/autism-spectrum-disorders-asd

12. Fetit R, Hillary RF, Price DJ, Lawrie SM. 2021. The neuropathology of autism: A systematic review of post-mortem studies of autism and related disorders. *Neurosci & Behav Rev* **129:** 35-62 DOI:10.1012/j.neubiorev.2021.07.014

13. Autism Speaks. Anxiety and autism: How common are anxiety disorders? https://www.autismspeaks.org/expert-opinion/how-common-are-anxiety-disorders-people-autism

14. DaWalt LS, Hong J, Mallick MR. 2019. Mortality in individuals with autism spectrum disorder: Predictors over a 20-year period. *Autism* **23**(7):1732-9. DOI: 10.1177/1362361319827412

ACKNOWLEDGMENTS

I want to thank Lorna Collins for carefully editing this manuscript. I also want to thank Barbara Hodges for her patience and creativity when designing the covers for my books.

My fellow writers from the now defunct Oak Tree Press, the Public Safety Writers Association (PSWA), and Croak and Dagger (the local chapter of Sisters in Crime) have provided intellectual and emotional support for my writing. I appreciate them as authors, advisors, and friends.

None of my books would be possible without the patience and love of my dogs: Bug and Elf.

ABOUT THE AUTHOR

J. L. Greger is a biology professor and research administrator from the University of Wisconsin-Madison turned novelist. The pet therapy dog, Bug, in her mysteries and thrillers is based on her own Japanese Chin. She includes tidbits about science, the American Southwest, and her international travel experiences in her **Science Traveler Series**.

The Flu Is Coming. In the first book in the series, a woman scientist traces the spread of a deadly new flu virus among the frantic residents of a quarantined New Mexico community. (New Mexico/ Arizona Book Award Finalist)

Murder...A Way to Lose Weight. A dean in a medical school helps police discover whether an ambitious young "diet doctor," disgruntled patients, or old-timers with buried secrets are killers. (Winner of the 2016 Public Safety Writers Association contest and New Mexico/Arizona Book Award Finalist)

Ignore the Pain. A woman scientist learns too much about the coca trade and too little about a sexy new colleague while on a public health assignment in Bolivia.

Malignancy. A woman tries to escape the clutches of a drug lord and accepts a risky assignment as a science consultant in Cuba. (Winner of the 2015 Public Safety Writers Association contest)

I Saw You in Beirut. A woman's past provides clues for the extraction of a nuclear scientist from Iran. The author's experiences as a science and education consultant in the United Arab Emirates and Lebanon are featured.

Riddled with Clues. A homeless man and a woman scientist are targeted by drug gangs after she listens to the strange tale of an undercover drug agent about his war experiences. The memories of an actual CIA agent in Laos during the Vietnam War are featured. (New Mexico/Arizona Book Award Finalist)

A Pound of Flesh, Sorta. The police and a woman scientist can't decide whether a package contaminated with the bacteria that causes the bubonic plague is a plea for help by a whistleblower or a threat from gang leaders awaiting trial. (New Mexico/Arizona Book Award Finalist)

Dirty Holy Water. A woman who usually serves as a science consultant for the FBI learns there is a thin line between being a victim and being a villain when she becomes the chief suspect in a bizarre murder case. (New Mexico/Arizona Book Award Finalist)

Games for Couples. Did lethal compounds in a cultured meat product—meat made in a test tube—kill a man in a clinical trial? Or did the toxic competition between biotechnology companies and spite of battling couples cause his death? (New Mexico/Arizona Book Award Finalist)

Fair Compromises. Sara Almquist and her FBI colleagues rush to find the culprits who endangered the lives of a hundred attendees at a political rally by poisoning the food with botulism toxin. Their target was a woman candidate for the U.S. Senate. (New Mexico/Arizona Book Award Finalist)

Bungle in the Jungle. The U.S. consular office in Manaus, Brazil, is a "Bungle in the Jungle." Can Sara Almquist and the new Acting Ambassador to Brazil figure out how the staff became enmeshed in the illegal international trade of drugs and cultural artifacts? (New Mexico/Arizona Book Award Finalist)

Escape from a Dark Cave. Sara Almquist, an FBI scientific consultant, investigates the murder of a young man near a historic cave in New Mexico. As she reconstructs the victim's

J. L. Greger

final days, she learns the autistic victim found the cave to be soothing. She finds the cave to be depressing.

J. L. Greger wrote a children's book in 2023 called, **_Come Fly with Elf._** In this picture book, a tiny Papillon dog called Elf dreams of flying in a hot air balloon.

See more at: http://www.jlgreger.com